A JACK FOR ALL SEASONS

Also by Lesley L. Smith

Temporal Dreams
Kat Cubed
Reality Alternatives
Conservation of Luck

The Space Operetta Series:
Book 1: *A Jack by Any Other Name*
Book 2: *A Jack in the Dark*
Book 3: *A Jack For All Seasons*

The Quantum Cop Series:
Book 1: *The Quantum Cop*
Book 2: *Quantum Murder*
Book 2: *Quantum Mayhem*

A Jack For All Seasons

By Lesley L. Smith

Quarky Media
Boulder Colorado

A Jack For All Seasons
Published by Quarky Media, PO Box 3332, Boulder, CO 80307
www.quarkymedia.com

ISBN: 978-1-950198-24-5 (ebook)
ISBN: 978-1-950198-25-2 (print)

A JACK FOR ALL SEASONS

Chapter One

On the *Shakespeare*, me and my friends and comrades in arms were hiding--in a courageous way--behind Quihiri's largest moon. That was the good news. Our new FTL drive worked, transporting our ship across the galaxy from Earth to planet Quihiri. Yay! The *Shakespeare* was the Terran Cultural Committee's flagship, spreading Earth's wonderful culture around the galaxy. And spying on other planetary cultures, of course.

The bad news was the Quihiri people were evil and had disabled all the other FTL drives in the galaxy. Hence, we were working against an entire planet by ourselves. And it was a planet of really mean sentients. In addition to the FTL drive sabotage, they were stopping many of their people from evolving into a more advanced species of energy-beings, the sldkfjfoisut. They'd also attacked the most awesome planet of them all, birthplace of The Bard and me (Jack Jones, magnificent lover-, singer- and spy-extraordinaire), Earth.

We were all peering at a giant image of the planet through the large viewscreen on the bridge of the *Shakespeare*. From space, it was a swirled blue-white marble--all oceans and clouds. "It looks like such a nice planet from up here," I said. "You'd never know they were the scourge of the galaxy."

"I'm open to suggestions, people," Gina, Captain Gomez, my wife (sort of), a voluptuous, curvilicious woman, said. She was an Amazon queen, able to melt hearts with her beautiful brown eyes or break you in half if you rubbed her the wrong way.

"A frontal assault would seem to be contraindicated," Commander Lu, the security chief, a tall, determined, crew-cutted by-the-book soldier, said.

"Agreed," Gina said. "We don't have the resources for it."

"Well, there's no way we can reverse the FTL drive sabotage without getting access to their systems," Commander Bello, the chief engineer, also a recently-young-again hottie, said.

"*I'll have grounds more relative than this--the play's the thing*," I whispered, still staring out the viewscreen.

"I like to play," Slid, a baby sldkfjfoisut, an energy being, also sort of my son, said. His body, now resembling a cloud, floating next to us, brightened with luminescent silver sparkles. "Can I play, too?"

"I think I understand what Jack's getting at," Addie, the sldkfjfoisut ambassador, Slid's mom, an awesome energy-being, and one of my lovers, said. "He wants to do a sneak attack." Her body, a multicolored cloud, phased into blue-gray--which I thought meant thoughtful and worried.

I held up a forefinger. "Exactly!" It was awesome how Addie understood me; we had a real connection. Of course, she'd sought me out because of my intragalactic reputation as an excellent lover and singer, so it wasn't surprising we hit it off.

"Ooh, I can help with that," Quinta, a newly-evolved sldkfjfoisut, formerly the Quihiri leader's wife and my special friend, said. "I know where everything is in the Quihiri embassy complex." Her multicolored cloud changed to the green-blue side of the spectrum--which I thought meant thoughtful and excited or possibly, horny.

"I don't know, Jack." Gina exhaled loudly. "I suppose you want to go?"

I nodded enthusiastically. "Of course."

"You are unusually lucky, but it sounds too dangerous," she added. Aw. She cared. "They know what you look like, and if they spot you, we lose the element of surprise. Right now, that's our only advantage." Ah. She cared about the mission.

But the play talk had given me an idea. "What if I go in costume?"

Addie, Slid, Quinta and I had successfully landed one of the *Shakespeare's* cloaked shuttles a short distance from the large government complex without being spotted. The plan was to sneak in the back door and creep undetected to the Aerospace Engineering Department of the University. Quinta claimed we could access the FTL drive control system there because that was where it had been developed and tested. And it wasn't guarded like the big official government control center was.

We all stood or floated inside the back hatch, getting ready to deplane.

"I want to look like a Keplarrian," I said. "They're strong and intimidating, like me. They look like giant snakes." The sldkfjfoisut could look like almost anything since they were made of energy.

Addie bobbed in front of me. Somehow, she gave off a vibe of careful consideration. "No. Your legs would be a problem. Slid can't cover them and your head, and we have to cover your head." Since I couldn't be human, the plan was Slid would shape-shift to become a mask for me.

"A Tau-Ceto-an?" I asked. The turtle-like sentients seemed powerful, like me.

"No," Addie said. "Slid doesn't have enough volume to do the big back. I think it will have to be an Alpha-Catoblepan. Their volume and physiology are most similar to humans." The Alpha-Catoblepans looked like giant mice.

Ah, well, the Alpha-Catoblepans loved me. They had excellent taste, so I might as well impersonate them. "I think we might have one of their translators here in the shuttle somewhere." I opened one of the storage compartments and started rummaging around.

"I've met an Alpha-Catoblepan," Quinta said. "And your hands are wrong. And your outfit. You need a tunic. But your boots are okay."

"Tunic and gloves," I said and came across a tunic and gloves immediately. "Huh."

"The *Shakespeare* is a ship of spies," Addie said. "I'm sure you're not the first person who wanted to blend in."

"Wow. you know a lot." I paused. "How do you know that?" I wasn't a very experienced spy, but one thing I did know was: spies were supposed to be covert.

"I know things," she said. I got a distinct impression of a smile, which was a good trick since she didn't have a mouth right now.

I finished searching the storage compartments in the back of the shuttle, and no AC translator. But I thought I'd seen one somewhere around here. I glanced toward the front of the ship. Yes. It was in one of the front storage compartments. I quickly retrieved it.

A voice in my ear said, "What's taking so long?" It was Gina over comms. On duty, we wore small earbuds for communication purposes.

"We're leaving now, beautiful," I said.

"That's Captain Beautiful to you, Ensign Jones," she said. I also heard a smile in her voice.

Someone else on comms sighed. I was guessing it was Commander Bello since he was the only other one on comms.

I put on the tunic and gloves and placed the translator around my neck under the tunic.

Slid bobbed up to my head and landed on my face. It felt ...different. It felt like I couldn't breathe. "Hey!" I tried to say.

"Honey," Addie said, "make sure not to cut off his air supply."

"Oops," my mask said.

Suddenly, it got easier to breathe. Yay. "What about you guys?" I asked.

They instantly transformed into two ordinary-looking Quihiri, big sentient gray octopus-looking creatures, namely, the bad guys. They were about the size of an average human, with three leg tentacles and three arm tentacles, each with a three-fingered hand. Their three-eyed, three-nostrilled, one-mouthed heads flowed into their torsos with no necks. Yeah, three was a real theme on Quihiri.

One thing our plan had in its favor was the Quihiri government suppressed all knowledge of shape-shifting energy beings. The average Quihiri didn't know that they themselves might evolve into one. So, any Quihiri we ran into should take our appearances at face value--no pun intended.

"Good job, guys!" I said.

Over comms, Command Bello said, "Can we get this thing started already?"

"Jack?" Gina said.

"Yes, Captain Beautiful." I fumbled with the back hatch

release in my gloves.

The hatch opened, and Quihiri air whooshed into the shuttle, bringing with it the faint smell of fish, seaweed, and ocean.

"Ah," Quinta said. "The smell of home." Her colors were swirling between black and the colors of the rainbow, indicating her roiling emotions. "I didn't realize how much I missed it until now." Until very recently, she'd been married to the Quihiri leader. Her transition to an energy being and her consequent rejection by her family had been tough on her.

"Don't worry, Quinta. This will all be worth it," I said. "*But he'll remember with advantages what feats he did that day. Then shall our names, familiar in his mouth as household words...be in their flowing cups freshly rememb'red.*"

We all exited the shuttle, stepping into the orange-ish sunlight, the setting sun on the horizon. We perambulated in the general direction of the embassy. We were on a rocky, sandy plain with large boulders scattered about. I could hear the crash of waves on a beach but could see neither waves nor beach.

"Addie," I asked, picking my way around smaller rocks, "why are the atmospheres on the planets we trade with basically breathable by humans? Do you know?" Sometimes we needed a rebreather, but none of the planets we visited were instantly deadly.

"Because you trade with them," my face, aka Slid, said.

"Slid's right," Addie said. "Humans trade with people that have similar physical and cultural environments. People living on worlds with sulfuric acid atmospheres or twenty times Earth's gravity, for example, would not appreciate what you have to offer, your culture. More importantly, humans couldn't survive on such hostile planets."

"Thanks." That made sense. Maybe I should have known that. It was probably somewhere in the Terran Cultural Committee (TCC) planetary briefing documents.

But in my defense, as a clone, I was less than a year old. But in my offense, Slid was less than a month old. I could learn a thing or two from Slid.

I pulled my fon out of my pocket. "Note to self: read all the TCC planetary briefings."

"Is that a Terran fon?" Quinta asked. "You shouldn't have brought that."

I glanced at it. Yikes. She was right. "Can I leave it in my pocket? Or take it back to the shuttle? Or I could leave it out here somewhere?" The giant embassy-slash-government complex towered over the next hill.

Over comms, Bello sighed.

Gina said, "Recall the mission plan. Stealth. Let's keep communication to a minimum. We don't want the Quihiri picking up our radio signals. And let's try to be as quick as possible. The longer you're there, the more likely you are to get caught."

"Yes, ma'am." I nodded. "I'll leave it here." I pointed at the ground. I knelt and put my fon on the ground and then covered it with a small flat stone and made a small tower of little rocks on top of it. I wanted to be able to find it after our successful mission. My life was on that fon if you counted my memory backups.

I stood. "Let's pick up the pace," I whispered.

In response, Quinta and Addie raced ahead of me.

I had to start jogging to keep up.

Me and my merry band stood outside the gargantuan Quihiri government complex at three exterior doors.

"Hopefully, these security codes still work," Quinta whispered.

Hopefully? But I didn't say anything. Yay, me. I was stealth-Jack.

Her tentacles flew over the security pad. Soon, the exterior doors opened with a deep whoosh.

As we entered, I quietly asked, "Your codes still work?"

She made a noise that sounded very much like a giggle. "No. They're my husband's codes. He didn't know I stole them." Since her husband was basically the leader of the whole planet, this code-stealing thing sounded pretty handy.

"Nice," I said.

"Shh," Addie said.

I shhed.

The three, well, technically, four, of us snuck along the dimly-orange-lit corridors. We didn't pass anyone. I didn't know what the local time was. Why was no one down here? Mealtime, maybe?

"What is this area? What's down here?" I asked Quinta.

"Shh!" Addie said.

"Shh!" my face said. It was a little disconcerting.

I didn't have to be told twice, er, four times. We tramped down the halls in silence.

Then, a security squad of four intercepted us. "Ambassador Quintavius, are you here? We detected your security code in use," the squad leader said. The translator on my chest was translating. Into English, not AC! I quickly turned the volume down to whisper.

"What are you doing down here, sir?" the squad leader asked.

Yikes. So, to summarize: sneaking, not so much.

Addie and I quickly stepped in front of Quinta. Hopefully, she was enough on the ball to change her appearance to look like her husband. Ex-husband? After someone suppresses your evolution into a higher life form and tries to kill you, doesn't that pretty much negate marriage vows?

"Stand aside, minions," Quinta said loudly and glided in front of Addie and me. She did look exactly like the Quihiri leader now--at least as far as I could recall.

I didn't know if she meant Addie and me to stand aside or the security squad. In any case, we all moved out of the center of the hall towards the walls.

"What's wrong with your voice, sir?" the security officer said.

She made a sound like a throat clearing. "Er, um, I have a cold."

"I thought you were in your quarters, with your new triple, not to be disturbed," the officer said. "You said it was special, private, family time. No disturbances, no matter what."

I could swear a couple of the other officers snickered.

Clearly, Quintavius had a new wife. Jeez, he didn't waste any time.

Quinta's color started veering into gray-black (sad, upset) but quickly veered back to green (horny). "What I'm doing is none of your concern."

"Yes, sir," the officer said.

The seven, eight counting my face, of us stood there in silence for a moment.

"So, sir, if you're not busy, can we escort you to the war council?" the officer asked. "They've been waiting for you."

Wow. Even a relatively inexperienced spy such as myself could tell this was a huge opportunity to find out exactly what the enemy was up to. But, even a relatively inexperienced spy such as myself could tell this could end very, very badly for us. I didn't know what to do.

Since Quinta didn't immediately answer, I was guessing she didn't know what to do, either.

"We wouldn't want to keep you from your very important duties, sir," Addie said, somehow conveying obsequiousness. She knew what to do; take advantage of the huge opportunity.

"Very well," Quinta said. "To the war council! Lead the way, minions."

The security squad turned around and started marching-slash-gliding down the hall.

Addie, Quinta and I exchanged worried looks but then turned and followed them.

In flimsy disguises, we were walking into a war council in the very heart and soul of enemy territory.

What could possibly go wrong?

Chapter Two

When I'd been in the huge Quihiri government complex before (in a previous daring stealth infiltration), I'd thought one of the rooms had led to an ocean. It turned out I was right. Addie, Quinta, Slid and I passed through a set of three large doors onto a beach led by the four Quihiri security officers. The room smelled strongly of ocean: seaweed, fish, salt. The water lapped gently against the shore. The orange sun beat down on us. I glanced up and saw a giant transparent greenhouse-type ceiling over the room.

The lead officer turned to Quinta. "Would you like the ceremonial boat, or would you prefer to swim, sir?" He pointed to a blob on the horizon. Where were we supposed to go? And exactly how far away was it?

Say, 'boat.' Say, 'boat.' I tried to send Quinta a mental message.

She said, "My AC minion can't swim. Bring the boat." I wasn't sure about being called a minion, but I was sure I didn't want to try to swim in my AC costume.

After a few moments, an elaborate water vehicle quietly approached. I didn't see anyone on board. Physically, it resembled a flat-bottomed barge, about ten feet wide and twenty feet long, but it was covered in extravagantly carved curlicues--in groups of three. And the colors were every color of the rainbow, and some I hadn't even known existed. The boat glided about a foot up the beach, and a piece of the side swung open like a door. I saw two more similarly hatched sections nearby.

The officer pointed at the opening with a flourish.

Quinta and Addie glided onto the boat, and I followed, suppressing a giggle. I was getting a definite pirate vibe. "*Oh, pour the pirate sherry...*"

As soon as the officer closed the door behind us, the boat set out across the water for the distant blob.

I glanced back at the officers on the beach, but they were already turning around and heading for the three doors. So, I guessed they weren't coming with us, and, yay, we hadn't raised any suspicions.

I stepped closer to my comrades-in-arms and glanced around the deck of the boat. We appeared to be alone. "So, what's the plan?"

"You're asking us?" Quinta asked in English in her normal voice. Her Quintavius disguise melted to her usual Quinta cloud.

"Is it safe to talk here?" Addie said.

"Safe enough," Quinta said.

"What about me?" my face, aka Slid, said.

"Sure, buddy," I said and waited for Slid to say something. He didn't.

"What's the plan, Jack?" Addie asked. Oh, right, I was supposed to be in charge of this mission.

The boat moved through the water, and we passed outside through a doorway set in a transparent wall. Suddenly, the boat picked up speed, and the wind blew on us. Since all my skin was covered, I could only tell by how my tunic was whipping back.

"I think we have to go to the war council and find out what's going on if we can, right?" I said.

"Are you asking us or telling us?" Addie said. I could detect some amusement in her voice.

"It'll work until the real Quintavius shows up," Quinta said. I could detect some sadness in her voice. Did she miss her husband? How could that be? He'd treated her so poorly, lying to her about evolving into a more advanced being. But I guess the heart wants what the heart wants--all over the galaxy.

"So, it's a plan," I said. "We're going to the war council. We'll find out what's going on with the war."

"Duh," Slid said.

"Until we get caught," Quinta said.

"So, I'm hearing we need a good escape plan," I said.

"A good escape plan would be good," Slid said.

"Ideally, the Quihiri wouldn't realize they'd been infiltrated,"

Addie said. "If there are two Quintaviuses in the same place and time, that would be hard to explain."

"You would make a good spy, Addie," I said.

She sparkled a little.

Okay. It was unanimous. We needed a good escape plan. I stared at the island on the horizon, coming closer and closer. Being on an isolated island did not seem conducive to a good escape plan...

"Jack?" Addie asked. "What's the escape plan?"

I glanced around us. But there was nothing to see but open ocean, a lot of open ocean.

How good a swimmer was I? Ack. Had I ever swum? No. Not in this body.

Over comms, Gina said, "Jack? Escape plan?"

Gina could not swoop down in the *Shakespeare* and get us. The ship was too big. And, oh yeah, it would reveal that it was here.

But Captain Wu could swoop down in the *Assyrian* and get us. "If things go wrong and we can't leave the way we're coming..." Ha. I smiled. "We'll need the *Assyrian* to swoop down and pick us up." The *Assyrian* was a small ship that had traveled to this system inside the *Shakespeare*.

No one answered me for a few moments.

Finally, Gina said, "Roger, that."

"We better go to radio silence," Addie said. "We're almost at the island." Sure enough, the barge had been moving very quickly and quietly through the water. I didn't hear any engine noise.

"How does this boat work, anyway?" I asked. "What's the power source?"

"We're being pushed by swimmers, creatures in the water," Quinta said and pointed a cloudy tentacle outside the boat.

"Think of them as aquatic horses," Addie said.

I carefully made my way over to the side of the boat, put a hand over Slid (so he didn't fall off), and looked down. Yep. There were a bunch of creatures, in groups of three, just under the water's surface pushing the boat. They looked like seals--with hands.

I jerked back. Could they have overheard our conversation?

I tiptoed back to Addie and Quinta. “Could those Quihiri selkies have heard what we said?” I whispered.

“They’re not selkies, Jack,” Addie said. “They look like Terran selkies. It’s called convergent evolution--”

I put my hand up. “Could they hear us?”

“No,” Quinta said. “They’re water creatures.”

“When we talk, sound waves travel through the air--” Slid started to say. How did such a youngster know how sound worked?

“I know how sound works,” I said. I was interrupted by a scraping sound as the boat glided up the beach of the isolated island. Small waves broke on the beach with a soft, roaring sound.

“Oops,” Quinta said and quickly morphed back to Quintavius. “How do I look?” she asked.

“Great,” I said. “Perfect. Good job, Quinta.”

Quintavius’s face wavered. “What?” she asked. “I don’t look like Quintavius?”

“No,” I said. “You do. Uh, Good job, Quintavius.”

Two Quihiri approached the boat from the interior of the island.

Quintavius’s face solidified again.

“*Hold Monsters! Ere your pirate caravanserie proceed...*” I couldn’t help singing quietly.

“Shh!” Slid said. “No singing, Jack.”

“Shh!” I said. “No talking, face.”

The largest of the newcomers opened the door at the front of the barge. “Your highness, exalted Quintavius, sire, welcome to the war council.” Judging by his large size and low voice, he must be a ‘he.’ Introductions were not made. I designated him Number One. His octopus-like body turned a little greenish--which I’d thought was horny but didn’t seem likely in this context. Did I need to reconsider what some of the Quihiri colors meant?

Quinta didn’t immediately answer him. Probably because she didn’t know what to say. Since she, like the rest of us, had no idea what was happening.

The second-largest Quihiri said, “Thank you for cutting your honeymoon short and gracing us with your presence. Was everything all right with your honeymoon?”

Number One said, "Quintavius, sire?" I wished I knew the governmental system on this planet better. They were treating him like a king, but when we were here before, he'd said he was merely an ambassador.

Quinta as Quintavius glided forward out of the boat and onto the beach. "You know you and the war are very important to me." Her tone of voice was odd. Like she was angry but trying to suppress it.

Now both the Quihiri on the beach were bright green. Maybe I didn't need to revisit it. Was Quintavius cheating on his other triple members with these two? On the other hand, I had no idea what the mating and/or marriage rules were for this culture. I reached for my fon to check the cultural info on the species, but of course, I didn't have my fon.

The two strange Quihiri followed Quinta up the beach and onto a path.

Addie and I trailed behind.

I scanned our surroundings. The large empty beach was pretty, with dark-blue waves breaking on the sugar-fine orange sand. I glanced up for a second. Of course, since the sun was orange, maybe the sand was truly white? If I wasn't undercover on a hostile planet in the middle of a war, it would be a perfect spot for a chaise lounge and a small table with some of those scrumptious little-umbrella drinks.

"Jack!" my face whispered.

The other five sentients were far ahead of us on the path.

I hurried to catch up. The path passed through a lot of orange sand, palm tree-like plants, and some six-foot-tall orange boulders. So, basically: nature.

Number Two said, "What exactly happened to your original wife, Quinta, sire?"

Number One looked back at them, seemingly fascinated by the answer. Could it be that these high-level Quihiri didn't know about the evolution of their species into energy beings? Or they did? I was having trouble reading them.

"It's none of your concern," Quinta said.

"As you wish, sire," Number One said. "Most of the others are already here." He led us to a large grayish-orange stone table in a clearing, surrounded by grayish-orange stone benches--most occupied.

Three large Quihiri already sat around the table, all mostly gray. Boredom?

Also, at the table: a member of the Tao-Cetoan turtle-like species in a brown tunic, a Keplarrian snake creature (green tunic), a Yeblypson chimp person (brown tunic), some kind of giant lobster creature (orange tunic) and a plant creature (green tunic) whose species I didn't recognize. It reminded me of broccoli.

The entourages of the various table-sitters sat behind them on the surrounding benches.

Crap. It was the evil version of the united federation of planets.

Also sitting at the table: another Alpha Catoblepan with dark gray fur (dark gray tunic). Not good. Not good at all. How many seconds would it take the AC to realize I wasn't really an AC? Not many, I was guessing. All he had to do was ask me a question in AC.

On the bright side, my tunic was spot-on.

When the others saw us, they all stood up and stared at Quinta. "Sire!"

So, Quintavius was the evil leader for everyone? Good to know.

Quinta somehow managed to wave her tentacles imperiously. "As you were."

They all sat down.

She glided up to the large stone chair and sat.

Addie and I sat on the bench behind her.

"Status report," Quinta demanded.

Number One said, "We weren't expecting you yet. We await one group."

"I don't care," Quinta said. "Give me the status report."

Number One made a sound like clearing his throat. "We believe all the FTL drives in the galaxy have been disabled--except for those in our ships, including present company."

"Believe?" Quinta asked. Jeez. She was good at being imperious.

"There might be a few," Number One turned and glared at the AC at the table, "that escaped the special upgrade." I knew that was true since my FTL drive still worked.

The AC looked a little sheepish, which was a good trick for a giant mouse. ACs sold the FTL drives.

"It's inconsequential," the AC said in his deep voice. "If any drives escaped the upgrade, they're owned by criminals. There's no chance a planetary ship like TCC's *Shakespeare* works."

I almost snickered.

Quinta nodded as if she believed him. "Speaking of Terra, what about it?"

"We await their delegation." Number One bowed his head. "But they put up an unexpectedly strong resistance. We do not yet have control." Wait. What? There was a Terran delegation to this war council? Traitors!

Quinta didn't miss a beat. "Who else has a status report?"

The Tao-Cetoan turtle man said, "The Tao Ceto government has surrendered already. My people are in power." He bowed. "We owe you a great debt of gratitude and stand ready to help you in whatever manner you desire, Emperor." Tao Ceto fell? Not good. And Emperor? Ick.

The Keplarrian hissed. "Ssss. We need additional FTL-equipped ships to gain control of the entire system. Keplarrians do not surrender easily."

"Hey!" the Tao-Cetoan said. "Tao-Cetoans don't surrender easily."

Bickering erupted amongst the sentients sitting at the table.

Quinta didn't stop them.

Number One got a call and answered his fon.

I scooted closer to him to try to hear him.

"What do you mean, this is Quintavius?" Number One said. "I don't know who you are, imposter, but I'm looking at the magnificent Quintavius right now!"

Uh oh.

And then, three humans strolled into the clearing. The twenty-something man in the front was exceptionally handsome, tall with curly dark brown hair, in great shape, with an amazing smile. And very, very sexy.

He was me.

Chapter Three

Number One angrily ended his fon call as Number Two greeted the new me in English. "Greetings, Ambassador Jax Jones."

Thus, I cleverly deduced the fake-me went by the name Jax. Several others around the table greeted him. He was apparently quite popular. He was so handsome, I wasn't surprised.

In the meantime, I scooted away from Number One and quietly talked into my comms. "Another me showed up. What should we do?" My mind was racing. We should take him prisoner and interrogate him--that's what we should do. But could we capture him and simultaneously learn what was happening at this meeting? And avoid blowing our cover?

"What?" Gina said over comms. "Speak up." She was no help.

I glanced at Quinta and Addie, and they somehow conveyed keen interest in what I was saying and doing without saying or doing anything.

"Quinta, Addie, if you can hear me, point one of your tentacles to the left," I said quietly over comms.

They both did so.

"Quinta, tell this Jax character you need to talk to him, and we'll grab him and take him back to our ship," I said. "Addie, you hang back a little and tell Number One that Quintavius has been having mental challenges. Tell Number One that Quintavius might not remember even being here now." Yay. If we handled this right, we could sneak out the way we sneaked in--with the added bonus of a new asset.

I stared at them, but they didn't react. "If you're good with the plan, wave a tentacle to the right."

Two tentacles moved slightly to the right.

Quinta made a throat-clearing sound. “Ah, Mr. Jones. Finally,” she said in English.

The interloper looked her way.

“I need to speak with you, Jones,” she said, pointing towards the beach with one of her tentacles.

He took a step towards her, followed by his two hangers-on. Uh oh. It would be much easier to capture one human rather than three.

“Without your minions!” Quinta added. Yay, Quinta. She stood and glided back towards the beach. Jax followed. When I didn’t follow immediately, she called back. “Come, AC minion.”

I stood and scurried after them.

Addie stood and leaned over Number One, speaking quietly.

Number One started looking alarmed.

I hurried after Quinta and Jax to the rocky area adjacent to the vast beach. We were out of sight of the table meeting area. Good.

“What’s this about, your royal highness?” Jax said, smirking.

I was glad I never smirked because it was not a good look on us.

“I know I’m awesome and all,” he said. “But if you want to have sex, no. Too bad, so sad.” He smirked some more. Jeez, was this guy irritating. I’d never met a more irritating guy.

Quinta gave me a look that said, ‘now what?’

Addie rushed up. “Number One got another call from Quintavius. He’s coming. Now.”

Looking at Quinta, Jax pointed at her. “Aren’t you Quintavius?”

Slid, on my face, said, “Bop him on the head! Bop him!

Addie gave my face a dirty look. “Violence is not the answer.”

“Wait a minute,” Jax said. “What’s going on here?” He leaned towards me, staring at my face. “You don’t sound like an AC. Something’s not right here.”

“Bop him with a rock!” Slid said.

I shrugged, leaned down and picked up a rock, and bopped him on the head.

He fell bonelessly to the ground.

“Huh. Glass jaw,” Slid said.

How did a newborn know so many Terran idioms?

"We have a problem," Addie said, pointing towards the water. Another one of those flat-bottomed boats was quickly approaching. That must be Quintavius--the real one.

"No time to lose!" I said. "We need to get this Jax character to our boat and get out of here before they land." I leaned down, grabbed Jax's arms, and tried dragging him towards the beach. He was h-e-a-v-y. There was no way I was this heavy.

We didn't go anywhere, despite my efforts.

"The boat's about to land!" Addie said.

A human called out from the table area, "Are you almost done, Jax?"

"Ack!" Quinta shrieked.

I started taking off my clothes. "Quick, get Jax's clothes off. I'll trade places with him." The ocean breeze felt cool on my skin.

Addie and Quinta quickly disrobed Jax.

Soon, both of us were naked.

He was definitely identical to me. (Lucky guy.)

"Slid, jump off," I said. "Jax is about to be an AC."

Slid jumped onto Jax's face.

The fresh air on my face felt refreshing.

We all started dressing Jax in my AC outfit as a boat landed and three Quihiri stepped onto the beach.

We'd just finished getting Jax dressed as an AC as the first Quihiri stepped off the beach about twenty feet from us.

"Quinta!" I hissed. "Change your disguise."

"Ack." But she morphed into a different Quihiri.

After a few moments, the three new Quihiri stopped next to us.

"What's the meaning of this?" Quintavius said in an imperious voice.

"I'm Jax Jones," I said.

"Yeah." He pointed his tentacles imperiously at the AC on the ground. "Who or what is this? Not an intragalactic incident, I hope."

"Nah." I smiled charmingly. "He just wanted to have sex. You know how crazy the ACs are for me. He tore my clothes off and wouldn't take no for an answer." I relaxed my smile. "I had to bop him on the head. Poor fella, but he'll be all right. The real scar will be my rejection."

Quintavius' color was swirling red and black. Anger, confusion. "And who are you two? I don't recognize you," he said to Addie and Quinta.

Quinta froze.

"We are at your service, sire," Addie bowed--as much an octopus can bow.

Quinta bowed, too.

"They're with me," I said quickly. "Part of my entourage. You don't need to worry about them, sir. They'll take our AC friend back to the embassy for medical care."

"This all seems very irregular," Quintavius said. "I need to consult with my committee."

"Yes," I said. "Great idea. Let's go to the big table." I should play this out and give them time to get away. Plus, I still really wanted to know what was going on at the table.

"Yes," he said, pointing at Addie and Quinta. "You two, stay put."

"Yes, sire," Addie said.

Quinta, seemingly tongue-tied, bowed again.

Quintavius started gliding up the path to the table, and I followed.

He stopped. "Clothes, Jax."

Oh, right. I was still naked. I quickly threw on my clothes and followed them.

I glanced back at Addie and Quinta. I'd have to trust them not to stay put, to get fake Jack back to the *Shakespeare* via our shuttle.

The real Quintavius, his two minions, and I glided back to the table.

I walked around and sat at the big table in front of the two humans. One of them leaned forward. "What did Quintavius want?"

"Shh," Quintavius said.

"Shh," I said.

"Are you, uh, all right, sire?" Number One stammered.

I thrummed like a plucked guitar string, ready to thwart the discovery that the previous Quintavius had been an imposter.

"Yes, of course," Quintavius said to him with a red swirl.

"Anyway, let's get this meeting started."

I was ready to jump up at the smallest provocation.

"Status report," Quintavius demanded. Wow. I was impressed with what a good job Quinta had done. "Let's start with the Alpha Catoblepans," he continued.

"Ah, sire?" Number One said.

"I'd like to hear the report from the Alpha Catoblepans," I burst out.

The sheepish AC said, "All the FTL drives in the galaxy should be non-operational, except for ours, of course."

Quintavius nodded.

"And what about Tao Ceto?" I asked quickly.

The Tao-Cetoan turtle man said, "My people are in power, sire."

"Keplarr?" I asked quickly. Hey, I was totally handling this.

"As I sssaid, we need additional FTL-equipped ssships to gain control of the entire sssystem," the Keplarrian delegate said.

"And what about Terra?" I asked quickly.

Everyone turned and stared at me. Why? I mentally reviewed. Ohh.

"Yes, what about Terra?" Quintavius asked.

Lie, Jack, lie. "I wanted to give my report. The Terrans are all but defeated. They have no ships capable of FTL-travel. Their morale is completely broken. Totally. They are beaten," I said.

"Uh," Number One held up a tentacle. "Our ships are still encountering resistance in the Terran system."

"Token," I said. "It's token resistance. The humans are beaten and broken."

"Uh," Number One held up another tentacle.

"Who would know more?" I asked. "A Terran who just came from the Terran system moments ago? Or some random Quihiri on an island in the middle of the ocean?"

"Uh," Number One said.

"Moving on," Quintavius said.

The chimp-person sitting at the big table said, "Things are under control on Yeblypso. With luck, we'll never have to interact with any of your species again. No offense."

Offense.

The lobster person sitting at the table said, "Same thing on

Xuphitov." I wondered where Xuphitov was.

"Ditto on Sapus," the broccoli creature said. I wondered where Sapus was.

"Excellent." Quintavius got a little sparkly, with a few silver and gold highlights on his torso.

"Sire!" Number One said. "Are you all right?"

I was guessing sparkles weren't typical. Could Quintavius be evolving as Quinta had? What an awesome problem for the jerk. I controlled my grin with difficulty.

Quintavius looked down at his torso and quickly turned black. "So, ah, as I was saying, it sounds like Mission Accomplished. We have successfully isolated our unique systems, protecting our peoples and cultures from outside influences. No longer will we be contaminated by other species." He paused. "No offense."

Offense. It was slowly dawning on me... These people were all speciesists. Not only did they refrain from having sex with other species, but they also didn't even want to interact with them.

"If your planets have any ...undesirable species, you can dispose of them however you see fit," he said.

Dispose of? They didn't want other species alive on their planets?

Oh no. My mood deflated like a pricked gas pod in Jupiter's atmosphere. Thousands, maybe millions, of people were in danger. I needed to do something. At the least, I should tell Gina so she could send out a warning.

But I didn't dare draw attention to my comms while I sat at the table.

"But, we ssstill need help on Keplarr," the delegate said.

"Fine," Quintavius waved his tentacles imperiously. "My people will deal with it. Talk to them." He stood up. "I, ah, need to get back to my honeymoon." Yes, he was leaving quickly. Yes, it was suspicious.

Uh... Now that my nerves about getting caught were fading, I realized I hadn't totally thought this through. The meeting was ending, and I didn't have an escape plan. Shoot.

My ride was gone. I didn't have another extraction plan.

I needed a new plan. The only thing I could think of was: to impersonate Jax and go with these horrible Terrans to find out what else they were doing.

I stood as well. “So, if this mission is completed, our alliance with all of you unsavory non-humans is dissolved. At last. Finally. I hope I never see another non-human again.” I stepped over the stone bench and gestured to my two human minions. I turned back to the folks around the table and smiled. “No offense.” Ha. Take that.

I quickly marched back in the direction Jax had come. My two human minions followed me.

Once we got over the small hill and out of view of the table, I slowed down a little to let them catch up to me. I didn’t know where their ship was or how to get into it.

“Yay!” one of them, the man, said, clapping me on the back. “We did it!” Sadly, I hadn’t even noticed him in the shadow of the other me. He was a pretty ordinary-looking Earthling, about five feet nine inches, with brown skin and brown eyes. He was not wearing a tunic. Instead, he wore brown leather pants, a jacket and boots. I liked his outfit.

“All right!” the female one said. She also looked ordinary, about five feet six inches, with brown skin, brown eyes, and also a nice leather outfit, hers in black. In fact, the two humans looked quite similar.

“Woo hoo!” I said, with two clenched raised fists.

“But the situation on Terra isn’t under control?” the woman said. “Why didn’t you ask for help?”

“We Terrans don’t need help from the likes of them, those octopus people. Ick,” I said.

“Well, you’ve led us this far, Jax,” the man said. “Whatever you think.”

“Hey, are you guys related?” I asked.

“Ha!” the man said. “That’s a good one. You know we’re twins.” He shook his head. “Jax. Always joking around.”

Over the next rise, a small spaceship came into view. It looked like, well, a flying saucer. It was saucer-shaped and had a dull metal exterior.

“That was a pretty horrible meeting with all those aliens,” the woman said, walking right up to the ship and opening the door.

The three of us stood outside for a few moments. I had no idea what I'd find inside, but whatever it was, I could handle it. *Then shall our names, familiar in his mouth as household words.*

"Blech," the man said. "I hate aliens."

We all entered the ship. It was galaxy-class but just barely. The walls, floors, and ceilings were all plain dingy metal. I already missed the *Shakespeare's* vibrant, colorful murals.

"We're aboard, Captain," the man said into some communications device. "Take off when ready."

"Yeah," I said. "Blech, aliens." But what I was thinking was: these humans were blech. I needed to talk to Gina. I could do that in my cabin. Probably. If I had a cabin.

I walked up to the woman and put my arm around her. "Why don't you come with me to my cabin, honey?"

She blushed and nodded. Of course. Who wouldn't want to come with me to my cabin?

She led me down the corridors until we stopped outside a closed door.

I put my palm on the security plate, and it opened up.

The woman, still snuggled under my shoulder, said, "Is it finally going to happen? Are we finally going to you-know?" She had such a look of hope in her eyes.

So... we hadn't had sex before? What was with this Jax guy? Better to be cautious until I figured it out.

"Sorry, honey, " I said. "I'll see you later." I stepped into the cabin and closed the door behind me.

Inside, the cabin looked significantly smaller than my cabin on the *Shakespeare*, with only a small bunk that looked like it folded down from the wall and a tiny toilet and shower area.

Of course, the most blatant difference was the dog lying on the bunk. He was medium-sized with big ears, a cute black nose, long fur, and an engaging half-white, half-black face. He was a border collie. And adorable.

I immediately ran to the bunk, sat down next to him, and started petting him. "Aren't you adorable? What's your name, buddy? Are you my new buddy?" Aw. I gave him a lot of rubbings on his head and along his back. His fur was thick and soft. Maybe this assignment wouldn't be so bad after all.

"Who the hell are you?" he asked. "And what did you do to

Jax?"

I fell off the bunk.

Chapter Four

"You can talk?" I sat on the floor of Jax's cabin. "Wow. You can talk?" This was every little kid's dream come true: a talking dog! I whispered, "*There are more things in heaven and earth...*"

In response, the talking dog(!) bared his teeth and growled a little.

"Ah, I mean, nice doggy. Nice, er...What's your name?" I giggled. This was amazing. "Fido? Rex? Spot? Buster? What's your name?"

He growled again and then said, "The fact that you don't know my name proves my point. Who are you? I won't ask again."

I scooted back a little on the floor. "I'm, uh, sorry, sir. Jax is fine; he's not in any danger. I'm his, uh, brother. My name is Jack Jones. And I'm happy to call you whatever you like. What would you like me to call you?"

His body language relaxed. He tilted his head a little as if thinking. "No one's ever asked me that before." He looked so cute that I had to fight not to pet him some more.

I looked for my fon to check the time. Darn. No fon. My fon'd been left in the middle of a rock field.

"You can call me Sir," he said. "No, Sire. No, King. No, Master. You can call me Master."

I swallowed. I'd asked, so I had to abide by what he said, right?" Yes, Master."

I glanced away from him. I still needed to warn Gina about the impending ethnic cleansings.

When I looked back, he had an expression that looked very much like a smile. "What happened to Jax?"

"He went on my ship, the *Shakespeare*," I said. "It's a good ship. He'll be fine there." People in the brig were fine. Mostly.

"Why are you here?" he asked.

"Ah, Jax asked me to take his place here on his ship."

Master narrowed his eyes. "The other humans won't accept a stranger even if he looks familiar."

"Right," I said. "That's why Jax asked me to pretend to be him. I'm just here to do whatever he would do. You don't mind if I contact my ship for a couple of minutes, do you?" I hoped my comms were still working.

"Can I talk to Jax?"

"Um, yes," I said. "Sure."

I fingered my comms, turning them on. "Gina? Come in. It's Jack."

"Jack? Are you all right?" she asked. "The others contacted me and--"

I interrupted her, talking very quickly. "I'm fine. I need to tell you the Quihiri goal is some type of ethnic cleansing. They want to execute the non-natives on all the planets in the federation, the ACs, the Tao-Cetoans, the Yeblypsons, the Keplarrians, the broccoli people, and the lobster people. I don't remember all the specific names. And the Terrans."

"What?" she asked. "Terrans are just going to execute non-Terran sentients on Earth? No. Impossible."

Suddenly a red light on the ceiling started blinking, and an alarm blared. Some public address system on the ship said, "Alert! Unauthorized transmission! Alert!"

"Ack!" I said. "I have to go! Warn the sentients on each planet!"

Someone knocked on the cabin door. "Jax! What are you doing in there?"

"Bye!" I ended communication with Gina and dug the tech out of my ear. I held it up. Shoot. Where could I put it that wouldn't be detected?

"We're coming in!" The door crashed open.

Master leaned over and gulped down the small communication device.

How was I going to get that back now? And would it even work? And, let's be honest--did I even want it back now?

My new female friend and a male friend I hadn't met yet,

barged into my cabin.

"We detected an unauthorized transmission from this location," the man said.

I leaned back. "Hi, babe." I smiled sexily at the woman.

She blushed.

"Hi, babe." I smiled sexily at the man.

He blushed.

"Gosh, that's a real mystery," I said. "I'm just here hanging out. I was thinking of getting naked and taking a shower. You know, after the tough mission down on the planet with those blech aliens." I rubbed my chest languidly.

"The sensor did identify this location," the woman said. "But could it have been a glitch?"

"That must be it, a glitch," I said. "Nothing going on in here, right, Master?" I looked at the dog.

He did not answer me.

"Oh, Jax!" the man said. "Always a kidder! As if the dog could verify anything."

They both snickered.

"Sorry about barging in, Jax," the woman said as they backed out.

"We're FTL-ing out in a few minutes," the man said.

They carefully closed the door on their way out.

I gave Master a long look. "So, the others don't know you can talk and are smart and stuff?"

"Not exactly." He sounded sheepish. "They wouldn't approve. They're speciesists. It was between Jax and me." He paused. "You won't tell on me, will you?" Now, he sounded hopeful.

"I won't tell on you if you won't tell on me," I said. "It's a deal. Partners. It's a pleasure to officially meet you, Master," I said, holding out my hand. "Ensign Jack Jones at your service. Do you shake?"

"Yes." He held out his paw, and we shook.

"Can I pet you?"

"Okay." His tail wagged a little.

I sat down on the bunk, pulled off my boots, and rubbed his tummy.

His tail wagged a lot.

I eventually got worn out from petting him and leaned back on the bunk next to him. “So, what’s your story, Master?”

He sighed. “Illegal cyber mods. I’ve got some chips in my brain as well as the voice synthesizer.”

“Did it hurt?” I asked.

“No.” He shook his head. “They did it when I was a puppy. I don’t remember any other way. Jax found me and rescued me. We’ve been together ever since.” He paused. “Until now.”

I tried not to feel guilty about separating them. “Where did the mods happen?” I asked.

“On the station, in an illegal genetic lab,” he said. “The same place Jax, and presumably you, were born.”

What was he talking about? “Sure.” I nodded in what I hoped was a confident manner. “Remind me...”

“*The Station*,” he said. “Hotbed of criminals, illegal gene mods, illegal cyber mods, basically the hotbed of illegal every kind of mods.”

“Oh, right, the station,” I said. I didn’t like the idea of illegal clones of me, or technically Old Jack, but I didn’t necessarily mind the idea of a giant free-for-all where anything went.

I was getting sleepy and leaned against the wall, closing my eyes.

“Hey, Jack,” he said. “I’m not a species-ist, but I don’t play like that.”

I opened my eyes.

He pointed his nose at a part of my anatomy, a part that was not sleepy at all. That was odd.

I shoved the pillow in my lap. “Sorry.” My mind was racing. That guy had said they were going to use an FTL drive, and my you-know-what was behaving unexpectedly. One plus one equaled eleven!

I jumped up. “Yes! My power’s back! My power’s back!” Yeah, I’d discovered I had a superpower--basically, I could take advantage of quantum improbabilities that leaked out of FTL probability drives. It enabled me to instantiate improbable realities.

“What is up with you?” he asked.

I needed to quickly think of some unlikely something. Shoot. I couldn’t think fast enough.

"My comms are not in Master's stomach!" I said.

"I don't feel so good..." Master leaned over and puked onto the floor.

"Jax Jones is rich!" I said. "He's got a million credits in his account. And I know what the account is and can access it!"

"What are you doing?" he asked.

"And I have an ansible to talk to Old Jack!" I looked around the room but didn't see any ansible.

"And I have an awesome new outfit." I looked around the room but didn't see any awesome new outfits.

I felt tired. I sat back down on the bunk.

"What was that all about?" Master asked.

"I have a superpower," I said. "Jax didn't have any special power?" I accidentally put my foot in the small spot of sick. "Ick."

"Not that I know of." He shook his head. "I'm not convinced you have a special power. What is it? Inappropriate boners?"

"No," I said. "Well, yes, sort of." I pointed at the floor where my metal comms tech glittered. "I made you puke, didn't I?"

He shrugged.

"How would I access Jax's credits?" I asked.

"There's an app on his fon." He pointed a paw at the drawer.

I opened it, found Jax's fon, powered it up, passed the biometric security screening, and opened the banking app. One million credits. I held it up to Master. Could he read? "A million credits. I bet Jax didn't have that before, did he?"

"No, he didn't," Master said quietly. "I don't think he did, anyway. How'd you do that?"

"It's my superpower." I jumped up and down a little in my one wet and one dry sock.

"Why'd you do it?"

Good question. "Money makes things easier," I said, quieting. "Whatever our scheme is, we'll probably need money to carry it out."

"What do you think our plan should be?" he asked.

"I'm not sure," I said. "What do you think?" I put the fon back and sat down.

"I'm not sure."

"From what I can tell, the people on this ship want to murder all the non-Terrans back on Earth," I said. "Murdering people just because they're different is not okay. I'm not down with that. I want to stop them. Will you help me?"

"Considering they'd probably murder me if they knew what I was truly like, I'm gonna say: Yes."

I flexed my toes in my soggy sock. "But right this minute, my plan is to take a shower." I stepped into the small bathroom, turned on the shower, stripped off my clothes, and stepped under the water. "Ah."

Once I'd gotten my hair all lathered up, I heard, "Jax, this is the captain," in a deep male voice from a speaker on the wall outside the shower stall. "Where are you? We're waiting."

Master stepped into the tiny bathroom. "There's a communications node on the wall. Just press the button."

I reached my arm out of the shower and pressed the button. "Hi, Captain. I'm sorry to keep you waiting. But I'm all wet and soapy right now. And naked. Do you want me to ...come," I grinned, "immediately, or can I finish my shower?"

The captain cleared his throat. "Ah, we can wait a few more minutes. Captain, out."

I finished my shower, taking my time, my mind racing. I had to go to the meeting to maintain my cover. Would they believe I was Jax? What would happen if they figured out I was an imposter?

What was the purpose of the meeting? Planning murders? Could I keep my cover under that circumstance? Could I keep my cool? I wasn't sure my spy skills were up to the task.

I dried myself with a big fluffy towel and exited the bathroom. The vomit was gone, and my comms earbud lay on the bed. How?

I looked at Master. I decided not to ask.

"If I were an awesome new outfit, where would I be?" I glanced around the small room. I opened the storage compartment and found black leather pants and a shirt. "Score! My power worked on this, too!"

Master lay on the bunk with relaxed paws stretched out in front of him. "Jax already had that outfit." He seemed amused.

"I'm a little worried about the meeting," I said as I put on the cool leather. "Do you know what's going on around here?"

"Yeah," he said.

"Can you come with me?"

He tilted his head. "I guess so. But I can't talk, remember?"

I found some socks and bad-ass leather boots that matched the rest of my ensemble. I sat to put them on. "What about a secret code?"

"That could work," he said. "I could give you a little nip when I disagree with something."

"Or, what about a little lick when you agree?" I said.

"That could work, too." He nodded.

I stood, clad head-to-toe in black leather. "Well, at least I know I'll look good whatever happens. Let's go, Master."

"Uh, about that," he said as we trotted out the door together. "In front of the others, you should probably call me Max. In fact, call me Max; it's my name."

"Yes, sir, Master Max, er, Max," I said and stopped. "Uh, where's the meeting?"

"Follow me." He bounded down the grimy hallway.

I followed him through the ship's cramped, plain corridors until he stopped outside a closed door. I whispered, "*Once more into the breach, dear friends, once more*." I opened the door.

Nine tough-looking humans, leather-clad and scarred, turned as one to stare at me.

I gulped.

Chapter Five

I stepped into the dimly-lit meeting room with my new best friend.

The biggest, scariest, scarriest man in the room said, “It’s about time, Jones.” He was also clad all in black leather. His longish black hair had some strands of gray, as did the stubble on his face.

“Uh, sorry ...Cap...” I started to say. I was an imposter, and any of these people looked like they could break me in half. I wasn’t nervous, not nervous at all. Not scared, either.

Max licked my fingers.

Max was right: I was Jack Jones. I was awesome; I could do this. I could do anything! “Sorry, Captain,” I said more confidently. “I had to take a long shower. Those aliens were horrible. Ick. Horrible.”

The twins who had been with me on the planet were nodding enthusiastically.

I found my way to the only empty chair. Max parked himself next to my leg.

“So, I assume the mission was a success?” the captain asked, staring at me. Since he looked like he could bench-press me, I had to force myself not to gulp at his attention.

“Totally a success.” I glanced down at Max. He didn’t do anything. “A huge big old success.”

A woman with very pale skin and no hair said, “What about getting some help subduing Earth? They’re still putting up a fight.”

“Nah,” I said.

“I’m with Jax,” the female twin said.

“Me, too,” the male twin said. “We don’t need the help of aliens.” He grimaced when he said the word ‘aliens.’

"Well, we'll find out soon enough," the captain said. "We're only a few hours out from Earth." He glanced around the table. We'll join the fight and finally remove all non-Terrans from Earth! Earth is meant for Earthlings. Those who oppose us will regret it! Or, rather, they won't live to regret it!" He snickered evilly.

Enthusiastic agreement broke out throughout the room. I heard a lot of 'Yeahs' and 'All rights.'

I said, "Yeah!" to blend in. I'm a good actor, so I'm sure it was believable. But, gulp. I didn't think I could fight people on Earth or in the TCC--no matter their species.

"Shouldn't we eat, rest, and generally get ready to fight, then?" I said. "It's already been a long day, and we need to be at our best to fight our best, right?" I had a brainstorm. "Maybe we should take eight hours or so to sleep?" Eight hours would give me time to figure out my next move.

Eighteen hard eyes looked my way.

"No." The captain scowled. "You've got three hours. Eat or whatever you need to do, but after that, we're joining the fight." Uh oh. That meant I only had three hours to come up with a plan.

Gulp. My mind raced. What could I do to stop them? My only external resources were a great outfit, a talking dog, and a lot of money... Of course, my internal resources were legion.

The meeting broke up. People exited the room.

The female twin approached Max and me. "Buy you dinner, Jax?" she asked, blushing. Wow. She had it bad for me. But I couldn't blame her. Even as Jax, I was pretty awesome.

And when was the last time I'd eaten?

In the meantime, Max was licking my fingers again.

"Sure," I said. "Me and Ma-ax would be happy to join you."

She took a step back. "Ah. Okay." She shrugged. "Let's go."

I followed her (the scenery, her behind, was lovely) and Max through the dingy corridors to a widening of the hallway, made into a rectangular kitchen area. One wall had counters, a sink, a small oven, and cabinets above and below. A rectangular metal-topped table sat in the middle of the space, surrounded by mismatched chairs and stools.

Two other crewmembers, both big burly guys, were there preparing food. Not knowing names was getting to be a real problem.

"Can I cook for you, Jax?" she asked.

The gentlemanly thing to do would be to cook *for* the comely maiden, but what would Jax do? I glanced down at Max.

He licked my fingers.

"Sure, babe." I smiled and sat in a chair. Max sat next to me on the floor.

As the cute female twin worked her kitchen magic, my mind raced. Three hours, I only had three hours to come up with a plan. That *should* be at least two and a half hours more than I needed.

"Hey, Logan!" one guy yelled. "Those are my mushrooms! Get your greasy mitts off them." He appeared to be a delightful smorgasbord of different human races and was one of the relatively smaller members of the crew (which on this crew wasn't that small).

"You snooze, you lose, Eli," the other guy, presumably, Logan, said and gave him a mean-looking smile. His muscles put the other guys to shame. He had very dark skin, and his skull was as smooth as a billiard ball.

Eli shoved Logan, and the container of mushrooms fell on the floor. Logan pushed Eli back. Wow. These guys seriously liked fungi.

While I didn't approve of crewmembers scuffling, I was appreciating all the name-calling. Now, I knew the names of Eli and Logan.

Max crept sneakily in the direction of the food on the floor.

Cute-female-twin-slaving-over-the-stove said, "Come on, guys. Soon we'll be back on Earth and have more food than we can eat."

"Shut up, Aria," Eli said. "This is none of your business." Ah ha. The tantalizing twin was Aria.

Max had almost reached the spill.

"Freeze, Mutt," Logan said. "Or, you'll feel my boot up your ass."

Max looked at me. Oh, right. He wasn't supposed to understand English.

"Here, boy," I said. "Come here, Max." I clapped my hands together.

Max came back to sit next to me.

Eli knelt and picked up his food. "I paid a lot of money for these," he muttered.

Ah ha. A plan was coalescing. What do criminals love more than anything else (besides possibly mushrooms)? Money. And who had a lot of money? Yours truly.

I just had to get each of them alone and bribe them with money or charm to do what I wanted them to do.

All I had to do was figure out what that was.

I needed more intel, and the only person I knew who could give it to me was Max. "Uh, Aria. I need to 'take Max for a walk,' if you know what I mean?"

"I know what you mean, Jax," she said. "Everyone knows what you mean. Go ahead. It's still a few minutes until the food is ready."

I stood up, said, "Heel, Max," and quickly walked back to my cabin. He followed, only nipping my fingers once when I took a wrong turn.

Once we were inside our cabin with the door closed behind us, he said, "Thanks, Jack. I do need to go."

"How does that work?" I asked. It wasn't like we had a handy tree around.

He tilted his head a little and somehow conveyed the idea that I was not the smartest homo sapiens he'd met. He walked into the tiny bathroom and climbed up on the toilet seat. "A little privacy, please?"

"Sorry." I turned away as he did his business, including flushing the toilet. How? At that point, I was wishing I had taken a peek.

"Okay," he said, now standing next to me.

"So, I'm thinking I can bribe all the criminals *not* to attack Earth. What do you think?" I asked.

"I think they love money and don't have any morals, so it should work," he said. "Except for the captain; he's like a dog with a bone." He paused. For a laugh? "We should get back to the kitchen."

"Does Jax have any special relationships with anyone? Sexual?" I asked, purely for the plan's sake, of course. "They'd be people to start with."

"No," Max said. "Jax doesn't have sex." He did a dog shrug.

"He says it's a sin."

"That's crazy!" I said. "Hasn't he ever heard of 'be fruitful and multiply?'"

"I don't know," he said. "It's a weird quirk, based on what he heard about the original Jack or something." He sounded sad. About Jax or himself? I was guessing a sentient dog didn't get a lot of opportunities to have sex either, poor guy.

"So, it's a clean slate," I said. "I could seduce everyone and win them over."

Max growled a little. "No. I think that would be dangerous. It's too out of character. Let's go back."

So, it would be a charm offensive without carnal delights. Challenging--but I was just the guy to rise (so to speak) to the challenge. And if charm didn't work (unlikely), there was all that lovely money.

Back in the kitchen, Eli and Logan each finished their meal preparations and took off in opposite directions to eat.

I petted Max and gave him some rubs as Aria finished cooking. She placed a plate of noodles in front of Max on the floor and in front of me on the table. It smelled delicious, like chicken and spices. I leaned over and sniffed deeply. "Mmmmm," I said.

She handed me some chopsticks and then sat down next to me with her plate.

I took a bite: citrus, sweet, but not too sweet, sour, peanuts, chicken. The bean sprouts were crunchy. "Yum. Pad Thai. Delicious. This is one of my favorites. Thanks, Aria."

She beamed. "Yeah, we like traditional Terran food on this ship."

I decided to put my charm offensive on hold for a few moments as I shoveled food into my empty belly via my gullet.

Once our plates were clean, Aria patted my hand on the table. "My mama always told me the way to a man's heart is through his stomach."

Charm offensive, back on. I leaned toward her. "Your mama is a very wise woman." I leaned closer. "And if she's anything like you, very beautiful, as well."

Aria blushed.

"In fact, you should come back to my cabin to discuss this

some more," I said sexily.

She stood up immediately. "Okay!"

Max nipped my fingers.

I glanced down at him. "You'll be okay here on your own, right, Max?" I quickly moved away from him.

Max growled a little.

"Good boy," I said. "I'll owe you."

I grabbed Aria's hand as we walked back to my cabin.

"It's cute how you always talk to him like he can understand you," she said.

"I think you'll find there are many, many things about me that are cute," I said in a sexy voice.

I pulled her inside and onto the small bed when we reached my cabin. The two of us did not fit on it without pressing all kinds of body parts together in a most delectable way.

She giggled. "Jax."

"*Shall I compare thee to a summer's day? Thou art more lovely*." I kissed her, and she kissed back enthusiastically.

She moaned. "Oh, Jax." We kissed for several glorious minutes. It was lovely.

Then, she pushed me away. "I'd do just about anything for you if you make love to me."

"Okay," I said sexily.

"What!" She shrieked. "Really? You want to get engaged? Oh, my God! That is so awesome!"

I must admit, at this point, I was just the tiniest bit confused. "So, we're engaged...?"

"Yes." She nodded. "You always said you could never make love until you were married. Maybe the captain can marry us right now!"

My spy skills were taxed to the almost-breaking point. "I, ah, am honored to be engaged to you, Aria, but what's the rush?"

"Sex is the rush, silly." She giggled. "And we're about to go into battle. We might die."

"You make excellent points, beloved, but I want to savor our engagement," I said. "I want to anticipate our love-making, to look forward to it."

"Oh, I know what you mean," she said.

We kissed some more.

I was getting slightly distracted. What was the mission? Oh yeah, dissuade Aria from attacking Earth. I pushed her away. “Beloved, perhaps since our love is so strong, we don’t need to attack Earth?”

She blinked at me. “What do you mean?”

“What if we sneak away when we get to Earth,” I said. “The two of us could go off, get married, and live our life together in peace.”

“But, the mission,” she said. “We’ve come so far already.” She scrunched up her nose. “We interacted with aliens.”

“You are more important to me than the mission,” I said. “Are you saying I’m not more important to you?”

She put her cute little hands on my chest. “Oh, you are. You are.”

“So, it’s decided, then?” I asked. “When we get to Earth, we both sneak away?”

She nodded and started to get off the bed. “Yes. Yes! I’m so excited! I have to go tell Aaron!”

I was guessing Aaron was her twin. I pulled her back down. “Maybe we should keep our engagement secret for now? We don’t want him or the others to get jealous of us, right?”

“Well, Aaron does have a bit of a crush on you, too,” she said. Very interesting.

“It’s decided then.” I nodded. “We are engaged, and it’s a secret. And in the meantime, we’ll act like nothing unusual is happening.”

She nodded, too.

“So, where do you think Aaron is now?” I asked casually. If a secret engagement worked on one twin, it might work on another.

“Probably in his cabin,” she said.

Someone scratched at my cabin door and then barked softly.

“Looks like Max got tired of waiting around.” Aria stood. “I should do some work for our cover story.”

“Good idea.” I gallantly showed her to the door. When I opened it, Max bounded in. Aria exited, and I closed the door.

“What’s up?” he asked.

“Where’s Aaron’s cabin?”

Chapter Six

I knocked on Aaron's cabin door. (I'd left my boon companion, Max, in our cabin.) Aaron was in for a treat: me! "*Journeys end in lovers meeting, every wise man's son doth know.*"

He didn't answer.

I knocked again.

No answer. Where was he? What I needed was to call him. I patted my pockets. Unfortunately, I had no fon. Egad. I felt naked--no, that wasn't it--I felt disconnected without it.

Just then, 'little' Eli clomped by. The size of his boots was impressive and made me wonder about his other proportions.

"Hey, Eli," I said charmingly.

He stopped and glanced at me. Sadly, it wasn't an overly-friendly glance.

I'd have to work on that. I smiled and stepped right up to him. "How's it going, Eli? Are you good, buddy? You look good." I said that last bit in a sexy manner.

"Fine, whatever," he said gruffly. When I didn't stop smiling, he added, "How's it going with you, Jax?"

"Fine." I stepped right up to him and gazed into his eyes. They were a warm brown, flecked with gold. Nice.

He didn't move away. Maybe I should try seducing him next?

He took a step away. "You looking for Aaron? He's in engineering." He turned and resumed clomping down the hall.

"Thanks, buddy!" I called after him.

Now, I just had to go to engineering and seduce twin number two. Easy-peasy. I examined the dingy, nondescript hall stretching out in front of me. I glanced behind me for more of the same.

Too bad I didn't know where engineering was.

I could wander around and find it--probably quickly, knowing me--but time was of the essence. I ran back to my cabin and popped inside, disturbing Max, napping on my (his?) bunk.

"Where's engineering?" I asked.

"Lowest deck," he said. "What now? Are you thinking of sabotage? Interesting."

I hadn't been thinking of sabotage.

Until now.

"Thanks!" I turned and ran back out of the cabin.

"Tick tock!" he said before the door closed. He didn't need to tell me I was running out of time.

I quickly made my way down to the lowest deck by sliding down the ladders. But no one saw my nimbleness. Too bad for them.

Engineering looked very similar to the engineering department on the *Shakespeare*. It was a large, dimly-lit room filled with large blocky equipment with loads of blinking LED lights in shades of green.

"Aaron? You down here, buddy?" I called out.

"Jax?" he called back. "Yeah. Over here."

I made my way around some equipment to find him kneeling on the ground over the FTL drive. He'd pulled it a little out of its niche, but it was still connected to the ship.

"So, how's it look?" I asked. "Ship-shape?"

"Ship what?" he asked, clearly confused.

Ugh. That was probably an old-fashioned idiom people didn't use anymore. (My original body was over fifty years old, but I'd lost thirty years of those memories.) I knelt next to him. "How's the drive look?"

"Fine," he said. "It's crazy how those creepy squids can make such great tech."

Technically, they were octopuses, not squids, but I didn't think telling him that would serve my purposes. And, oh, yeah, technically, not real octopuses, just convergent-evolution-octopuses. Focus, Jack. I shook my head.

"So, ah, thanks so much for going down to the planet with me," I said. "I appreciated having you as backup. You're so big and strong." I rubbed his arm. "And handsome." He was handsome. I gazed into his eyes. His dark brown eyes were flecked with lighter brown. Nice.

A flush rose under his brownish skin, and he looked like he might giggle at any moment. I leaned in and pressed my lips to his.

He threw his arms around me and enthusiastically kissed me back. We fell to the floor. When we finally came up for air, he said, “I can’t believe it finally happened! You don’t know how long I’ve been waiting to do that.”

Judging from his enthusiasm, I was guessing it had been a long time. “Well, the main thing is we connected now.”

“Getting married! It’s a dream come true. What changed your mind, Jax?” He gazed into my eyes. He was quite adorable. But I did not understand this marriage-crazy, no-premarital-sex aspect of Jax at all.

“I guess *there is a tide in the affairs of men which taken at the flood, leads on to fortune,”* I said. *“Omitted, all the voyage of their life is bound in shallows and in miseries. On such a full sea are we now afloat, and we must take the current when it serves, or lose our ventures.*”

He grabbed me again, and we rolled around, kissing and hugging. It reminded me of some very energetic, if very friendly, wrestling.

It was all going quite swimmingly until an alarm went off. ‘Warning. Warning. Leaving FTL space. FTL drive failure.’

We both sat up and glanced over at the FTL drive. Wires trailed behind as it had been pushed far from its cradle.

“Oops,” I said and grinned.

“Oh, no!” Aaron said. “This is bad. Oh, no!”

“We can just reconnect it,” I said.

“But no one on board knows how to connect it!” he said. “And what if it’s broken! Oh, my God! The captain’s going to kill me.” When he looked at me, there was real fear in his eyes.

“Surely, he won’t actually kill you,” I started to say.

“What about Oliver?” he practically shrieked. “The chief engineer before me? The captain threw him out of the airlock! Oh, my God!”

“Aaron! What did you screw up, now!” a deep voice, the captain’s voice, boomed out from the top of the ladder.

We both stood up.

"You have to hide!" he said. "Hide!" He pushed me further into the dimly-lit space. "Please! If anything happened to you, I'd never forgive myself."

I heard boots descending the ladder.

"But I don't want anything to happen to you, either," I said. I didn't. "I can talk to the captain."

"Hide!" he said. "If you care about me at all, hide!" He pushed me toward the back of the room.

The poor man was genuinely terrified. What kind of a den of thieves had I gotten myself into?

As the captain strode into the room, I slipped behind a big boxy piece of equipment. He looked like an angry ambulatory mountain.

Eli followed behind the captain. Eli looked like an angry ambulatory hill. They were both scowling. I'm not gonna lie; in their black leathers, with their scars, they were on the intimidating side. How did Jax fit in with these people?

"What happened to the FTL drive?" the captain asked.

Aaron stood in front of him, quivering. "Uh, sir, uh, I was, uh…."

The captain drew a fist back and sucker-punched him in the jaw. "When I ask you a question, answer me!"

Aaron fell to the ground, clutching his jaw.

All right, this was too much. I stepped out from behind the machine. "Captain. Eli." I nodded at each of them in turn. "The drive just stopped working," I said. "We *just* now pulled it out to check on it. That's it, Cap, I swear."

Eli's face seemed to relax when he saw me.

The captain also seemed to simmer down some. He glanced at Aaron on the ground at his feet. "Is this true, Aaron?"

"Uh, yes, uh, sir," Aaron stammered through lips already starting to swell.

"It was probably those horrible aliens," I said. "The drive's from them. They probably double-crossed us. Right, Eli?" I gave him a look that said, 'Go along with me now, and I'll make it worth your while later.'

"That's true. You can't trust an alien, Cap," Eli said, nodding.

Yay, Eli!

"Damn them!" The captain clenched his fists. "Those damn squids!"

Not squids.

Aaron scrambled to his feet. He glanced at me and said faintly, "Damn squids."

"What are we going to do about the drive?" The captain pointed at the mess that had been the FTL drive.

"We'll just have to find someone to fix it," I said. "Where are we? Any planets nearby?"

"We are near the station, Cap," Eli said. "Maybe someone there can help."

Someone here could help: me. But I was all about stopping the brigands from reaching Earth. "Good idea, Eli."

"Shit." The captain turned and strode to the ladder. "This shit is the last thing I need. Come on, Eli, Jax. We'll need to arm up for the station and devise a strategy." He turned around. "Aaron, try to fix this mess."

Still clutching his jaw, Aaron nodded.

The captain started climbing the ladder. Eli followed.

After patting Aaron's back and whispering, "Bye, Aaron," I followed them up the ladder. I followed them through the next level's hallway to a large storeroom chock full of weapons.

They both started putting on some armored vests. I stared as they moved on to armor for their shins and thighs.

"Why are you just standing there, Jax?" the captain said. "You know better than anyone how dangerous the station is." Me? How did I know? Jax must know. I needed to consult Max ASAP.

I whispered, "*On such a full sea are we now afloat*," as I followed suit and started putting on my own armor.

Once we were armored up, Cap passed out various non-projectile weapons: an electromagnetic pulse gun, a taser, and knives of various kinds. I watched them slip each into various pockets and holsters and did as they did. Briefly, I thought of beautiful Eva, the *Shakespeare*'s self-defense expert, who could probably tell me how to use all of them. I hoped she and the *Shakespeare* were okay.

"You ready, then?" the captain asked us.

Eli glanced at me. "What's the strategy?"

"We're finding someone to fix the FTL drive," the captain said. "Obviously. And we'll get them to help us, whatever it takes."

Eli and I both nodded.

"I should bring Max," I said quickly. I needed backup now if I ever did. "I have contacts on the station." I was guessing. "And they'll expect Max to be with me." I was guessing.

"Yeah," the captain said. "Hurry up. Meet us on the bridge."

"Yes, sir." I hurried to my cabin.

When the door slid open, Max took one look at me and sighed. "We're going to the station?"

"Yeah," I said. "I need your help."

"I don't suppose I can talk you out of it?" he asked. What was the deal with that place?

"No," I said. "I don't think the captain would go for that. What's his name anyway?"

"Captain," Max said. Obviously, that was a joke. "He only lets us call him Captain." He jumped up off the bed. "This is not going to be pretty. We weren't supposed to stop there. Why did we come out of FTL space? Did you sabotage the drive?"

I was pretty sure I could trust Max, but I didn't want to admit I broke the ship by rolling around on the floor with Aaron. "Those darn squids must have double-crossed us."

He said, "Huh," somehow conveying disdain.

"Can you tell me anything about this station?" I asked.

"It's exactly as bad as you've heard," he said.

I hadn't heard anything. "Oh?" But I said it in a worldly way.

"A lawless zone, full of illegal gene mods," he tilted his head for a moment, "criminal enterprises, including all manner of drugs, gambling, mercenaries, murder and anything else for hire, and ...slavery."

"Slavery!" I couldn't believe it in this day and age. "*This thing of darkness*." My nervousness had morphed into sadness. "Sentients shouldn't own sentients. That's just wrong."

"I agree with you there," he said. "And I know you, of all people, feel that way." Why me? Was he mixing me up with Jax? Did Jax have experience with slavery?

We stood there in silence for a moment. "The captain's waiting," I said. "We should go." I grabbed Jax's fon.

The two of us raced to the bridge. The captain and Eli were sitting in the pilot and co-pilot chairs. As soon as Max and I entered, we flew off with a jerk. Max and I scrambled to sit down. I had to strap him in. (No hands was a significant disadvantage.)

I had nothing to do as we flew to the station but think. I didn't want the bad guys to fix their FTL drive. But it was unlikely anyone on the station could do it. What then? Arrest the whole crew on behalf of TCC? That would be a good trick. How? And put them where?

Honestly, I was having trouble focusing on the captain and his crew of bad guys because I couldn't stop thinking about slavery. Max must have been a slave, poor guy. I petted his warm furry back and scratched his tummy. He seemed to like it.

As we approached, through the viewscreen, the station looked like a haphazard group of spaceships and space debris stuck together.

And what had he meant by 'me of all people'? Could Jax have been a slave? Poor guy; that would be horrible. I realized I really, really did not like slavery. All too soon, we were docking at the station.

The four of us walked to the airlock, ready to disembark.

"It's night, local time," Eli said.

The captain said, "You will never find a more wretched hive of scum and villainy." Then, he smiled and opened the door.

Chapter Seven

I stepped onto the station with Max, Eli, and the captain. A short hallway opened onto a bustling, dimly-lit, colossal space filled with carts, booths, and stores. The busy marketplace was big enough for a sizable spaceship to fit inside; maybe it originally had another purpose? At any rate, now, all manner of sentients whisked back and forth. It smelled musty, like machine oil and sweat. "Maybe we'll cover more ground if we split up," I said.

"Good idea, Jax," the captain said and hiked off immediately.

"Uh, I guess I'll see you later, then, Jax?" Eli asked.

I smiled sexily. "Sure."

He walked off, as well.

Once they were both out of sight, Max said, "What's your plan, Jack?" So, he wasn't afraid to talk here. Interesting.

"I need to buy a fon," I said.

"Why don't you just use Jax's fon?" he asked.

"I don't want the captain to listen to my conversations or track me." Yes, I'd learned some lessons in my short life. "And I need a private place to use my new fon."

"You should rent a room," he said. "Come on. I know a good place for both." He quickly led me to a dingy storefront where I purchased said fon and then to an equally dingy bar. The bar was a large room with a high ceiling and a sad collection of mismatched fake-woodgrain tables and chairs, a staircase along one wall, and a hallway leading somewhere in the back corner.

"Rooms upstairs," Max said, gesturing at the stairs with his cute nose as we walked inside. He led me to the bar proper along the back wall.

"What'll you have?" the bartender asked. He seemed to

be one of the lobster species I'd seen at the meeting on Quihiri. What were they called again? He scanned my armor and weapons.

When I didn't immediately answer, he said, "Well?"

"A room," Max said.

"For the two of you?" the bartender said. "Never mind. No judgments. Ten credits an hour. The first ten are payable now. Food and drink, extra."

"And a fon," Max said.

"A hundred credits," the bartender said.

I sent him the credits via Jax's fon.

He handed me a package, pressed some keys on his fon, and said, "Room ten, first floor."

Max and I adjourned to room ten. It looked the same way motel rooms look all over the galaxy: a bed, a table, a chair, and a small bathroom, albeit on the small and scruffy side.

Max jumped up on the bed and lay down, sniffing everything. I tried not to think of what might be on that bedspread.

"They must have room service here." I took a couple of steps and then sat down next to him. "You want something to eat or drink?"

"Sure," he said. "Water and steak, very rare."

I set Jax's fon down next to him. "Can you order it?" I wasn't entirely sure what talking dogs could do.

"Yeah," he said. "Voice activation."

"Good. Water and steak for me as well, but medium."

"Okay." He leaned over Jax's fon and started talking into it.

I stood up, walked into the tiny bathroom, put the toilet seat down, and sat on it. There was some other plumbing apparatus next to it that looked sort of like an empty sink on the floor, which I couldn't identify.

I had to work hard to unwrap my new fon from its plastic packaging, but I finally yanked it out. I called Gina, getting her voicemail, of course. She was probably at least several light minutes away from me.

"Hi, Gina. It's Jack. I'm okay. I'm still with Jax's crew. We had to stop at the station for repairs to their ship." I paused. "Something happened to their FTL drive, somehow." I snickered.

"So, anyway, they're out of commission. Call me back at this number and let me know where the *Shakespeare* is and how I can help. Hopefully, the Quihiri have been foiled by now. Hopefully…" I trailed off. I didn't like to think of sentients all over the galaxy being murdered. "Please call me back right away." I stared at the fon for a few moments. She didn't call me back right away. There was nothing else to say until I knew what was going on, so I turned it off.

I sat in the bathroom for a few moments ruing the fact I couldn't do a memory backup since I didn't have my memory app. It had been hours and hours since I'd backed up my memories. It made me feel uneasy.

I went back into the bedroom where Max and Jax's fon still lay on the bed.

"Don't trust me, huh?" Max said.

"Huh?" I said intelligently.

"You went into the bathroom to make your call," he said.

"It was in case room service came; I didn't want the employee to hear me," I said and sat beside him.

"Oh, okay," he said. "They didn't come yet." He'd been surprisingly helpful already.

"I'm thinking I need to move Jax's money," I pointed at his fon, "somewhere where the captain and the rest of them can't find it. Untraceable." I held up my new fon. "Do you have any ideas?"

"Yes," he said. "Give me your new fon." He started talking into one fon after the other, back and forth.

Soon, he said, "It's done." Wow. I was glad I'd asked him.

"Thanks, Max," I said. "You would make a good spy."

His tail was wagging, and he seemed to smile.

Just then, there was a knock on the door. "Room service."

While I ate, I pondered what to do next, but I decided I didn't know until Gina got back to me.

"So, now what?" Max asked once he'd finished eating.

"Good question," I said. "Is there anything you'd like to do? You've been super helpful. I'd be happy to help you with something if you need it."

His mouth fell open. Finally, he said, "Really?"

"Yes." I nodded.

"I would like to try to see my parents," he said. He sounded sad and wary.

"They're here on the station?" I asked.

He nodded. "They were. I was born here. In a lab."

That didn't sound good. "You think they're okay?"

"Doubtful," he said. "They weren't okay when I knew them. They were prisoners...." He choked up.

"Well, we better go find out and help them!" I stood up. "Just tell me where."

"It might be dangerous." He stood up on the bed.

"Danger knows full well that Caesar is more dangerous than he," I said. "My middle name is Danger." Huh. I didn't think I had a middle name. Maybe it should be Danger. Or, Caesar.

"If you're sure," he said.

I nodded.

"Well, it is the night shift here," he said. "The lab should have a skeleton crew."

"Sounds like just the kind of thing Jack Jones, superspy, would do. Let's go!" Besides, we had armor and weapons, right?

I deliberately left Jax's fon in the room in case my new crew was tracking it.

Max led us to the lowest level of the station. My footsteps echoed on the metal flooring of the dark hallway. I didn't know what it was, but it felt like walking through a graveyard.

We stopped in front of a door with a lighted security panel.

Max didn't say anything for a moment.

"Max?" I whispered. "You okay, buddy?"

But he just said, "I might know the security code if they haven't changed it." He rattled off a stream of numbers.

"Wait," I said, reaching out to the pad. "Say it again, slower." He did, and I input the numbers, appreciating my fingers. The door popped open.

"Be careful!" he said.

I peeked my head in. The room just inside the door looked like a science lab. A snoring human in a uniform sat in front of a computer.

I stepped inside and tased him. "Sorry, dude."

I waved Max inside.

He walked in cautiously, sniffing, and looking every which way. "He's the only guard. Come on." He walked to a windowed door in the back with another security pad.

I glanced through the window and saw two large dogs and several puppies in cages. This was not going to be good. They were all border collies with long fur, mostly white, with various black or dark brown patches.

Max gave me the code, I input it, and the door snicked open with a puff of equalizing air. I smelled dog. We entered the inner lab, and I closed the door behind us.

Immediately all the dogs started barking. The adorable puppies jumped up, tails wagging. The adult dogs did not stand up. Not good.

Max barked a lot and ran up to the adult dogs.

I followed him more slowly.

The biggest dog looked ancient, hooked up to medical machines, covered in scars with strange metal devices attached in various places, and held down with straps. I'd never seen anything like it; it was horrifying.

Despite the seemingly happy puppies, this was not a good place.

"Max, Max, is that you?" the big dog asked in a robotic voice.

The other adult dog, a female, whined. She was also hooked up to machines, covered with scars and devices, and held down by straps. Also horrifying.

"Yes, Dad, it's me," Max said, tears in his voice. "Mom. I came back to save you, to save all of you."

The adult female whined louder. Poor thing.

The male glanced at her. "No, Max. You need to get out of here. It's too dangerous."

The female whined again. Ugh. My heart hurt.

"And it's too late for us," Dad said. He paused, gave Max a pleading look, and then looked directly at me. "Young man, you have to help us. Please, kill us. We've been here for years. Much longer than a normal lifespan. They'll never stop experimenting."

Stunned, I couldn't speak.

"Can't lose you…." Max stopped talking, seemingly

overcome with emotion.

"Forcing us to make new children they experiment on and sell," Dad said. Left unsaid was, 'like you, Max.'

Mom whined loudly.

"No," Max said. "I'm getting you out of here, all of you. All of you."

"If you disconnect us, we'll die," Dad said. "Please do it."

Max fell onto the floor, whining, head down, covering his nose with his paws.

I felt tears on my cheeks, and my brain rebooted. "I can do it."

"No, no," Max said.

"Please," Dad said. "I'm begging you. Put your mother and me out of our misery."

"I ...think it's the right thing to do," I said. "We need to stop this--" I waved my hands around. "Once and for all. No one should be treated like this." I felt sick. Being tortured was horrible, but being forced to create children who were then abused was unspeakable. This needed to stop.

My mind raced. I could euthanize the adult dogs with an electromagnetic pulse; it would be instantaneous. And actually, that would probably work on the computers, too.

I went over to the cage of puppies and unlatched it. They bounded out and ran to Max lying on the floor and started jumping on him and licking him. I opened the other cages.

After several moments, he lifted his head.

"I'll take care of it, sir," I said. "And destroy the computers. Max, you get these pups out of here to safety."

Mom barked, and the puppies ran to her, barking, jumping, and licking. She seemed to tell them something, and they started whining, but then they went to the door and stood there.

"You have to destroy our bodies afterward," Dad said. "We don't want there to be a chance they could clone us and start the whole process over."

My blood froze at the word 'clone.' Hadn't Jax been born here on the station? Had it been in a lab like this? "Everything will be destroyed," I said grimly. "You have my word."

"There's a biological hazard system for the lab," Dad said. "To destroy pathogens. Very high-temperature flames inundate the entire room."

"I'll do that, sir," I said.

Max still lay on the floor, whining a little.

"Come on, puppies. Be quiet now." I led them into the other room near the outer door. "Stay." They stayed.

I pulled one of the computers from the desk, carried it, wires dangling, into the back lab, and set it on the floor. I sprayed it with the electromagnetic pulse. "Say your goodbyes, Max."

He slowly got to his feet as if he was an old man. He walked right up to his mom's cage and barked something. She barked back. His head hung down.

I went into the outer lab, sprayed everything with an electromagnetic pulse, and got the other computer. The guard continued snoring, lucky for us.

Dad was saying, "I'm depending on you to take good care of your brothers and sisters, Max. I know you can do it."

After I put down the second computer, I sprayed all the electrical equipment in the inner lab with an electromagnetic pulse.

"I will, Dad," Max said, voice breaking. "I love you."

"I know," Dad said. "Me and Mom know. We love you. Now get out of here. Quick."

Max hesitated a moment but ran out of the room. I heard him giving instructions to the puppies. "We're going out into the station...."

I held up the blaster. I cleared my throat. "This will be instantaneous."

"Do it," Dad said.

Before I could lose my nerve, I blasted Mom. She instantly stilled, now at peace.

"*To sleep, perchance to dream*," I whispered.

"Thanks..." Dad was saying. He stopped talking mid-sentence when I blasted him. He was at peace. No one could ever hurt him again.

"*Good-night, sweet prince; and flights of angels sing thee to thy rest*."

I ran out of the room, closed the door, and pushed the big red button. Fire immediately engulfed the air-tight room. I ran through the outer lab, where the security guard was still slumped in his chair and right on out the open door into the hallway where Max and eight adorable puppies stood.

I punched the door closed behind us. "We have to get out of here!"

Max said, "Run!"

Chapter Eight

On the villainous space station, once me and Max and his eight brothers and sisters were well away from that horrific lab and what I'd done, we all stopped in a deserted hallway to catch our breaths. Just before dawn, here on the lowest levels, no one was stirring. The puppies all flopped onto the ground, panting.

I couldn't remember ever feeling so grim. Things on the station had definitely taken a bad turn.

"What now?" Max asked.

"We need a safe place to hide out and plan our next move," I said.

"Back to your room?" he asked.

"No." I shook my head. "I don't think that's secure enough. We need a secret place."

"I might know somewhere," he said. "But secrecy will cost you."

I shrugged. "It's worth it. Lead on."

Max led us to a much more seedy area of the station and inside a nondescript-looking doorway. He gestured with his nose towards the check-in area, surrounded by a clear plastic barrier.

As I approached the desk, the night clerk stirred. "What do you want?"

"I want a room with two beds and a bathroom," I said. "And I don't want anyone to know we're here."

The employee, one of those orange-brown fur-covered monkey-resembling species, looked us over. "I don't want any trouble. Privacy costs extra."

I nodded once. "Of course."

He quoted a price twice what I'd paid for the other room, and I paid it. He gave me two keycards, and we all trudged to the room.

When we got inside, the pups perked up, running around sniffing everything. Personally, I was unimpressed with the room. This place made my other accommodation look luxurious. Had this room ever been cleaned?

One pup tried to jump up on one of the beds, but he didn't quite make it. I leaned over and placed him gently on top.

Max jumped up on the bed as well. "These youngsters need to sleep. They've had a tough night."

"You've all had a tough night." I started scooping up puppies and putting them on the bed. Soon, all nine dogs were on the bed. They were enjoying smelling the smells on the bedspread.

Max barked something, and they all lay down. "They are all riled up."

I knew just what they needed. I cleared my throat and started singing softly. "*Lullaby, and good night, in the skies stars are bright. May the moon's silvery beams bring you sweet dreams.*" As I sang, their eyes got heavy and closed. Soon, they were all breathing regularly.

"*Hush, darling one, sleep through the night. Sleep through the night, sleep through the night.*" The only sounds in the room were the quiet ins and outs of tiny breaths as little puppies slept, safe and sound.

Out of this nettle, danger, we pluck this flower, safety.

I quietly poked Max in the shoulder. He'd also been breathing regularly. He opened his eyes and gave me a look that said, 'What now?'

I put my finger in front of my mouth in the universal shush gesture and pointed at the bathroom.

He nodded and very carefully extracted himself from the bed.

The two of us went into the bathroom and closed the door behind us.

"We need some rest, too," he said.

"I know, but I think I need to check in with the captain and Eli," I said. "I don't want them to think I've abandoned the ship."

"Haven't you abandoned the ship?" he asked.

As far as I knew, the ship we came in on was the only one with a working FTL drive on the station. "I need the ship. We need the ship. I don't think you and the puppies are safe here on the station. We need to get you guys out of here."

Of course, I also had my concurrent earlier-assigned missions, namely foiling my current crew of thieves, saving Earth, thwarting the evil Quihiri, and winning an intragalactic war.

An FTL-capable ship would come in handy for all of that.

"But where would we be safe?" he asked.

They would be safe on the *Shakespeare*--except for that pesky intragalactic war. I shouldn't take a bunch of youngsters into a war zone.

"Back on Earth?" I said. "There must be some places there safe from the war. And there are a lot of humans who love dogs."

He growled. "I don't want to be someone's property again."

"No, nothing like that." I held up my hands. "You won't be property. I think it's the best shot for all of you."

He quieted, seemingly thinking. "Well, maybe you're right," he said softly. "I do need to consider my brothers and sisters."

"Of course, I'm right," I said. "For now, you go rest up with the others, and I'll meet with Eli and the captain and try to figure out our next step." I opened the door.

"Thanks for your help, Jack," he said quietly. "I appreciate it." He jumped up on the empty bed and closed his eyes.

I closed the bathroom door again and accessed my fon. There was a message from Gina. Yes!

"It was good to hear from you, Jack," she said. "Your twin has been very forthcoming about the crew of the *Whydah*." That was the name of my new ship! "Apparently, they are not a friendly bunch. Watch your step. And he was very concerned about someone named Max. Take care of him. Anyway, Jax says his crew was working with the Quihiri. They planned to murder all the non-human sentients on Earth." Her voice was grim. "The last I heard, TCC was holding its own against the Quihiri space attack. But--" She drew the word out. "If humans are working against them in secret, TCC might not realize it. You have to stop them, Jack. You need to go to Earth and warn them." She paused for a moment. "Take care, Jack. Good luck."

"You take care, too, Gina," I whispered.

My to-do list was getting rather long. Of course, I was just the man to save the day!

I stood up. I needed to get control of the *Whydah*, one way or another.

When I walked into the commodious central space of the station, the lights were turning up, starting a new day. There were even more carts, booths, and people than when we arrived. The hustle and bustle were pretty amazing. I hadn't seen so many people and so many wares since I'd been back on Earth.

I yawned as I entered the bar-slash-hotel I'd checked in to when I first got to the station. When was the last time I'd slept? I couldn't even remember.

"Jax!" Eli called out from the bar.

The captain, scowling, sat on a stool next to him. They both had drinks in front of them.

As I approached them, I couldn't seem to stop yawning. "Hi, there." What was I supposed to be doing? Oh, right, looking for an FTL-repairman. "Did you guys have any luck?"

"What have you been doing, Jax?" the captain growled.

"I'm sure he's been chasing down leads, right, Jax?" Eli said.

"Yeah," I said. "Chasing down leads. I've got a good one." I yawned again and sat down next to Eli.

"How about you guys?" I asked. "Did you come up with anything?" Please, no.

The captain shook his head. "Why'd you get a room here, Jax? You aren't trying to jump ship, are you?"

"It's part of my cover." I leaned towards him. "And how could I jump ship? No one's going anywhere with all the FTL drives out."

In answer, he merely took a sip of his drink.

"What's your lead?" Eli asked.

"I'm still tracking it down," I said.

The captain stood. "I'm heading back to the ship. You guys coming?"

I pointed at the stairs. "I need to be here in case my contact contacts me." I yawned again.

"I'll, uh, stay here," Eli said. Left unsaid was, 'and keep an eye on Jax.' Maybe he wanted to hookup with Jax, i.e., me? No doubt that was it.

"Whatever," I said, standing.

"All right, keep me posted. I'm gonna move the ship." The captain turned and strode away.

Eli stood. "Do you really have a lead?"

"Yeah." I nodded. "But right now, I need some shuteye." I stood and started walking for the stairs.

Eli followed me.

I woke to find Eli lying in bed with me, watching me sleep. Was it creepy or flattering?

My subconscious had been working hard while I was asleep, and I knew what I needed to do.

In the meantime, I lifted the covers and glanced down. I was still clad in my underpants. So, we hadn't had sex. This Jax was difficult to understand. "Morning." I smiled sexily.

He said, "It's the beginning of the night cycle," but didn't smile.

Did he know why Jax eschewed physical affection? Sadly, I couldn't ask him. It would blow my cover as Jax, and I didn't entirely trust Eli. "Evening, then." I gently brushed my hand along his jaw. It was a genial jaw.

He slapped my hand away. "There's something strange about you…."

"What? Do you think I'm not Jax, er, me?" I grinned sexily and gestured at my excellent naked chest. "That's crazy. Am I not sexy enough?"

He flushed. "You seem different somehow," he said. "And your hair is longer." He pointed in the general direction of my hair. I did not recall that from when I saw Jax earlier--but then we were in a hurry, and things were pretty jumbled.

"It grew?" I said.

He reached out for the night table and grabbed his gun. "Try again." Well, this was not a good development.

On the nightstand next to me, Jax's fon rang. I held up a finger. "Just a sec. Hello?"

Max answered. "We haven't heard anything from you in hours. Is everything okay?"

"Hello, there, lead," I said. "Thanks for getting back to me. Yes, everything's fine on our end. How about with you?"

"We're fine," he said. "The pups are getting a little bored."

Various answers flashed through my mind, 'Take them out for a walk,' 'Teach them their letters,' 'Teach them computer programming.' Exactly how smart were they? But I couldn't say any of that. "Yes," I said. "I can meet you to discuss your, ah, price. When and where?"

"So, you're not alone," Max said.

"Bingo," I said. "See you then and there." I ended the call and put Jax's fon on the night table. I leaned back, putting my hands behind my head. I grinned some more.

"I'll put a pin in our discussion, but it's not over," Eli said. "Did you find someone who can fix our FTL drive?"

"Of course," I said. "*My dear dear lord, the purest treasure mortal times afford is spotless reputation--that away, men are but gilded loam, or painted clay. A jewel in a ten-times barr'd-up chest is a bold spirit in a loyal breast.*"

Eli frowned. "Huh?"

"Yes," I said. "I found a guy who can fix the drive." My mind raced. Where should I set up the fake meeting? Singing to the pups last night had been delightful. I missed singing.

"Who?" Eli asked. "Where are we meeting? When?"

"At that place where they sing…" I said suggestively. Hopefully, there was someplace to sing on the station.

"At the karaoke bar down the street?" he asked, seeming incredulous.

Who knew criminals like karaoke? "Yes!" I said. "We're meeting them tonight."

"Them?" he asked. "Them who?"

I thought fast. How could I get all the crew off the *Whydah*? And how could I make Eli think it was his idea? "The FTL drive engineer and his guards," I said. "The engineer has a rep as being paranoid, especially now with all the troubles. He has a huge security detail, like, uh, twenty people. All armed and dangerous." I acted worried. "Gosh, I'm worried. Super worried. I don't see how just the two of us can handle it."

Eli was already reaching for his fon. "I know who can."

So far, so good.

While he was on his fon, I went back into the bathroom and called Max with an update. I walked back into the bedroom just as Eli was ending his call.

"The crew is in," he said.

"Good," I said.

Now, all I had to do was sneak away from the scary space pirates, retrieve nine exceptional dogs and get them through the station without being detected, and finally steal the *Whydah*.

I resisted the urge to say, 'What could possibly go wrong?'

Chapter Nine

Gagopa, the karaoke bar, was a massive musty room with a foot-tall stage along one wall. All the tables and chairs and the bar itself looked like they had seen better days, much better days. It smelled like old beer.

Eli, I, and everyone else had to surrender our weapons to enter.

The captain nodded at us as he strode in like he owned the place. "Is he here yet? Your contact?" He carefully checked out the whole room. He'd come back to the station, along with what looked like the entire crew. Good.

"Not yet," I said.

Aria rushed right up to me and tried to kiss me. It hurt me to gently push her away. "We're on a mission, babe," I said.

"Oh, right," she said and giggled a little.

Aaron was giving his sister and me a weird look when he came up right behind her. Once she had walked out of ear range, he said, "Are we still okay?"

"Of course." I smiled sexily.

"Maybe I should tell Aria about us," he said. "She seems to have a crush on you."

Of course. But I said, "Nah. Let's focus on the mission right now, okay? It's important."

"All right." He walked off to join the rest of the crew, clustering around a couple of tables in the back.

Eli was talking to one of the crew members I hadn't officially met yet. Hopefully, he wasn't telling him I was suspicious.

I approached the captain.

"Do you see the FTL guy?" he asked quickly.

"Not yet," I said. "I'm just wondering where the ship is, you know, for when we rush him over to it."

He stared at me for a moment. "We docked the *Whydah*."

I waited for him to say which dock. He did not. Darn it.

He loomed over me sufficiently that I was not inclined to press him. Oh well, I'd solve that problem when I got to it.

Night had officially fallen on the station, and people, primarily humans, were streaming in. Evidently, not every species was physically able to sing or enjoyed Terran music. Their loss!

I had been worried my adopted crew would stand out like a broken thumb, but many people on the station wore leather, scars, and tattoos. The *Whydah* crew fit right in.

Since I still had a lot of money from my wish, I planned to bribe the Gagopa employees to keep the *Whydah* crew here as long as possible, maybe by encouraging/forcing them to sing.

I approached the most strapping guy in the club, standing, arms crossed in front of the stage. "So, I'm here with my crew." I turned and waved at them. Aria and Aaron waved back. The captain and the rest frowned. "And they want to sing. A lot. They've been talking about it for weeks. But they're afraid."

"Why's that my problem?" The guy grunted.

"I was hoping you guys could help them overcome their nerves, get them on stage. Even if they don't seem to want to get on stage, they really do. I promise."

He stared at me. "Are you trying to ditch them or something?"

Yes. "No," I said quickly. "Of course not."

He grunted again. "Because I could make that happen for the right price. Slip something in their drinks…."

"Just out of curiosity, what would be the right price?"

He quoted a figure, a very high figure. But it was a figure I could meet.

"Yeah, okay." I got out my fon but held it out at hip level.

He held his fon at hip level, and I transferred the funds. He saw the amount on my fon. "Guess I should have asked for more."

"Thanks for your help, sir. I appreciate it." I smiled at him.

"Not so fast." He grabbed my arm as I turned away. "What are you drinking?"

"Uh..." Think fast. What would none of the *Whydah* drink? "A Shirley Temple."

He guffawed.

"Is that it then?" I asked. "Do we have a deal?"

"No." He pointed at the stage. "You have to sing." He said it like it was a big imposition.

The man that hath no music in himself…

"Well, gosh, if I have to, I have to." I immediately jumped on stage and quickly accessed the song computer. They had just about every ancient Terran song there was. Score.

In the meantime, burly-bouncer-guy turned down the room lights and put a spotlight on the stage.

Ooh. I found the perfect song.

The first notes rang out, and I sang, "*I've been really tryin', baby, tryin' to hold back this feeling….*"

As I sang, I watched a cute waitress bring my crew a tray of drinks, including a bright red Shirley Temple. I could tell they asked her about it because they all looked at me and started laughing.

I kept singing.

Everyone in the place turned and watched me. That was more like it. They were mesmerized.

When I finished the song, I got a standing O.

Of course.

I joined my crew at our tables and threw back my Shirley Temple. No one was laughing now.

The waitress kept the drinks coming, and after another round, the *Whydah* crew seemed quite drunk, slurring their words and slumping at the table.

That was my cue. I met the eye of the bouncer guy and nodded at him.

He nodded back at me.

I made my escape.

Outside, I pulled out my fon and immediately called Max.

"It is time?" he asked.

"Yes. The crew's disabled. I'm coming to get you. Any trouble on your end?" I had considered asking Max to bring the pups to the ship but decided it would be too dangerous for them. Someone was bound to be angry about the lab's destruction and might be looking for dogs.

"Nope," he said. "We'll be ready for you."

"If you get a chance, please look up which dock the *Whydah*'s at." I had no idea what his hacking skills were, but it didn't hurt to ask.

"Okay," he said.

I took off for the seedier section of the station.

I unlocked the motel room door and slipped inside to find nine dogs baring their teeth, growling at me.

I held up my hands. "It's just me. Calm down."

They calmed and started wagging their tails.

"Sorry," Max said. "We didn't know it was you until you opened the door, and we smelled you."

Belatedly, I realized we should have set up some secret knock or something. Oh well, live and learn.

"You guys ready?"

"Yeah," Max said. "And we got a couple of big boxes and an anti-grav cart to travel in."

"Great idea!" I said. I wished I'd thought of that. "Ah, how did you get it?"

He shrugged. "Basically, room service."

I quickly assembled the boxes and put them on the cart.

"Okay, jump in, everyone," Max said right before he jumped in one of the boxes.

The pups followed suit.

I loosely closed the boxes.

A couple of the puppies whined.

Max said, "I know it's dark, but we're safe now, and we'll be even safer when we get to the ship."

I powered up the cart, and it lifted off the floor. I glanced around the room. Was that everything? It was.

I took a step towards the door.

And someone knocked on it. Oh no. I looked out the peephole.

It was the grungy night clerk I'd just passed on the way in. He knocked again. "I know you're in there, Mr., ah, Smith."

I opened the door, quickly stepped into the hall and closed the door behind me. "What can I do for you, sir?" He was a young but fat human. It looked like he rarely left his chair.

"There have been inquiries about some dogs." His voice had an unpleasant oily quality to it. "Don't you have some dogs with you?" He knew I did.

"What do you want?" I asked.

He held out his fon. "Extra privacy costs extra." Ah ha. He was extorting me. Well, that was a lot better than turning me in. I didn't want to face the kind of monsters who would torture those poor dogs like that. I shuddered.

"How much extra?" I asked. I decided this was not the time to haggle.

He named a figure, and I paid him.

He practically rubbed his hands together in glee when he checked his fon. "Tomorrow, you might need even more privacy."

Tomorrow we would be long gone. But as long as he thought we'd keep bribing him, he'd keep covering for us. "We, er, I mean, I, do like my privacy."

"Until tomorrow, then." He waddled off to his chair.

Inside the room, Max had poked his head out of the box. "Everything okay?"

"Close enough."

"Hey, cut some kind of hole in the side here, so I can see what's going on," he said.

I did and closed his box back up.

"Now, we're going to play the quiet game," he said. "Whoever can stay quiet the longest time wins a prize."

The puppies started snuffling and barking excitedly.

"Don't worry, it's a good prize," Max said. "Okay, we're starting now. Be quiet."

I waited a few moments, and the puppies quieted.

We exited the room and exited the motel through a side door. No one seemed to be around, so I didn't think we'd been spotted.

I quickly pushed the cart in the direction of the docks.

Everything went fine until we got to the large central station hub, filled with sentients and all manner of things for sale. One of the pups barked.

"Hey, you, what's in those boxes?" someone called.

I didn't stick around to find out who. I started running.

"Get him!" someone yelled.

I heard several feet pounding behind us.

"Hurry!" Max said as I pushed the cart through the crowd.

It was so crowded the people chasing us had trouble catching up. I ran and ran to the docks.

"Dock three," Max said. Thank goodness he was a decent hacker.

I ran right up to dock three, to the *Whydah*. I skidded to a stop and glanced behind us.

I could just make out a small crowd of humans running our way. Shoot. One of the people looked familiar, but when I tried to get a better view, I lost sight of him.

"Hey!" Max said.

I turned back to the ship.

"Biometric lock," Max said.

I touched it. Nothing happened.

The group chasing us got closer.

Max said, "Lick it!"

I put my head down and opened my mouth, stuck out my tongue, and it scanned my eye.

The ship's outer door clicked open.

I quickly shoved the cart inside and punched the door closed behind us.

Through the small door window, I could see the people chasing us stopped at the outer door, stymied by the lock. They cursed and said a bunch of stuff I couldn't hear.

I punched the inner air-lock door open and pushed the cart inside. I slapped the door closed behind us and took a breath. It smelled stale, like sweat.

We made it.

I powered down the cart, and it sank to the floor. I opened the box tops, and the pups and Max jumped out, tails wagging. Now, it smelled like dog.

"Phew," Max said. "That was a close one."

"We should get the ship out of here," I said. "I'm going to the bridge."

I ran for the bridge, and Max and the puppies ran after me.

Soon, we were all on the bridge. I sat in the pilot's chair and punched in the commands to power up and move away from the station. Luckily, human spaceships all over the galaxy were fairly similar. We flew away from the station.

The puppies started barking cheerfully and wagging their tails even more. They were adorable.

Max, seemingly helpless to resist, joined them in a joyful bark, his tail wagging happily.

I laughed and got down on the floor next to them. They all piled on, and we had a puppy party. I couldn't stop laughing. We were safe. We were all safe. Hallelujah.

After several minutes of that, I stood up. (Darn.) "I need to go to engineering and reconnect the FTL drive."

I casually strolled over to engineering. It looked the same as ever. I walked right up to the FTL drive, still lying unconnected where we'd left it. I knelt and picked up one of the wires.

"Freeze," an unfamiliar voice said.

Chapter Ten

What is it about the word 'freeze' that makes a person turn and look? Whatever it was, I turned and looked.

The man holding the ray gun on me was handsome in a T'Challa kind of way, regal and powerful. I smiled sexily and sat down on the floor. "Hi there."

"What are you doing with the FTL drive?" he asked. "And where's the captain?" The way he talked, this guy was clearly part of the crew.

Behind the stranger, Max crept up, tiptoeing on four paws, head down, snout out.

I smiled at the stranger again. "Relax, buddy. The captain gave me instructions on how to fix the FTL drive." I pointed at the drive. I lowered my voice. "He's sending us on a secret mission."

The ray gun didn't waver from my chest. "What secret mission? Why didn't I hear anything about it?"

"Duh," I said. "It's secret."

He narrowed his eyes and reached for his fon. "I'm calling the captain." I was pretty sure the captain was passed out and wouldn't be able to take his call.

I met Max's eyes and pointed my chin at the fon. "If you wanna call the captain, call the captain, by all means."

Max lunged and knocked the fon and the ray gun out of the guy's hands. That was not what I was going for, but I could improvise. I stood up.

"Oh, no, Max," I said. "You made him drop his stuff. This is my friend. He wouldn't hurt me. Please don't hurt him."

Max growled and darted around, generally acting like he would hurt my friend.

I pretended to dart after him. In the confusion, I stomped

hard on the stranger's fon. "Oh, no." It broke into several pieces. "Down, boy! Down, Max!" I stomped on the ray gun. It experienced significant crackage. "Oh, no! Now, look what I did. I'm sorry."

For his part, the stranger seemed incredulous that all this was happening.

Max calmed down some. I petted him on the head. "Thanks for protecting me, boy. But I wasn't in danger."

"Give me your fon, Jax," the guy said. He seemed suspicious of me for some reason.

"Gosh, sorry, buddy," I said. "I don't have my fon with me."

He whirled and started walking for the door. "I'm going to the bridge to contact the captain."

Shoot. That didn't sound good. "Of course you are. Good idea." I quickly scanned engineering, looking for something to solve my problem. What to do? If I hadn't broken the ray gun, I might have been able to stun him.

Max pointed his nose at a smallish piece of equipment on top of another piece of equipment.

I grabbed it and ran after my obstacle, now walking quickly down the hall.

Max followed us.

I hit the stranger pretty hard on the head with the piece of equipment. He crumpled to the floor. I felt guilty.

Max said, "Why didn't you just hit Dion from the beginning?" Ah-ha! Dion was his name.

"I was trying not to hurt him," I said. "You didn't need to lunge at the poor guy. The captain can't answer his fon. He's down for the count. I was trying to tell you that."

"How would I know that?" he asked. "You pointed at his fon."

"I was pointing to say, 'let him call,'" I said. Apparently, my nonverbal communication skills needed some work. "What should we do with him now? Sick bay?"

"If you don't want to space him, locking him in sick bay is as good a place as any," Max said. I was pretty sure he was joking with his 'space him' comment. Pretty sure.

I dragged Dion to the small sick bay and carefully placed him on the cot there. I put a bottle of water and some painkillers next to him. I exited and locked the door behind me.

I marched back to engineering. This time there were no interruptions, and I successfully connected the FTL drive.

I walked back to the bridge, where I found Max and the puppies.

I sat down in front of the FTL drive controls. I promised Gina I'd check in with TCC back on Earth and warn them about humans working with the Quihiri. I laid in a course for Earth and leaned back in the captain's chair. It felt good. "So, we're going to Earth on TCC business. I have important orders," I said. "Do you want me to drop you and the puppies off there, Max?"

"Where's Jax?" he asked. "Is he on Earth?"

He was likely still in the brig on the *Shakespeare*. "Uh, he's probably on my old ship, uh, filling in for me."

"I want to go meet up with Jax," Max said. "I miss him. He's my family."

"I don't think the *Shakespeare* is safe for you or, especially, the puppies," I said, pointing. They were all on the floor, sniffing each other, jumping on one another, or rolling around. "We're at war. The puppies are depending on you to keep them safe."

"I know what my responsibilities are, Jack," he said, voice filled with anger. "Do you?"

We know what we are…

I started to bristle. "What's that supposed to mean?"

I exhaled, trying to calm down. If I genuinely respected Max as a sentient creature, as a person, I should listen to what he wanted for himself and his family, shouldn't I?

"The *Shakespeare* is supposed to be in the Quihiri system," I said.

"Then that's where I want to go," he said. "That's where we need to go." He pointed his nose at the puppies.

I sighed. "All right. I will take you to the *Shakespeare*, but first, I need to go to Earth. I promised I would go there. I was ordered to go there."

I input the Earth coordinates, engaged the FTL drive, and away we went.

I leaned back in the chair some more, watching the black- and white-furred pups. Wow, they were cute. I was glad I wouldn't have to say goodbye to them immediately.

"What do you plan to do about Dion?" Max said after a few

moments.

I sighed loudly again. I still felt bad that I'd hit him. "I wish Dion had been on the station with the rest of the crew." Something about that was important. I sat up straight. Did I just accidentally utilize my special skill to send Dion to the station?

"What?" Max asked.

I jumped out of the chair. "I need to go check on our prisoner." I raced down the halls to sick bay. I unlocked the door. Empty, it was empty. And the small space had no place to hide. "Shoot." I really needed to do better than waste my special skill like that. *"I am constant as the northern star."*

At my elbow, Max said, "What happened to Dion?"

"He's on the station," I said.

"What?" he asked.

"He, uh, needed medical treatment."

"But how'd he get there?"

"It was my special skill," I said.

He gave me a blank look.

"Remember how I got all that extra money on Jax's fon?" I asked. "The money that I've been throwing around right and left?"

"You were serious about that?" he asked.

"Yeah." I nodded.

"That doesn't make any sense," he said.

"I know." I nodded again. "It's something about the FTL drive and quantum possibilities."

"Why not wish for intragalactic peace?" he asked. "Or at least all the FTL drives to be fixed?"

Shoot. I really should have thought of that. "I wish for intragalactic peace, and all the FTL drives to be fixed!" I said.

Max glanced around us. "Nothing seems different."

"Come on," I said. "Let's go back to the bridge."

Back on the bridge, I didn't see any signs of intragalactic peace or all the FTL drives fixed, either.

Soon, we exited FTL space near the Earth system, behind the moon. Yes, I was that good. The moon looked like a giant gray dusty ball. Earth looked like a lovely blue marble flecked with fluffy white clouds. Beautiful. I exhaled. Home.

I couldn't see anything amiss near us through the bridge's

viewscreen. Promising, but not conclusive.

I activated the sensor array to gather data. Was the battle for Earth still raging? Several large Quihiri ships had been firing on Earth the last time I was here. I examined the sensors' data.

The puppies barked softly, jostling and wrestling with one another on the floor of the bridge.

"What's happening?" Max said.

"Just a minute," I said. "I'm trying to figure that out." There were multiple radar signatures on the other side of the planet: three large ships and many, many smaller ships. The battle for Earth must still be on.

If I had a crew, I would join the fight.

I glanced at the puppies. I shouldn't put children in danger.

Keeping my eye on the radar display, I activated the communications array. "Terran Cultural Committee Command, this is Jack Jones. Come in, TCC Command."

"Jones? Is that you?" a familiar voice asked. "Why are you using unsecured comms?"

"TCC Command, this is Jack Jones," I said. "I don't have access to secure comms. Who am I speaking with?"

"This is Lieutenant Singh," he said. "Stand by for secure comm codes."

Something on the *Whydah* bridge beeped, and a light on the console in front of me started blinking. I pressed it.

"TCC?" I asked.

"Yes, Jones," Singh said. "What ship are you on? It's not TCC."

"I, uh, appropriated the *Whydah* for the war effort," I said.

"I'm not familiar with that ship," he said. "But what do you want? We're busy fighting the Quihiri menace."

My spirits sank. Still? "This is Jones, reporting for duty. How can I help?"

"What's your weapons compliment?" Singh asked.

Max interrupted. "Didn't you get previous orders, Jack?"

He was right. I had intelligence I was supposed to impart. "Ah, actually, Lieutenant Singh, I have some vital intelligence."

"What is it?" he asked, sounding impatient.

"There are human enemies of TCC," I said. "They're fighting with the Quihiri, but their ultimate aim is to exterminate all non-humans on Earth."

"Humans fighting with the Quihiri?" he asked. "Against TCC? Dammit. You better come down to the surface. I'll send you the coordinates."

"Roger that," I said.

Max nipped my hand.

"Ouch." I withdrew it from his reach.

"I don't want to take the pups anywhere near that battle," he said softly. Since the *Shakespeare* was at war, this seemed inconsistent with what he'd said earlier, but stressed people weren't necessarily consistent.

I glanced at the pups still cavorting on the floor.

"We will definitely avoid the battle," I said.

Using their coordinates, I laid in a course for Earth's surface. I kept a close eye on the radar, however, prepared to change course if we got close to the battle.

As directed, the *Whydah* swooped up to the west coast of France and flew close to the ground towards Paris. But the coordinates led us to a place named Versailles, with a large green space area, gardens, several bodies of water, and an extravagant light-colored stone building. It was beautiful. This must be the famed Versailles Palace I'd heard about. "Huh…"

We were directed to a large plaza area, and I landed the ship.

I pointed at Max and the pups. "You guys stay here where it's safe."

"How long will you be gone?" Max asked.

"I'm not sure," I said. "But we'll go find Jax right after I'm done."

I stood and strode purposefully towards the exterior door.

Despite the circumstances, aka war, I was glad to be back on Earth, breathe fresh air, and feel the sun on my face. I had a spring in my step as I opened the exterior airlock.

Right up until I saw a phalanx of TCC security forces pointing large rifles at my face.

"Ack." I may have stumbled a bit, but if so, it was in a graceful way. I put my hands up. Palms out. "No need for guns. I'm Jack Jones, TCC Lieutenant Junior Grade. I swear." I experienced a strange mix of nerves and déjà vu all over again.

Lieutenant Singh stepped up, pointing his large rifle at my face. "If you were the real Jack Jones, you'd know he's only an ensign." He scowled at me.

"Uh, crap," I said. "Yes. I'm only an ensign. I was demoted. I forgot for a minute."

"Not a likely story," Lieutenant Singh said.

"Well, having a bunch of rifles pointed at your face is a little distracting," I said. "Sorry."

Singh got closer and stared into my face. "He looks like Jones. But what with shape-shifters and clones, who the hell knows what he is."

Uh oh. How did a person prove he was himself? My nerves ratcheted up. "We met before, er, not in person, but we talked before when I flew to TCC headquarters on a TCC shuttle. And before you said I had to be interrogated...." I trailed off. Even I could tell this story didn't sound so good.

"Search the ship," he said.

Uh oh. Now, I'd put Max and the puppies in danger. Not good. Not good at all.

"I swear I'm TCC Ensign Jack Jones," I said. "I'm on your side. I have important intel related to the war. I'm alone. There are, uh, no other people on this ship."

He pointed his gun at me. "Take him into custody."

Chapter Eleven

I was on Earth, my home planet. Yay! But I did seem to be under arrest. Boo! The weather was lovely, with the sun shining down and a light breeze blowing. Yay! I did smell something burning, wafting over from the direction of Paris. Boo! It must be a remnant from the recent battle. I didn't hear any evidence, like explosions, of a current battle, however. Yay!

During all these observations, my mind was racing. Clearly. How to prove I was me? Maybe I could sing something? I stopped for a moment to savor the sun's rays hitting my skin. Yay, Earth! "*Presto il biglietto...Figaro! Figaro! Figaro!*"

"What?" Singh said.

I shook my head. Who did I know on Earth? There was a certain lady-love, a luscious duplication engineer, Sophia Olsson. There was also Old Jack, who should still be in the TCC holding cells. Old Jack should be geographically near, but there was no love lost between us. What if he didn't feel like identifying me? I had basically stolen his life, after all.

Lieutenant Singh was leading us away from my, ah, appropriated ship when I heard a lot of barking. *Bark, bark, bark.* Darn. I'd told the dogs to hide.

I stopped short. "Please don't hurt my dogs. They haven't done anything wrong."

"We treat dogs fairly." Singh craned his neck, looking back over his shoulder at the ship, which still had the exterior door open.

"Lieutenant Singh, we found nine border collies here, an adult and eight pups. What should we do with them?" one of his officers said over the radio.

"They're good dogs," I said. "Really good."

Singh gave me a long look. “If you’re truly TCC Ensign Jack Jones, you know dogs have rights on Earth.”

“I am!” I said. “I know. They’re protected from physical harm, including assault, murder, kidnapping.”

“And if they’ve been enhanced,” Singh continued, “they have the right to life and liberty, freedom from slavery and torture, freedom of opinion and expression, the right to work and education, and more--like all enhanced animals.” I didn’t think I recalled that. It must have happened sometime in the last thirty years (which I couldn’t remember).

“Yes!” I said. “They’ve been enhanced. They deserve all the rights.” Then, I felt a little guilty for a few moments. Did Max want me to keep the enhancements secret?

“We’re coming,” Singh said into his radio. He pointed back at the ship with his gargantuan gun.

We all traipsed back across the crushed-stone roadway to the *Whydah*. The faint smell of something burning was a little disquieting.

The officer left behind was standing in the doorway in front of Max and the pups. Crouching, the dogs all had their teeth bared and were growling fiercely. The officer was pointing his rifle at Max.

“Stop!” I ran up.

The officer pointed his rifle at me.

“Er, I mean, stand down, sir. Please.” I turned to Max. “It’s okay. You guys have the same right as homo sapiens.” I turned to Singh. “Right? Sir?”

“Yes,” Singh said. “If they understand those rights.”

“Go ahead, Max,” I said. “Tell him.”

Max’s posture relaxed; he barked once and sat. The pups instantly sat down calmly.

“It wasn’t your information to tell, Jack,” Max said. “But, yes, Lieutenant Singh, we all have the sentience of homo sapiens.”

The TCC officer standing next to him was startled and almost dropped his rifle.

“Well, this puts a different spin on things,” Singh said. “Are you willing to answer some questions? Do you support the mission of TCC? Can you vouch for this supposed Jack Jones and his activities?”

"Yes," Max said.

"Will you come with us to TCC headquarters?" Singh asked.

"Yes," Max said.

"Please stand down, men," Singh said. Why did Singh believe Max and not me?

The officers quit holding their guns in our direction. Yay!

"This way, please," Singh said. He led us in the direction of Versailles Palace.

Unfortunately, we didn't go inside the palace. We went through an unobtrusive door in an outbuilding and then down some stairs. The pups were having a little trouble, and officers scooped them up and carried them down the steps. At the bottom of the steps was what looked like a subway stop.

Soon, a train whisked us away; I watched the bland underground scenery and cogitated on a plan. Within minutes we stopped at a subway platform almost identical to the first one. Darn. I thought I'd have more time to devise a plan to prove I was me.

The eleven of us ascended via an elevator. After a short walk down a rather nondescript white hallway, we entered a much larger nondescript white room. Everything was bright white; walls, desks, uniforms, electronics. And there must have been over fifty TCC officers sitting in front of the latest bleeding-edge computers hard at work. Me and the others not wearing white stuck out like bloody thumbs.

I knew exactly where we were. I grinned. If my old friend Katarina was here, we were home free. "Welcome to TCC Headquarters, Max, pups." We needed to give the puppies names.

For their part, the dogs were sniffing everything and looking around, trying to take it all in.

A uniformed, older man with white hair and a smooth white beard approached us. "Report Singh," he said in a gravelly voice.

"We apprehended these ten individuals en route to TCC headquarters--" His voice, on the other hand, was a little squeaky. "For what purpose, we don't know." He glanced at his fon. "Their ship is the *Whydah*, registered out of Johannesburg, South Africa, here on Earth. Traders. The dogs are purported to be sentient."

The puppies barked softly and wagged their tails a lot. Max looked wary.

At the doggie commotion, a grin flitted across Singh's face. "They're probably sentient." He pointed at me. "This claims to be TCC ensign Jack Jones."

The man took a step forward and scrutinized my face.

"Uh, hello, sir?" I said. "Is Katarina here, perhaps? She knows me." When he didn't answer, I added, "Ensign Jones reporting for duty, sir. Here to help the war effort in whatever way I can. I have intelligence about the crew of the *Whydah* and the war."

"I thought you were the crew of the *Whydah*," the man said right in my face.

"Uh, not exactly," I said. "I'm not part of the *Whyda*h crew. I borrowed their ship. They're bad guys. They're working with the Quihiri against TCC."

"The Quihiri!" he said. "So, you're admitting you're in league with the Quihiri? Singh, take them to holding."

"But I'm a TCC officer!" I said. "I'm not in league with anyone! I'm here to help!"

The pups stood and yipped.

"All of them, sir?" Singh asked, watching the puppies.

"Yes," the man said, now sounding tired. "Interrogate them."

Singh frowned but said, "Yes, sir." He pointed back to the elevator with his rifle.

The puppies, still standing, now started whining.

The TCC prison looked the same in every respect as it did every other time I'd been down here--a dimly-lit nondescript hall with sound-proof cells. And, yes, it was a sad commentary on my short life that I'd been to the TCC prison more than once before.

When we walked past Noah's cell, he perked up and waved and yelled stuff at us. But, of course, we couldn't hear anything because of the soundproof forcefield. I glanced at him as I went by. I did feel a little bad for him since his only crime was helping Old Jack with his nefarious scheme. So, essentially, Noah's crime was he was too good a friend.

Sitting on his bed, Old Jack just looked at us and shook his head a little as we walked past his cell.

Singh opened a cell and gestured the ten of us inside.

The puppies immediately ran all around, sniffing everything. Max stood next to me.

Singh closed the door but didn't initiate the forcefield.

"We don't belong here. Singh, you have to help us," I said. "Captain Gomez of the *Shakespeare* ordered me to gather intelligence on the *Whydah* and its crew. I fulfilled my mission. I have intelligence!"

"I'm listening," Singh said.

"We first became aware of them at a war council on Quihiri, which three *Whydah* crewmembers, Jax Jones, Aria, and Aaron, attended," I said.

"What are these other crewmembers' last names?" he asked.

"Uh..." I said. "I don't know." At least I did know telling him Jax was another me, and I was engaged to Aria, and Aaron was not a good idea.

At my blank expression, he added, "What other crew did you meet?"

"Eli and Logan and the, ah, captain," I said. "And Dion! I also met a guy named Dion."

His expression was not amused. "What happened at this war council?"

"First, they said all the FTL drives in the galaxy were offline except for theirs, the sentients at the council," I said. "These groups want to isolate their species. They don't want to trade information and culture, and well, trade. And they're willing to kill to do it. There were emissaries from all our closest allies: Alpha Catoblepas, Tao Ceto, Yeblypso, Keplarr,...." I was blanking again on some of the species' names. "The, ah, broccoli people, the lobster people...."

"I can jump in," Max said. "The Sapus, the Xuphitov."

Now, Singh looked a little sad. "If this is true, we didn't know the conspiracy was so widespread."

"The *Whydah* should have documents and communications with more specifics," Max said.

I pointed at him. "Good point! Yes. The *Whydah* must have records."

He nodded. "We already dispatched a team to download

everything from the *Whydah*." When did that happen? (Singh had been with us the whole time.) He continued. "We seem to be having some trouble with passwords and security clearances, however."

"I can help," Max said. "No one pays attention to a dog. I can tell you about the crew. And I know a lot of passwords."

One of the pups barked.

Max glanced at him. "Any chance we could get some food?" he asked.

Singh observed the puppies and grinned. "Yes." Then he observed me, and his grin morphed into chagrin. "How do I know anything you say is true?"

"It's all true!" I said. "I'm Jack Jones! I'm a TCC ensign!"

"Prove it," he said.

"Katarina knows me," I said. "She can vouch."

He made no move to get Katarina. "How do I even know you're human?"

"I am!" I said. "Old Jack knows me." I pointed at him. "He'll tell you." I hoped he'd tell him. There was a minor possibility Old Jack was still mad about our previous encounter. I'd promised him some music and hadn't delivered.

While I was waving my hands around, Max managed to nip one of them.

"Ouch!" Several drops of blood beaded on one of my fingers and dropped onto the floor. Two of the puppies ran over to smell it.

"He's plainly human," Max said, then pointed at the blood with his nose. "Human blood."

Singh leaned over and looked at the blood. "Okay, he's human." He straightened up. "Thanks for the assist. But that doesn't mean anything else he's said is true. Or that what you've said is true."

"Snacks?" Max asked.

"Okay, for the puppies' sake," Singh said. "Sit tight." He turned and stalked away.

"Was that necessary, Max?" I stuck my bleeding finger in my mouth.

He somehow conveyed the impression of a shrug. "I'm hungry. And the pups are, too. That was taking too long."

I suddenly felt exhausted. When was the last time I'd slept? Or eaten? I turned around and went and sat down on the cot.

How to prove I was me? I glanced over at Noah and Old Jack. I probably couldn't depend on them. Even if they said I was me, TCC thought they were unreliable--they were in TCC prison, after all.

I wondered where Katarina was. Busy with the war effort? I knew she was a bigwig, some kind of Commander, but I hadn't heard exactly what.

And how was the war going? Ugh.

So, all that left was my favorite duplication engineer, Sophia, to verify I was me, but she was at the TCC medical facility, which was not here in France.

My mind went around and around.

Eventually, Lieutenant Singh reappeared, arms full of paper bags.

I stood up and started singing, "*Three little maids from school, are we….*"

He only said, "I wasn't sure what kind of snacks to get, and we didn't have any dog food on site, so I got a bunch of burgers from the commissary."

"Don't you recognize the famous voice of famous singer Jack Jones?" I asked. No one answered.

Max seemed to smile at Singh. His tail wagged a lot. "Burgers will work."

The puppies stood up and started their tails wagging energetically.

Singh opened a tiny door, placed the bags on the floor, and pushed them inside the cell.

I smelled the somehow uniquely-Terran scent of fast-food burger, greasy fried meat. Ah, the smell of home. Okay, I gave up. Food now. Worry about my identity later.

All the dogs had run up and were nosing around the bags.

"A little help, Jack?" Max asked.

I leaned down and unwrapped a bunch of burgers. The dogs fell on them like, well, wolves.

I'd just reached for one for myself when Singh said, "You, not yet."

"Why not?" I asked. With difficulty, I forced my attention from the bags of food and the delicious scents wafting from them and turned my attention back to him. "What?"

"The *Shakespeare* missed its last check-in," he said quietly. My spirits sank. Oh, no. It would kill me if my friends were hurt or worse.

"We're very worried about them," he said. "If you're who you say you are, do you have any way to get in touch with them?"

"Besides the regular communications network?" I asked.

He nodded.

There was something… "Hmm." What was it? Something to do with Old Jack. "I think…

He leaned towards me. "What?"

"I think Old Jack might have an ansible," I said. At least, he used to. "And the other end of it is on the *Shakespeare*."

Singh's mouth hung open. "An ansible? Why is this the first I'm hearing about this? Do other TCC officers know about this?"

I shrugged. "So, I need to talk to Old Jack."

"Okay." He nodded and reached out to unlock my cell's door.

I glanced back at the dogs chowing down on burgers. Didn't I get a burger? Apparently not.

I stepped out of our cell.

Singh and I walked over to Old Jack's cell. Singh pressed some buttons on the security pad, there was an almost imperceptible whoosh, and I caught the faint scent of sweat.

Old Jack stood up and walked right up to the front of the cell. He crossed his arms in front of himself. "What do you want now?"

Singh pointed at me. "Go ahead."

I stepped up to the cell. "We need your help. The *Shakespeare* is in danger."

"Why should I help you?" Old Jack said. "Why should I help any of you?"

I still felt a little bad about promising him music and then not delivering several months ago. I walked right next to Singh and whispered. "Can't we give him some music?"

Singh exhaled loudly. "Fine." He turned his attention back to Old Jack. "We'll give you some music."

"*I believe in music*," I sang. "*I believe in love. I believe in music*."

Singh must be considered reliable because Old Jack didn't question the promise. "Okay. What do you want?"

"Do you remember that time I talked to you via an ansible?" I asked.

A smile flitted across his face. "It was kind of memorable, now that you mention it."

Singh exhaled again.

"How did that work?" I asked. "Did you have some kind of equipment?"

"Yes." He grinned, savoring the moment. "It appeared out of thin air." Then, he turned around and went back to his bed. He lifted the mattress and pulled out what looked like a data cube. He walked to the front of the cell and held it out. "But it hasn't done anything since."

Singh pointed at the small airlock door, and Old Jack put it in. Singh extracted it. "How does it work?"

Old Jack shrugged. "Beats me." I concurred, but I wasn't about to say it.

I took the device and held it in my flat palm. "Come in, *Shakespeare*. This is Jack. Come in."

Gradually, a small scene appeared, floating over the cube.

We all leaned towards it.

I heard a faint alarm blaring.

"What is it?" Singh asked, wrinkling his brow.

I couldn't quite make it out. I saw straight lines and maybe a metallic finish covered in dust or something. The whole scene was jerking back and forth. Overlaid over it all was a red flashing light. Oh, no. That couldn't be good. "I'm not sure," I said. "But whatever it is, I don't think it's going to talk to us."

The *Shakespeare* was definitely in trouble.

Chapter Twelve

At TCC Headquarters, down in holding, Katarina had finally shown up. Her hair was escaping its bun, and her white uniform was wrinkled and sweat-stained. “This better be good, Singh. We’ve finally got the last of the bastards on the ropes.”

“Commander Devi!” Singh straightened.

Her comms chimed, and she pressed a device in her ear, turning it on. “I’ll be back in a few moments.” She pressed the device again, turning it off. “What, Singh?” She smiled. “Hi, Jack.”

I smiled sexily back at her and waved with my free hand.

Singh sputtered. “How do you know this is Jack Jones? Our Jack Jones?”

“I don’t have time for twenty questions,” she said. “He just is. What do you want?”

Singh pointed at the image still floating above the cube in my hand. “This is a real-time image from the *Shakespeare*.”

Katarina leaned towards it, squinting. “How do you know it’s the *Shakespeare*? You can’t truly see anything. And, in real-time, no. That’s impossible.”

“It’s possible, ma’am,” I said. “I promise. This is one end of an ansible. The other end’s on the *Shakespeare*.”

She froze for a moment, staring.

“Ooh.” It hit me what we were looking at. “This is an image of the, uh, service tunnels. But it looks like they’re under red alert.” The scene jerked. “With failing artificial gravity.”

Now, she was frowning. She straightened. “Even if that was true, what do you expect me to do about it?”

“Just let me go to Quihiri to help them,” I said.

“You can go to Quihiri?” she asked. “You have a working

FTL drive?"

"Yes," I said. "But unfortunately, the *Whydah* is a small ship. It doesn't have room for many crew."

From the holding cell, Max said, "Can't you just move the drive to another ship, Jack?"

Katarina, or, rather, Commander Devi, seemed just now to notice the dogs in the cell behind us. "Why are these dogs imprisoned? Most of them are puppies. This is not okay."

"Uh, Commander Abara told me to...." Singh faltered.

"Let them out at once," Commander Devi said, steel in her voice.

Singh quickly went over to the cell and opened the door.

After finishing demolishing the burgers, the puppies ran out and clustered around her, tails wagging, barking, and jumping.

She leaned down and petted them, laughing. They frolicked all around her.

Time seemed to stop as the rest of us watched her and smiled.

Then, Old Jack said, "Hi, Katarina," and the moment was broken.

She stood and glanced at Old Jack but didn't answer him. Instead, she pointed at Singh and me. "You two transfer the FTL drive to the *Agincourt*. It's under the command of Captain Wright. Leave for Quihiri immediately to assist the *Shakespeare*. I'll contact Wright."

"Me?" Singh squeaked.

"You help Jack," she said. "Whatever he needs." Nice.

"I'm going, too," Max said. "And the puppies. I'm Max, by the way."

"Not the puppies," she said. "They're children. That's non-negotiable. Max, you can stay here with them or accept a TCC commission and join the *Agincourt*, your choice."

The puppies whimpered. I got a definite sense of sadness.

Max said, "Uh...." He was clearly conflicted. Among other things, I knew he wanted to reunite with Jax.

"I have a friend here, Sophia Olsson, who can take care of the puppies." I didn't know for sure Sophia would take care of them, but come on, puppies.

"You all work it out," Katarina said. "Jack, give me the

ansible."

I handed her the ansible.

"I have to go." She turned around and left, touching her comms. "Captain Wright--" she said as she walked back down the hall.

"She's a whirlwind, that one," Singh said, breathless.

"That's Katarina for you," Old Jack said, also sounding a little in awe.

We all nodded.

The puppies seemed restless. "What are you thinking, Max? Stay here or leave the pups with my friend Sophia?" I asked.

The pups chirped and wagged their tails.

"They want to stay with me," Max said.

"Maybe you all could stay with Sophia," I said. "She's super nice. And very pretty." Brainstorm. "And she works at the TCC Research Medical Center."

Now, the pups were back to barking and jumping up and down.

"Medical Center?" Max said. "Could she give the pups voice synthesizers?"

"Sure." I didn't know Sophia could do it for sure but come on puppies.

Singh touched his ear, turning on his comms. "Yes, ma'am." He touched his ear again, turning them off. "You're supposed to report to the *Agincourt*, Jack."

"No." I shook my head. "Not until my friends are taken care of." I pointed at the dogs. "Loan me your fon, Singh."

Singh handed his fon over, and I called Sophia and convinced her to meet me in the TCC Headquarters cafeteria. Yes, I'm that charming.

After Singh got Old Jack some music, I convinced him to go shopping at the commissary to get me a new fon and uniforms, miscellaneous clothing, toiletries, and a memory rig. You know, minor necessities of life. It was pretty awesome having an assistant. That probably wasn't what Katarina had in mind, but I wanted to make the most of it before Singh wised up.

I'd eaten two burgers and a bunch of fries in the cafeteria. Nice.

The dogs had partaken again, and Max was taking them for a walk outside.

I leaned back in a chair and rubbed my stomach. Now, I was super tired.

"Jack?" a luscious female voice asked.

I stood up and accidentally knocked my chair over. My former lover, Sophia, still looked like an athletic Scandinavian goddess--just as delicious as I remembered. I held my arms out, and we embraced. She *felt* just as delicious as I remembered.

We kissed.

Someone said, "Ahem." It was Max. The dogs were back from their walk.

Sophia and I separated, and she squeaked in surprise. "It almost seemed like this dog said something."

Max looked at me with an expression that said, 'This one's not too bright.'

"Sophia, this is my comrade-in-arms, Max, and his eight brothers and sisters. They're all genetically enhanced," I said. "Max, puppies, this is the brilliant and beautiful Doctor Olsson. She works at the TCC Research Medical Facility."

"Nice to meet you, ma'am." Max exhibited appropriate respect.

She immediately kneeled and stared at his neck. "Can I touch it?" There was a bulge on his neck that I hadn't noticed under all the fur.

"Yes," he said, sounding wary.

She commenced studying his voice synthesizer. "Nice work," she said. "But you didn't get this done on Earth, did you?"

"No," he said.

Then, she couldn't resist and, smiling broadly, started petting him. "You're pretty awesome, aren't you?"

"Yes," he said, now sounding smitten. "And the pups, too."

She glanced over at them. Then, we repeated the beautiful woman's puppy party as she rolled around on the ground, and the puppies jumped on her, barking, licking, and wagging.

"Ahh." I loved my job.

I glanced at Max. He seemed to love his job, too.

I stepped over to him. "What do you think?" I asked quietly. "Can she take care of them?"

"Definitely," he said, tail wagging.

"What about you?" I asked. "Are you staying?"

"No," he said, now sounding serious. "I'm worried about Jax."

Finally, the puppy show ended. "Do they all want voice synthesizers?" Sophia asked.

Each puppy barked once.

Max said, "Yes. Can you do it?"

"Yes," she said. "I can. And don't worry, they'll be safe with me."

When Singh, Max, and I stepped onto the Agincourt, a man in a captain's uniform was standing there waiting by the door. "They're aboard," he said over comms and closed the inner airlock door behind us with a bang. The ship hallway was pristine and functional, all business. "Let's go." The ship jerked a little as it pulled away.

He turned his attention to the three of us. "I'm Captain Wright." He stared like he wanted to reprimand us for making him wait. In truth, I felt a little bad about it. The *Shakespeare* was in trouble, and I'd spent an hour eating dinner (?), lunch (?). What was that meal? And taking care of the puppies.

"Which one of you is Jack Jones?" Wright finally said.

I held up my hand.

"Please come to engineering now," he said.

Singh held up his hand. "What about us?"

"I don't care," Wright said, already walking away.

I handed Singh my bag (yay! I had enough stuff to need a bag!). "Figure out our quarters. I'm taking a nap after this." I couldn't remember the last time I slept.

I ran after Wright.

"Good luck," Singh said, standing still.

"Good luck!" Max called, running after me.

Engineering on the *Agincourt* looked almost identical to engineering on the *Shakespeare,* with lots of complicated-looking machines with blinking lights. Wright marched me through the crowd to the featureless spherical FTL drive lying disconnected on the floor in front of an FTL drive-sized space.

I lay down and stuck my head in the space. It was dark. "Can someone shine a light in here?" A light appeared. I connected my FTL drive to the *Agincourt*. I turned it on, and a tiny green light lit up.

I stood up. "It's done." I brushed my pants off.

The *Agincourt's* crew were peering at me and the FTL drive. They started clapping and cheering. "Woo hoo!" "Yeah!"

I held my hands up over my head, drinking it in. Yeah, I loved my job.

"I should make a wish," I said. No one seemed to notice; they were still cheering.

Max bit my finger. I glanced down at him. I shouldn't make a wish?

"Set a course for Quihiri, fastest possible speed," Wright said. "Everyone back to work or assigned relief shift. Be ready for battle when we get to Quihiri."

"What would you like me to do, Captain?" I asked. Sleep, sleep, sleep. I hoped he liked me to sleep.

"You're on relief shift until we get to Quihiri," he said. "Get some sleep." Yeah!

A tongue caressed my cheek. *Mmm.* A large, raspy tongue that smelled like old meat. I opened my eyes. Max lay next to, and partly on, me on the bunk. Both of us didn't really fit on the small bed.

I pushed his face away. "Okay, okay. Thanks for the wake-up lick." I sat up.

"We're almost at Quihiri," he said. "You taste different from Jax."

"I guess that's not surprising?" I said. "We're different. The old nature versus nurture thing."

"I guess," he said. "You smell different, too."

Even I could smell myself at this point. I glanced around the tiny metal-walled, metal-floored, metal-ceilinged room, just a fold-down bunk and a couple of wall hooks. No sign of a shower. "Do you know where the showers are?"

"Yeah." Max jumped down and walked for the door. "Open." The door opened.

I grabbed my bag and followed him.

The large communal shower area was empty but for Max and me. Too bad for the *Agincourt* crew.

Soon, I was showered. I even had enough time to record my memories. *Ahh.* I felt better than I had in days.

"Jack? Where are you?" It was Singh's voice coming out of my new fon.

"In the showers," I said. "Do you want to come to join us?" Now that I thought about it, Singh was a nice-looking guy.

"What?" he asked. "Really?" he sounded honored. "No. We're coming up on Quihiri. The captain wants you on the bridge."

The crew quarters on the Agincourt might be smaller, but the bridge was definitely bigger. It was massive, with metal walls, floors, etc., and metal consoles with computers. There must have been several dozen uniformed crewmembers here as well, standing or sitting in chairs around the edges. They were all focused on the huge viewscreen in the front.

"Cap?" I called out. I couldn't find him in the crowd.

"Here," he said. The crowd parted to reveal the captain sitting on a big chair, kind of like a throne, in the middle of the space.

"I would come up on Quihiri behind their biggest moon," I said.

He glanced at me, and it was as if he was restraining himself from saying something like, 'Duh.'

"Any sign of the *Shakespeare*?" I asked.

"No," he said. My heart crumpled. We were too late.

"Wreckage?" I asked, peering into the screen. I should have hurried.

"No," he said.

"Other ships?" I asked.

"There are some Quihiri ships," he gestured at the screen. I could see some dots off in the distance. "According to sensors, the Quihiri ships have taken heavy damage. They haven't detected us."

"What about the surface?" I asked. I could only see ocean from this distance.

"There's damage on the surface, too," he said.

"No, I mean, does the surface know we're here? What's

their weapons situation?" Had we jumped from the frying pan into the war zone?

"We're cloaked," he said. "I have defense handled. And the offense, for that matter. Your job is to find the *Shakespeare*. Where is it?"

I had no idea. "Uh, do you have the ansible?"

"Lieutenant!" Wright barked out. A man I hadn't met yet ran up with the ansible. He handed it to Wright. Wright gave it to me.

I activated it.

The scene was the same as before. Failing gravity. Alarms. Red flashing lights.

No signs of life.

This my hand will rather the multitudinous seas incarnadine, making the green one red.

Chapter Thirteen

Everyone was looking at me on the bridge of the TCC warship Agincourt. Crew-cutted uniform-wearing TCC officers surrounded me. This crowd seemed much more no-nonsense than I was used to. No fun-loving thespians or spies here. I gulped.

I was supposed to be able to find the missing TCC ship, the *Shakespeare*. Unfortunately, I didn't know how to find the missing *Shakespeare*.

"Jack?" Max asked, standing at my side. "Where's Jax? You need to find him."

They all stared at me.

I stared back.

From the corner of my eye, I noticed Singh check his fon. That reminded me…

"Captain," I said.

"Yeah, Jones," he said from his captain's throne.

"I need to go down to the surface of Quihiri to retrieve some equipment," I said. Said equipment was my much-missed fon. "I think the *Shakespeare* left me some information." I hoped they left me some information.

Captain Wright gave me a steady look. "Commander Devi has a lot of faith in you, Jones." He paused, and I imagined he was thinking, 'I don't know why.' But he said, "Fine. I can give you a cloaked shuttle to go down to the surface. But the name of the game is stealth. I can't help you if you get into trouble. Lieutenant Commander Horvat, come here."

A white-skinned, dark-haired human officer seemed to magically appear next to him. "Yes, sir," he said. I realized most TCC officers were human.

"You're going to the surface of Quihiri with Ensign Jones

here--" Wright said.

"And my crew." I wasn't going to be separated from Max. And Singh. I waved at Singh, and he walked closer to us.

"And his," Wright smiled, "team. Retrieve his equipment. Do not be detected. Do not lead Quihiri forces to the *Agincourt* under any circumstances. Do you understand?" Now, Wright looked grim.

Horvat's mouth was pressed into a thin line. "Understood." He saluted Wright, then turned on a dime and marched towards the door. At the door, he stopped and looked back. "You coming, Jones?"

Max nudged my leg.

I hopped to it. "Uh, yes, sir. Come on, Max, Singh." I raced after Horvat, Max ran after me, and Singh raced after Max.

Captain Wright said, "Resume searching the planet's oceans for the *Shakespeare*'s transponder signal."

My heart caught in my throat. I hadn't even thought of that. Maybe the reason we couldn't see the *Shakespeare* was she was underwater.

Outside the bridge, we all walked quickly away. "So, who's your team?" Horvat asked.

"Max, here," I said. "I guess he's an ensign?"

Max barked.

"And Lieutenant Singh, here," I said.

Singh waved. "Hi, sir."

"Do you all have combat training?" Horvat asked as we walked down the corridor. I assumed he knew where he was going.

"Basic combat training," Singh said. "From the TCC academy."

Horvat nodded.

"Don't worry," Max said. "I can handle myself." He bared his teeth. I had to struggle not to jerk back from him. His black-and-white long-haired cuteness was transformed into formidableness. I'd never seen this side of him.

"Jones?" Horvat asked.

"I, uh, got combat training at the academy." Thirty years ago. "And I've been training on the *Shakespeare*." Of course, I was more of a lover than a fighter.

"Good," Horvat said. "We're stopping at the armory."

Several minutes later, in a shuttle, the four of us were pulling away from the *Agincourt*, armed for bear. The shuttle cloak was on. As we got away from the ship, I finally got a look at it from the outside. It was huge, a gray multi-story ovoid, stretched much longer than it was tall. Armament ports and sensors bristled from it every few feet. It looked like the progeny of a giant metal watermelon and a giant metal porcupine.

Horvat must have seen my amazed expression because he chuckled. "Yeah, it's impressive, isn't it? The biggest TCC ship. We've got all the latest tech, 3-d printers, including bio-matter and holographic communications. Projectile and energy weapons. We've never been seriously threatened until…." He stopped. I knew he was thinking they'd never been seriously threatened until the recent attack by the Quihiri.

"Did you guys have any casualties on the *Agincourt*?" I asked.

"No." He shook his head. "We were way out by Jupiter, and our FTL drive was out. By the time we returned to Earth, most of the fighting was over." He paused, pressing his lips together again. "But there were a lot of casualties, good men and women." He puttered to a stop.

Now I realized what his tight-lipped expression earlier meant. It meant he was willing to die rather than endanger his crew. Glancing at Max and Singh, I gulped. What had I gotten them into?

Singh looked ashen. "Yeah, things were …challenging at headquarters."

"I'm sorry to hear of your losses," Max said.

I petted his head. It was soft. I wanted to snuggle and pet him and rub his tummy, but it didn't seem like the time. He didn't seem to be in the mood.

I was able to direct Horvat to my previous shuttle landing spot in a deserted area of Quihiri. Had that only been a couple of days ago? "*The time is out of joint – O cursed spite*," I whispered.

We landed, and Horvat turned off the engine.

"Did you turn off the cloaking?" I asked, peering out the front viewscreen. It was overcast. I couldn't see anything but wet gray rocks and wet gray ground.

"No," he said. "The cloak has its own power supply. It'll stay on."

We, humans, strapped on many weapons, complete with holsters; it wasn't as empowering as I'd imagined.

We exited, and outside, the humidity was smothering.

I picked my way through the rocks to where I thought I'd left my fon.

I found my fon pretty easily. It was under some rocks right where I'd thought it would be. Honestly, I was a little surprised things had gone so smoothly.

As I knelt to pick it up, something moved in the corner of my eye.

Max started growling.

Someone shrieked, and I heard a thump.

"Jack?" a familiar female voice asked.

I turned to see a medium-sized gray-skinned Quihiri. She resembled a man-sized, three-legged, three-armed octopus.

I also saw Horvat lying on the ground, aiming at her with one of his many weapons.

I stepped in front of his gun. "No, Horvat. She's a friend."

"She's a Quihiri!" he said. "Get out of the way, Jack."

"What *is* that?" Singh asked, pointing with a look of horror on his face. "It was just a rock! I swear!"

"Calm down, everyone!" I said. "She's a friend, a shape-shifting energy being." I'd decided not to try to pronounce her species' name.

Horvat lowered his gun.

"Addie?" I stepped towards her.

"Yes." She bobbed up and down a little and then transformed into her energy form, a cloud of sparkles. "Where did you guys come from?"

"Cloaked shuttle." I couldn't help smiling. "Addie!" I rushed up to her. How do you hug an energy being? "I'm so glad to see you. I'm glad to see you're okay. I'd hug you if I could."

"We could merge again if you want to, but maybe now isn't the time," she said.

"Where's Slid?" I asked. "He's okay, isn't he?"

"He's supposed to be on the *Shakespeare*," she said.

"What about the others?" I said. "The *Shakespeare* crew? Jax?"

"They're all on the ship," she said. "I don't know if they're safe. I hope so. We haven't had contact in a while."

"What are you doing here, Addie?" I asked.

"Amazing," Max said, sniffing loudly. "I didn't smell anything but rocks, sand, and water."

"What's going on?" Horvat asked, now back on his feet.

"I don't understand what's happening," Singh said.

Oh, yeah. We're on a secret mission. "Let's go back to our shuttle, where we can talk," I said.

Back in the still-cloaked shuttle, I made introductions. "Everyone, this is my old friend, Addie. She's been helping TCC and the crew of the *Shakespeare*."

"Addie, this is Lieutenant Singh from TCC headquarters," I said. "Commander Devi assigned him to help me. This is Max; he was on the crew of the *Whydah*--"

She interrupted me. "Are you Jax's Max?"

"Yes!" Max jumped up. "Do you know Jax? How is he?"

"He was fine," she said.

I interrupted her. "Let's circle back around to this. Addie, this is Lieutenant Commander Horvat from the TCC warship, the *Agincourt*."

Addie bobbed up and down. "Sir, nice to meet you. Nice to meet all of you."

"Uh, hello," Horvat said. "What species are you? I'm not familiar with shapeshifting energy beings...."

Addie said, "I'm a sldkfjfoisut."

My new friends were crowding around my old friend. This looked like it could take a while. I decided to take a break and let them chat for a few moments.

I got some water and accessed my fon. It needed a charge. Darn it. If it did have any info I needed, I'd have to wait for it. I plugged it in and rejoined the group.

"What do you mean you had a baby with Jack?" Singh was saying. "How?"

"The usual way," Addie said. "Mostly. Sex."

Everyone turned and looked at me. I smiled and waved. "Yes, I helped Addie have Slid. He's an awesome little shapeshifting energy being."

My new friends seemed very surprised if their expressions were anything to go by.

"My baby is on the *Shakespeare*," she said. "It was hard to leave him, but Quinta and I are on a secret mission, and we thought it might be too dangerous for Slid."

"Where's Quinta?" I asked.

"Where is the *Shakespeare*?" Singh, Horvat, Max, and I all asked simultaneously.

"It's not back yet?" she asked.

"Back from where?" Horvat asked.

"They got a distress call from a ship running out of oxygen," she said. "They went to help them. They're not back yet? Oh no. Slid!" Her energy form started turning black, and she sank towards the floor.

"That's why we're here," I said. "Don't worry. We're going to save the *Shakespeare*. The *Agincourt* is an awesome ship; it can save stuff, for sure. We'll save the *Shakespeare* and everyone on board."

"What else can you tell us about their mission?" Horvat asked.

"That's all I know," she said, now inky all over.

"We will save them, I promise." I held my hands up. "Right now, can you tell us anything else about your mission? Are you with Quinta? Where is she?"

Just then, we heard, "Addie? Where are you? Oh, no! Addie?" via the external sensors. The voice got more and more panicked.

We all rushed to the front viewscreen to see what appeared to be a Quihiri, mostly. Every few moments, she'd get blurry on the edges.

I punched the button for external communications. "Quinta? It's Jack. You're saved!"

She seemed to be looking all around. "Why can't I see you? Are you a sldkfjfoisut now, too?"

What? "No. Just come around to the back of the shuttle so we can let you in," I said.

"The back of what?" she said. "I don't see anything." She morphed into her energy-being form, a cloud of energy particles.

I jogged back to the door, opened it, and stuck my head out. "Over here, honey."

"Thanks." She quickly floated to me and came inside.

I closed the door.

Then, we basically repeated the previous scene, only the gang told Quinta what was going on.

"But wait a minute!" she finally said. "I have news, too. I found the Quihiri underground!"

"The what now?" I asked.

"The Quihiri underground," she said. "We heard there were some good Quihiri who don't want to kill everyone."

Addie floated up. "Yes, they were rumored to be open to the whole sldkfjfoisut evolutionary process."

"Yes!" Quinta seemed excited now, sparkling with shades of silver and gold.

"This sounds excellent," I said. "Can you try to get them to help with the FTL drive situation?"

Now Addie was sparkling, too. The sldkfjfoisut were kind of awesome, the way they wore their hearts on their sleeves--so to speak. I felt like I was sparkling, too.

"Yes!" Quinta said again.

"This all sounds like good news, I guess. But..." Horvat said.

"It sounds like you guys should continue your mission," Singh said.

"It doesn't help us find the *Shakespeare*," Horvat said.

"The *Shakespeare*'s not back yet?" Quinta stopped sparkling. Addie stopped sparkling. Aw. I felt like I had stopped sparkling.

Max looked at me. "Jack? What was that tech you picked up? Does it have any info?"

Oh, right. Our actual mission. "Sure," I said. "I'll just get it." I walked back to my fon. It had enough charge now to show I did have a message. I accessed it.

A small holographic head of Gina appeared in the shuttle. "If you get this, Jack, something must have happened." She looked serious and not sparkly at all. " I appended our planned course to this message, and we'll keep pinging it while we're in range. The *Shakespeare*'s in trouble."

"I'm coming, Gina!" I said. "*Once more unto the breach, dear friends, once more*!"

Chapter Fourteen

It was difficult saying goodbye to Addie and Quinta, but they said they needed to continue their mission on Quihiri working with the underground. Our ultimate goal was to defeat the bad Quihiri and restore all the FTL drives to working order, after all.

"*Parting is such sweet sorrow*," I said.

"*Farewell: my blessing season this in thee*," Addie said.

We all looked at Quinta.

"Goodbye, forsooth, good parting something something," she said. "Sorry, I don't know your Terran quotes."

"Don't worry about it," Singh said, straightening his uniform. "Only nerds go around quoting stuff."

Max barked, presumably in agreement. "*I had rather be a dog, and bay the moon…*" he said. So, he did like quotes?

Anyway, Addie and Quinta exited the cloaked shuttle.

Horvat said, "Take off in ten seconds. Back to the *Agincourt*." He was already sitting in the pilot's seat. When did that happen?

The rest of us scrambled to sit down. I belted Max into the seat next to me.

"So, after we rendezvous with the *Agincourt*, we're going to Jax and the *Shakespeare*, right?" he asked.

"Sure." Hopefully.

We zoomed away from the planet. But the artificial gravity worked fine, so it didn't feel like zooming. It didn't feel like anything.

"Do you think people ever turn off artificial gravity?" I said quietly to Max.

"What? On purpose?" he said. "Why?"

I guessed that was a no.

"Stay on mission, Jones," Horvat said, turning around.

Possibly I was a little too scatterbrained. I couldn't even remember the last time I'd had sex. There was something relevant there… I glanced around the small shuttle and realized my sex options were currently pretty limited. Singh was about it. I looked at Max.

"What?" he asked.

Focus, Jack! "Uh. Nothing."

I grabbed my fon and started scrolling through the new data. The distress call from the stranded ship seemed legit. The *Shakespeare*'s course through space seemed clear.

I glanced at Max again.

"Why do you keep looking at me?" he asked.

"Oh!" Palm plant on forehead. In the back of my mind, I was thinking about that moment in engineering when he nipped me. "My wish! You prompted me to save my wish."

Max leaned toward me. "Are you gonna use it now? What do you wish for?"

"I wish we were next to the *Shakespeare*!" Belatedly, I realized if they were under fire or underwater, things could get very dicey very soon.

But the scene out the viewscreen was the same: space. I glanced around the shuttle. Same boring walls, floor, and ceiling. Same boring seats. Same sort of boring team--except for Max. I didn't think a talking dog would ever get boring. And me--I'd never be boring, either, of course.

"It didn't work?" Max asked, also looking around.

Maybe it just seemed like nothing was different. "Commander Horvat, what's our position, sir?"

"We're almost to the *Agincourt*," he said. "Why?"

"No sudden position changes?" I asked. "Nothing's different?"

"No," Singh said. "Why?"

"No reason," I said, mind racing. Why didn't my power work?

We docked with the *Agincourt*. Horvat and Singh immediately started striding purposefully somewhere since they knew where they were going. I strode purposefully with them.

Max trotted after us purposefully.

Soon, we stepped onto the giant bridge. Ah ha. We'd been striding towards the bridge.

"Report," Captain Wright said.

"We retrieved the tech," Horvat said, holding out his hand and staring at me.

"What?" I said.

"Give me the fon," he said. "It's got the *Shakespeare*'s course."

"No. It's my fon," I said. "I need it." It had my memories on it. It had my contacts, pictures, music and, well, my everything. "And you don't need my fon. I know how to take us directly to them. Just turn on your FTL drive and make a tiny jump."

"A jump where?" Wright said.

"It doesn't matter," I said. My new hypothesis was my special power only worked while the FTL drive was actually operating. In hindsight, it was obvious. It depended on the probabilities of the quantum drive. I couldn't believe I'd been so stupid as to think I could postpone my wish. I resisted another palm plant with great difficulty.

"We can't just jump." The *Agincourt*'s navigator snorted. "We need to know where to jump."

"No, we don't," I said. "Just jump an inch or whatever."

"Give me the fon, Jones," Wright said. "Get it, Horvat."

And then, Horvat grabbed it out of my hand and started quickly walking to the giant captain's chair.

"Hey!" I ran after Horvat and tried to grab my fon back. He easily dodged my efforts.

"Stand down, Jones," Wright said.

"Give me my fon back!" I said.

Max started barking.

"Get that dog out of here," Wright said.

All the attention in the room focused on Max.

As one of the crewmembers approached Max, he bared his teeth, flattened his ears and growled.

The crewmember flinched back.

"Thanks, Max, buddy," I said. "But you need to calm down." I turned back to the captain. "Leave Max alone. And listen to me. Just jump. And give me back my fon."

But Wright didn't give me my fon. Instead, he accessed my fon. He must have a captain's password override.

He sighed. "You two stand down." He pointed at Max and me. "You're confined to quarters. Jones, I'll give you your fon if and when I'm done with it. You better shape up, or you're going to the brig." He scowled at us. "And the next stop is the airlock, so don't tempt me."

What kind of ship was this? Airlock? He'd murder us? That didn't sound legal, but I immediately shut up.

"Singh, escort them to quarters and then guard outside," Wright said.

Singh looked as shocked as I felt. "Uh, yes, sir." He didn't want to go out of the airlock either. He pointed at the door to the bridge, swallowing a lot.

As the three of us exited the bridge, Wright said, "Navigation, follow the *Shakespeare*'s course."

Singh led Max and me to the same quarters we'd woken up in only a few hours ago. He opened the door. The bed was still rumpled. "So, here we are," he said. "Get inside. And no guff." Guff? What was guff?

"Do you think you can make us do anything?" Max asked.

Singh gulped and said quietly, "Airlock?"

Max growled but walked inside.

I followed him.

Singh closed the door behind us.

Max and I sat down on the bunk.

"I don't like these TCC assholes," Max said. "Why are they such assholes?"

"They aren't usually," I said. "At least the crew of the *Shakespeare* isn't. The crew of the *Shakespeare* is awesome. But then, we're primarily a ship of entertainers, not soldiers."

"I hope Jax is okay." Max lay down, resting his head on his paws.

"I hope so, too," I said. "The crew of the *Shakespeare* will take care of him." If they can.

"I can't believe Wright was so uncooperative," I said. "My captain always does what I want." Eventually.

"Aren't you married to your captain?" Max asked.

"Yes." Huh. I didn't realize how unusual Gina was. She

deserved a lot more love from me.

We lay on the bunk and sulked a little.

Finally, I said, "Do you think the *Agincourt* is using its FTL drive now?"

"I'd say it's likely," Max said. "Are you going to use your power?"

"I'd say it's likely." I grinned.

He grinned. "Good luck."

I pressed my eyes closed and concentrated. "We are next to the *Shakespeare*. We are next to the *Shakespeare*. We are next to the *Shakespeare*." I really concentrated.

Then, I opened my eyes and looked around. Everything in the small room looked the same. Did it work?

"Did it work?" Max asked.

I shrugged and then popped up out of bed and went over to the door. "Singh, are you still out there?"

"Yeah," he said through the door. "Why?"

"I think we're next to the *Shakespeare*," I said through the door.

The door whisked open. "Huh?" he said. "Next to the *Shakespeare*? How?"

"Can you check?" I smiled sexily at him.

He seemed caught in my handsome smile for a few moments. "Huh? What?"

"Can you go check on our location?" I batted my eyelashes.

"Uh, no," he said. " That doesn't make any sense."

We stood there looking at one another for a few moments. I'll admit it, he looked good. And, of course, I looked really good.

Finally, I said, "Really? You don't believe me?"

"No," he said, looking like he didn't not believe me.

"Do you want to come inside and talk about it?" I asked.

"What about guarding the room?" he asked.

"Max will guard the room," I said. "Plus, that will give us some privacy."

From inside, Max cleared his throat. "Sure. I can stand outside in the hall and keep an eye on things." He walked up to us and wagged his tail. "No problem."

I took a step back from the door and gestured Singh inside. "Come on in. It's gotta be more comfortable in here rather than standing in the hall."

Singh looked conflicted.

"I don't think I even know your first name," I said. "What is it?"

"Aarav," he said.

"Beautiful," I said. "Isn't it beautiful, Max?"

"Yes, beautiful," Max said.

"I guess it wouldn't hurt to come inside for a couple of minutes," Aarav said.

Aarav stepped inside, and Max stepped outside. I closed the door. Then, I went over to the bed and sat down and patted the empty space next to me.

Aarav came and sat down next to me.

"You are a very attractive man, Aarav," I said. "You don't mind me saying that, do you?"

"Uh, no," he said. "I don't mind."

"Your lips look very kissable." I leaned in. "You don't mind me kissing them, do you?" I whispered.

"Uh, no," he said. "I, uh, don't mind."

We kissed for a few moments, and it was delicious. He appeared to be a novice kisser, but that made it all the sweeter.

Time passed pleasantly.

We were rudely interrupted by a loud barking noise coming from the hall.

"Max?" I asked. "What's wrong?"

More barking.

Reluctantly, I got off the bed and went and opened the door. Max was definitely worked up about something. When he saw me, he said, "I hear soldiers coming." He pointed his nose down the hall.

Plot twist! I straightened my uniform and plastered on a smile.

When the armed soldiers reached us, I said, "What can I do for you, gentlemen?"

"Grab him," the leader said.

One of the minions grabbed my arm and started dragging me back the way they'd come.

"Get the others, too," the leader said.

At least Max was armed to the teeth. Ha.

Other minions approached Max and Aarav, but then I couldn't see anymore because I was being dragged down the hall. I had to struggle to keep on my feet. "What's up, brothers? I'm happy to help. We're all in TCC together. Yay, Terra!"

They didn't answer and instead kept dragging me down the hall.

Eventually, they dragged me onto the bridge, thrusting me forward. I stumbled.

Captain Wright glowered at me from his large captain's chair. "Where the hell are we?" he thundered. "Something weird happened; we aren't where we're supposed to be. For some reason. I suspect you had something to do with it, Jones."

I looked out of the large viewscreen to see an unfamiliar star system. The central star was slightly bigger and oranger than the friendly yellow sun I was used to. I spied several terrestrial planets and one huge greenish-yellowish gas giant. I didn't see the *Shakespeare*. "I, uh, think we're next to the *Shakespeare*," I said. "Did you scan for her?"

"Scan for the *Shakespeare*!" he bellowed. Then he got up out of his chair and strode towards me. "Where are we? This was not the course we laid in."

I could not for the life of me recall who knew about my special skill and who did not. It was supposed to be secret. I said brilliantly, "Uh…."

"*Shakespeare*!" one of the crewmembers said. "I detect the *Shakespeare*."

"I guess you did help, Jones." Wright turned quickly and stalked back to his big chair. "Red alert. Full shields. Approach the *Shakespeare*."

"Yay!" I jumped up and down and clapped my hands.

Max said, "Yay." I hadn't realized he was standing slightly behind me.

I also saw Aarav, who I didn't realize was behind me. I smiled sexily at him. He blushed.

We flew past a jungle planet covered in green plants and wispy white clouds, and then the *Shakespeare* appeared on the viewscreen. She seemed to be floating listlessly on her side.

"Closer!" Wright said.

We got closer. The *Shakespeare* had scorch marks on her.

"Oh, no!"

"Report!" Wright said.

"She's taken significant damage, Captain Wright," one of the crewmembers said.

"No life signs on the ship," another one said.

"No!" My knees collapsed, and I fell to the deck.

Chapter Fifteen

I'd found the *Shakespeare*, but I was too late. I felt empty, totally hollowed out. Was the oxygen level getting low?

"Commander Horvat, take a small team and check it out," Captain Wright said.

"Yes, sir," Horvat said.

I thrust my hand into the air. "Request permission to join the team, sir! I know the ship."

Wright nodded. "Yeah. Good idea, Jones. "

Max said, "Request permission to join the team, sir!"

"No," the captain said.

"We don't have any spacesuits that would fit you," Horvat said.

Max bared his teeth and started growling.

"Chill, Max," I said. "If Jax is there, I'll find him. And if he needs help, I'll help him. I promise."

He relaxed a little. "You better."

Horvat was already at the door to the bridge. "Come on, Jones."

A little later in the spacesuit-putting-on-room Horvat made introductions. "Jones, this is Patel and Nguyen. Guys, this is Ensign Jones."

Unfortunately, I was having a little trouble remembering how to put on a spacesuit, so I wasn't paying attention. Had I, personally, ever been on a spacewalk? I didn't think so. Of course, I'd had the training at the academy when I was a teenager. Or, at least, I remembered having it.

I managed to get my body inside the suit, but then I could not figure out how to get the helmet to make an air-tight seal.

"You okay there, Ensign?" one of the other team members said. He had on a bright-blue spacesuit instead of my boring standard-issue white one with a clear faceplate.

"Uh," I said. "I mean, of course, I'm awesome. But I'm having a little minor trouble with the helmet."

He reached over and pressed something, and whoosh, my helmet indicator was green. Air-tight.

"Thanks," I said. When I checked out the rest of the team, one had on a bright red suit and one bright yellow. I couldn't see any faces through their mirrored helmets. "Cool suits."

"Yeah," Blue said. "They're special." So, the radios were working, and I was tuned to the right channel. Good.

"We're part of an elite team deployed for special missions," Red said. Was that Horvat's voice? I thought it was.

"Three people doesn't sound like much of a team," I said.

"There's more of us," Blue said. "They'll be deployed if needed." He seemed to be an alpha male.

"So, you're a virgin?" Yellow snickered. Was he the clown of the group?

The rest of them also snickered.

I was torn between bragging and being a gentleman. "*Can one desire too much of a good thing*?" I smiled sexily.

They all laughed.

"That's a yes. We're talking about spacewalks, Jones," Yellow said. He put his arm around my shoulders. "Don't worry, virgin. I'll take good care of you."

I gulped.

The four of us approached the *Shakespeare* in a shuttle. The way she floated listlessly there on her side was sad. But I had no one to blame but myself for not finding her earlier. *I have that within which passes show, these but the trappings and the suits of woe.*

I hoped I wasn't about to find a ship of ghosts. *I am dying, Egypt, dying.*

"Jones?" Red said. "You with us?"

I shook my head. Okay, too many quotes, even for me. "Yes, sir."

"We're coming up on the shuttle bay," Blue, our pilot, said.

"Doors open. Forcefield down." He glanced at the co-pilot, Red. Why? I didn't think they could see each other's faces.

Yellow, sitting behind Red, turned to face me. No doubt, he could read my expression, and it wasn't good.

No one needed to say anything further. Open doors and no forcefield were bad.

We flew right into the shuttle bay and parked. Only the red emergency lights lit the vast expanse.

Blue turned off the shuttle.

They all jumped out of their seats and checked the weapons and ammo strapped to their suits. Cool.

I had no weapons or ammo strapped to the outside of my suit. Bummer.

"Come on then, virgin," Yellow said as Blue opened the hatch. We all turned on our exterior suit lights.

The four of us stepped into the shuttle bay. They drew their weapons. My boots clicked a little as the magnetic field in my boots reacted with the metal floor. Since we were inside the ship, I didn't know if this actually counted as a spacewalk.

"Should we close the doors or turn on the forcefields?" I asked. Now the team looked dark red, purple, and orange. I glanced down; I looked pink.

"We'll see," Red said. "Where's the closest control console?"

"No shuttles or other ships," Blue said. That was true. The bay was empty.

"Jones, console?" Yellow said near my side.

I pointed to the door to the interior of the ship. "Near the interior door."

The four of us clicked our way up to the door.

Which stood open. Oh no. Vacuum on the ship. I realized I'd been holding on to a shred of hope that things weren't quite so dire. A tear escaped my eye and started floating around the inside of my helmet. I blinked the rest back.

"I'm sure this is tough, but you need to keep your head in the game, Jones," Red said.

He was right. This might turn out to be the most challenging thing I'd ever do, but I owed it to my friends--or their memories--to be competent. And that was the last non-mission thought I would have.

I marched up to the console and input my passcode. It worked. I accessed the exterior door controls to close it. No, go. I accessed the forcefield controls. Nope. What was going on here? I accessed the ship's main control dashboard. Ah ha. "No fuel."

The Color Rangers all looked over my shoulders.

"No oxygen." I punched some more keys. "No water. No food." I stepped back from the console. "Weird. Why would everything be at zero?"

No one answered my question. Instead, Red said, "Can you check the logs and the detector data from here?"

I shook my head. "No. We need to go to the bridge for that."

Yellow took a step back and held his arm towards the open interior door.

It was eerie clicking through the empty red-lit ship. All the murals looked washed out in shades of red, brown, and gray. It all reminded me of my childhood dreams of Mars, the red planet. Of course, when I went to Mars on a high school field trip, it wasn't all red.

Here, some dark black scorch marks were on the walls as if there'd been a battle. In the gloom, they also seemed eerie.

One thing that wasn't eerie: no bodies. Thank the stars.

The four of us clicked to the bridge. It was empty as well.

"No bodies," Blue said.

"Yeah," I said. "I noticed."

Red was already at one of the control consoles. "Locked down," he said. "Only crewmembers can access ship systems."

"Good thing you brought me along," I said, walking up to one of the consoles.

"Good thing we brought you along," Yellow said.

I accessed the system with my unique passcode and turned off the emergency alerts. The ambient light turned from dim red to dim white.

A giant image of Gina appeared on the screen. She looked beautiful (of course) but very stressed out. "If you're seeing this, Jack, you found the ship. And, unfortunately, you did not find the crew." She paused, seemingly gathering her wits. "I can't believe

I'm about to say this, but space pirates have attacked us."

Space pirates? Oh no.

"The distress call we received was fake, a trap," she said. "When we arrived, heavily-armed pirates boarded us." In the background, I heard what sounded like pulse rifles. She glanced in their direction. "We managed to hold them off to get the crew into shuttles or escape pods and get away." They might be okay! Yay! "I've locked down the ship's system so they can't take the ship itself." The shooting sounds got closer. She picked up her pulse rifle from off-camera. "Hopefully, TCC can find us, or what's left of us, in this planetary system." An energy beam flew past her, and the recording ended. It didn't look good for Gina. Boo.

"The pirates must have drained the ship of resources," Blue said.

"Makes sense," Red said.

"You okay, Jones?" Yellow said.

I had to be okay. My friends were still in trouble. "I want to access internal sensors and ensure no one's trapped behind an airlock or anything." There was a minor chance someone could still be alive if they were onboard.

"Download the data," Red said to Blue. "Especially any info about these pirates."

I didn't detect any life signs. Not even any sldkfjfoisut--I checked carefully. "No life signs."

Yellow was watching me and nodded.

"Should we scan the planetary system for human life signs?" I asked.

"Better to do it on the *Agincourt*," Red said.

What about Jax? He wasn't officially part of the crew. Would Gina evacuate him with the others?

I had a very bad thought; I had to sit down. Weren't Jax's crew on the *Whydah* space pirates? What if the *Whydah* crew was looking for me? Trying to get revenge on me for stealing their ship, for stranding them on the station?

No. It couldn't be them. How would they find the *Shakespeare*? How could they get way out here? We were many light-years away from the station.

"You okay?" Yellow asked. "You look like you might be sick. Not a good idea in a suit, I gotta tell you."

"Uh," I said. "We should see if the *Shakespeare*'s FTL drive is still here."

"Good idea," Red said. "Can't you tell from here?"

"Right." I input some commands. "Oh, no. It says the FTL drive is off-line."

"What does that mean?" Blue asked.

"Off-line could be off-line," I said. "Or it could mean it's gone, stolen. That would not be good. It still worked." The *Whydah* crew would know the value of a working FTL drive.

If it were the *Whydah* crew, Jax would have recognized them. I stood and scanned the computer for messages or anything else from Jax. Nothing. On second thought, that made sense; he didn't have access to the *Shakespeare*'s system because he wasn't part of the crew.

Could Jax still be in league with the *Whydah*? I couldn't believe he'd betray Max.

At any rate, if he'd been staying in my quarters, he might have left me a message there. "I have to go to my quarters!" I said.

"Now is not the time to pick up your toothbrush, Jones," Red said.

"No," I said. "I think there might be a message there for me."

Red pointed at Yellow. "Go with him, Patel. We'll meet you back at the shuttle bay." Ah-ha: Yellow was Patel. That meant Blue was Nguyen.

"Stop by engineering," I said. "See if the drive is there."

Red, er, Horvat, nodded.

I turned and started running towards my quarters. Mistake. Somehow, I must have lost all direct contact with the floor because I floated away. I flailed around with my arms and legs, accomplishing nothing.

Patel walked quickly after me and grabbed my arm, dragging me back down to the floor.

"I can't believe I was just talking about how fun no artificial gravity would be," I muttered.

"Come on," he said. "Where are your quarters?"

We quickly walked over to my quarters. I used my passcode to open the door, heart in my throat. What if Jax's body was in here?

The door whooshed open, and my quarters were empty. That was a relief.

There was something scrawled on the wall. All the pictures (of Old Jack) had been removed. I walked inside. The message said, 'The *Whydah* crew is here! They're after me! They're after you, Jack!'

Oh no. I sank down on my bunk. The *Whydah* captain, especially, and the others had seemed ruthless.

Patel walked up to the wall. "Is the *Whydah* a ship?" He peered right at the message. "What is this written in?" He reached up one gloved finger, wiped the final exclamation mark, and held his finger up to his faceplate. "Is this makeup?"

I nodded. "Yeah. Probably." It had the look of my favorite eyeliner.

Over the radio, Horvat said, "You were right, Jack. The FTL drive is gone."

I leaned back. My actions had put everyone I cared about in serious danger.

This was my worst nightmare.

I wished I was dead.

Chapter Sixteen

Back on the *Agincourt*, Max met me at the door to the shuttle bay. The rest of the team was still on the shuttle doing official-type things. As soon as I stepped onto the ship, I unlatched my spacesuit helmet. Ship air rushed in, smelling of sweat and shuttle fuel.

"Did you find Jax?" Max asked. "Is he dead?"

I took off the helmet. "We didn't find any bodies. We think the crew abandoned ship in shuttles and escape pods. Jax left me a note."

"What'd it say? How is he?" Max was very bouncy, quivering with excitement. He'd never seemed so much like a regular dog to me before.

"He said the *Whydah* crew attacked the *Shakespeare*."

Max yelped.

"Yeah," I said. "You don't need to tell me. The *Whydah* crew is bad news."

"You need to tell Captain Wright about it," Horvat said, appearing next to me, red helmet under his arm.

Patel stepped onto the ship and took off his helmet. I hadn't gotten a good look at him before. He was dreamy; he was exactly as I'd imagined Aladdin. He could rub my magic lamp anytime. "What's that look?" he asked.

"Nothing," I said and cleared my throat. "Good mission."

Blue, Nguyen, walked past us with his helmet off. He was as super-hot as the superhero Lightning. I couldn't believe I'd made a not-awesome first impression; it wasn't like me--what a lost opportunity.

"Get your head in the game, Jack!" Max said, prancing in front of me. "Let's go see Captain Wright. Now. We need to find

Jax!"

He was right.

"Your dog is bossy," Nguyen said and nodded. "I like it."

Max ran off towards the bridge, and I followed him.

"Suit, Jones!" Horvat called after me. He pointed towards the spacesuit-putting-on-room.

I ran (sort of, it's hard to do in a spacesuit) to the room and quickly took off my suit. The rest of the Color Rangers still beat me to their skivvies. If things hadn't been so dire, I would have wanted to hang out and take in the scenery, but I didn't. My friends from the *Shakespeare* needed my help.

I turned around and dashed to the bridge to talk to Captain Wright. Max was ahead of me the whole way.

On the bridge, Captain Wright seemed surprised to see me for some reason. "Let's, ah, go into the wardroom, Ensign Jones." We entered the room next to the bridge, and he pointed at one of the chairs around the large table.

I sat, panting a little from my run.

Max nipped my finger lightly.

I pulled a chair out for him, and he jumped into it.

Captain Wright sat down and steepled his fingers in front of him on the table. "You're out of uniform, Jones."

I glanced down. Oops, I was naked. "This couldn't wait, sir," I said. "The *Shakespeare* was attacked by the crew of the *Whydah*, a group of space pirates that I've had ...dealings with in the past." I turned to Max. "Max used to be part of the crew. Did they know you were sentient?"

"No," Max said. "They thought I was just Jax's pet."

I said, "We need to scan the planetary system for TCC tech, shuttles and escape pods, as well as human life signs. We think the crew of the *Shakespeare* abandoned ship."

"That's not procedure," the captain said. "TCC officers are supposed to stay and protect their ship."

"The *Whydah* crew is ruthless," Max said. "And Jack here has them all riled up. They would have done brutal things to the TCC crew. Jax must have warned them."

"All riled up?" Captain Wright's eyebrows rose on his forehead. "Why riled up?"

"I, ah, may have accidentally stolen the *Whydah*," I said.

"And sort of abandoned its crew on the station."

Nguyen, Patel, and Horvat, all wearing plain black uniforms, walked in quietly and sat at the table.

"It's not like I threw them out the airlock!" I said. "They shouldn't be that riled up, right?"

"No, they're riled," Max said. "Definitely riled." He nodded.

"This *Whydah* isn't on my radar," Wright said. "They sound small-time. TCC doesn't consider them a threat."

"They should," I said. "They were in league with the Quihiri in the war."

"We're getting off-track!" Max said. "Look for Jax!"

"Yes, he's right!" I said. "Look for the *Shakespeare*'s crew. They're in danger!" I did not add, 'And it's all my fault.'

"Captain Wright, I can't believe I'm about to say this, but I agree with the dog," Horvat said. "TCC doesn't leave sentients behind. We need to find them."

"Yes." Wright put his palms on the table and stood. "Okay, we'll focus on finding the *Shakespeare* crew."

Max jumped down and ran after him to the bridge.

I stood.

Patel came over and put an arm around my shoulders. "I'm liking this new uniform."

Was he too much? Oh, no. Was this how it felt for other people when I flirted with them?

"Stand down, Patel," Horvat said with disgust in his voice. "Jones, go get dressed."

Dressed, back on the bridge, I tried to pant quietly (a lot of running around).

Patel caught my eye and winked. The wink seemed inappropriate, given the circumstances.

The captain was saying, "No technology detected. No human life signs. Initiate search pattern beta on the second planet."

Wright glanced my way. "The second planet can best support human life, so it's our best shot."

Did the space pirates know that? "Any sign of the space pirates?" I asked with a small, very small, wobble in my voice.

"No," Wright said as if he wanted to find a sign of the space pirates and wreak vengeance on them. I gulped. He continued. "We thoroughly scanned the system, and there are no other spaceships here."

An officer at the sensor controls turned around and faced us. "I'm not detecting any technology on this planet, TCC or otherwise, Captain," she said.

I gulped again. "But if they powered everything down, you wouldn't detect the shuttles and escape pods, right?"

Captain Wright looked at me with pity. "That's not procedure. They should at least leave on a beacon wherever they landed."

"But space pirates were after them!" I said. "They're hiding from the pirates." And, no, those were not sentences I ever expected to utter.

Standing next to me, Horvat said, "It's more likely the pirates intercepted their pods and captured them."

"Begin life scans of the rest of the system," Captain Wright said.

Max barked. It was as if he got more doggy when he got more upset.

"No!" I said. "If this planet best supports human life, I think they're here. We need to go down there and look for them. We have to."

"It's a whole planet, Jones," Horvat said. "If the sensors aren't detecting anything from up here, there's no way a landing team could find something."

"I can find something! Do you detect life signs, intelligent life, on the planet?" I asked the sensor officer. I had a gut feeling my friends were here.

"Yes." She nodded. "A lot of life signs. This planet is rich in indigenous life, plants, and animals. They even have a low-tech sentient species."

"It makes more sense to survey the rest of the system, Ensign," Captain Wright said. "And maybe we can detect a sign of the pirates' ship before they went to FTL space." He frowned. "Assuming they went to FTL space."

"They stole the *Shakespeare*'s FTL drive," Horvat said. "So, however they got here, they can access FTL space now."

Max barked again. I glanced down at him. "I hear you,

buddy." I looked at the captain. "Me and Max are taking a shuttle and looking for the *Shakespeare*'s crew on this planet."

"No," the captain said.

Max growled quietly.

"I know they're down there!" I said. "We have to find them! Do you want to find them or not?" I wasn't starting to get hysterical.

"I can lead a small away team, Captain Wright, sir," Horvat said.

"I'll keep an eye on Jones," Patel said. I didn't want him to come, but I probably needed all the help I could get.

Wright exhaled. "All right, Horvat, Patel, Nguyen, Jones--"

Max growled.

"And Max!" I said. "We need Max. He can sniff Jax out!"

He barked in agreement.

"I thought you were Jack?" Horvat said to me.

"No, Jaxxxx Jones," I said, trying to emphasize the x.

Horvat started to ask another question.

Max barked.

"We don't have time for this!" I said and turned and started running back to the shuttle bay. Max was right behind me. The others followed.

The five of us, this time without spacesuits, pulled away from the *Agincourt* in a shuttle. Nguyen was piloting again.

"Jones?" Horvat asked. "Any ideas on where to go?" We approached the planet. From the air, it looked like one big, green jungle.

My mind raced. The *Shakespeare* crew would want to blend in with the indigenous life in case the pirates were still after them. "Head for the biggest city."

"No cities," Nguyen said.

"The biggest town, then," I said. "The biggest farm, whatever. Wherever the most sentients are."

In stealth mode, we flew over a large village. It was after dark, but we could tell there was some kind of gathering or festival. "There!" I said. "They'll be there, somewhere."

Patel exhaled. "No doubt they'll be hiding. It won't be easy to find them among all those sentients." I didn't agree; I knew my people.

I petted Max's head. "That's why Max is along."

He sniffed loudly. "Right. I can find Jax, no matter what." Ah. He could smell him.

We parked the stealthed shuttle in a small clearing away from the largest village. When the back door opened, humidity roiled in. I immediately broke out in a sweat.

The scents of green growing things, rotting leaves, basically nature, filled the air. The atmosphere was full of the calls, clicks, and thrums of forest creatures. And something else…

"Is that music?" I asked. Very faintly, I thought I heard some familiar strains.

We walked stealthily in the direction of the town. I smelled the faint scent of wood smoke. As we walked on a path through the forest, nearing the town, I definitely heard some familiar music. Terran music! They were here! My friends were here. They had to be here! I couldn't help smiling.

Patel touched my shoulder. "What's that sexy smile about?"

"Let's focus on the mission. And call me Ensign Jones."

He backed off.

I reached down to touch Max's head. He was trembling.

Max looked up. "He's here! I smell him! He's here!"

"Yes!" I said. "But we need to be careful. We don't know what the situation is. Be cool." Not easy to do in this humidity. I was already sweating a lot.

We walked through some trees and came to a clearing. A wooden stage had been erected in the middle, surrounded by bonfires in containers. The natives, reminding me of bipedal tigers, stood around the stage, enraptured.

In the center of the stage stood Gina in an impromptu cat costume. She sang, "*Touch me, it's so easy to leave me, all alone with the memory...*"

Other *Shakespeare* crew members on stage, also dressed as cats, were humming along in accompaniment. Hurray! I found my friends! And they were all right! Hurray! I may have jumped up and down slightly.

And they were doing *Cats*! Glancing around the cat-like crowd, I couldn't say I was exactly surprised.

In my ear, Commander Horvat whispered, "Is that Captain

Gomez on stage? What is she doing?"

"*Cats*!" I whispered back, grinning.

She kept going. I hadn't appreciated before what a good singer she was, her voice deep and melodious.

The hummed accompaniment died out gracefully.

There was a moment of silence, and then the crowd of actual cats started making chirping noises.

"I smell Jax!" Max said, next to me. Before I could stop him, he ran up on stage and jumped on Jax--whom I hadn't recognized with his fake whiskers, makeup, cat ears, and crude brown tunic and tail. Clearly, Jax was no longer a prisoner. The crew of the *Shakespeare* must trust him now.

For his part, Jax was thrilled to see Max and immediately dropped to the stage. The two of them rolled around together, and Max licked him enthusiastically.

Eventually, Jax and Max and the rest of the cast surrounded me.

Jax nodded to me.

I nodded to him. It was much more awkward than I'd been expecting. Maybe it had something to do with the fact that Max seemed to prefer Jax.

"Thank you for taking care of Max," he said.

I glanced down at Max. "It was a pleasure."

"You got here sooner than we expected," Carter (*Shakespeare* First Officer Carter Nillion, Gina's other husband besides me) said, standing next to me.

"What are you doing?" Horvat asked him.

"*Cats*!" I said.

He threw me a dirty look."*Why* are you doing *Cats*?" he asked Carter.

"We don't have anything," Carter said, keeping his attention directed towards the stage. "We had to sing for our supper. And it seemed to be working--until you showed up. Uh, oh." Fumbling, he pulled a small machine out of his pocket.

A large native, wearing an elaborate belt with several tools, approached us. He (?) bared his sizable sharp teeth and said something--I had no idea what--in a low, raspy voice.

Out of Carter's little machine, we heard, "What is this new prey?"

Chapter Seventeen

I stood in the middle of a verdant jungle on a strange planet surrounded by menacing cat people with giant carnivorous teeth. Great, right? I loved my life! My friends were okay, so I could face anything.

I bared my teeth and said, “Greetings, Esteemed Leader! It’s an honor to meet you. Please consider me your faithful servant.” I bowed. I ad-libbed a little song, “*Hello, hello, hello*.”

My words came out as cat noises from Carter’s translation machine.

Then the cat-chief made a noise that sounded suspiciously like purring.

Carter whispered, “Thanks, Jack.”

“I like this kit,” the cat chief’s words were translated. “He will sit next to me at the feast.”

“Uh, sir,” Carter said. “Now that our tribe has found us, we were hoping to leave with them.”

“You asked to partake of our feast,” the cat chief said. “You paid for your part. I gave you my word. You don’t want to dishonor me, do you? You will attend the feast. “ He bared his giant teeth again.

“Uh, yes, sir.” Carter’s teeth-covered expression said he was terrified.

I felt a hand on my back and turned to see Gina in her impromptu cat costume. “It’s good to see you, Jack.” She glanced at Carter and opened her mouth--no doubt to ask where our ship was.

“We are all staying for the feast,” Carter said.

Gina was an excellent spy and knew how to roll with the unexpected. She bared her teeth in a big smile and said,

"Wonderful."

Thus, several minutes later found me sitting on a dais at a large table at the right hand of the chief of the cat-people. Gina, with Carter's translator, sat at his left. Several other non-elevated tables formed a large rectangle. We were all in a large clearing in the jungle. A big fire in the center illuminated the scene, along with torches set every few feet along the perimeter. I was getting a kind of Terran Hawaiian vibe. In the center, around the fire, the cat children sat. The cat-children were super cute, resembling giant sentient kittens. I wanted to take some of them home with me.

Carter and a few others from the *Shakespeare* had been relegated to the kiddie area. I saw several of the *Shakespeare* crew sitting at the tables. I did not see my buddies, the Color Rangers, or Max and Jax. I briefly wondered if Max-the-dog was deliberately being kept away from the cat people. Probably. I grinned.

Gina and the cat chief were chatting via the translator. The chief looked bored, as if he'd rather be anywhere else doing anything else with anyone else. Or did cats always look that way?

I leaned back in my chair, sniffing the scents of lush jungle, wood smoke, and grilling meat. I glanced over at Gina. I was so relieved the *Shakespeare* crew was all safe and sound, I grinned again. This was turning out to be a good night.

A female (?) cat walked up and held out a crude jug.

I nodded and smiled widely, showing my teeth.

She poured some liquid into a crude cup on the table in front of me.

I grabbed it and took a sip, almost choking. Woo! That was some potent potable. I grinned. Correction: this was turning out to be a great night.

Leaning over the cat chief's plate, Gina frowned and shook her head at me.

I grinned back at her.

She frowned again and pointed at the cup, shaking her head.

"Too late, babe!" I said and smiled.

The chief took plenty of alcohol from the cat waitress. Gina did not.

I sipped the cat beverage, and a warm glow spread from my chest and stomach. I liked this cat planet.

The chief leaned towards me, baring his teeth, and meowed something.

"What?" I said.

He meowed again.

"What?" I said.

He held his hefty hand/paw out for Gina's translator. She handed it to him, and he gave it to me. I placed it on the table in front of me.

The cat meowed again. "I see you appreciate our festival drink," the translator said.

"I do," I said. "It's lovely."

He leaned towards me. "Why does your female not partake? Is she with child?"

I almost spit festive festival drink all over the chief. "Uh, no, sir. Not with child. She's just serious. Careful."

"I once had a female like that." He shot her a glance. "She was not fun."

I resisted the urge to ask what happened to un-fun cat females when they were no longer wives. A cat waitress brought us a platter of grilled meat. The chief ate it with his fingers. Technically, they probably only looked like fingers, what with convergent evolution and such, but I was gonna call them fingers. Anyway, I followed suit. I had no idea what the meat was, but it tasted like …chicken.

The chief and I had an excellent time chatting, eating, and enjoying the festival drink. He told me of his many conquests on the battlefield and in the bedroom. I told him of my many conquests on the battlefield and in the bedroom. Yes, some of those conquests were imaginary, but I was a good storyteller if I did say so myself.

At some point, I realized Gina was no longer sitting next to him. I glanced around the feast. The center fire had burned down, and the cat kids had presumably gone to bed. Most of the folks at the tables were gone, including the *Shakespeare* crewmembers. Did that mean they'd gone up to the *Agincourt*?

The shuttle would have had to take several trips to ferry them up.

"I like you, Jack," the chief said. "You are my favorite alien."

"Thank you, chief," I said. "You are my favorite alien." At the moment, anyway.

A thought made its way through my festive festival-drink fog. "Have you met a lot of aliens?"

"Your group today…" he said, slurring his words slightly.

I nodded.

"And those octopusesss a while back." He swayed back and forth a bit.

"Wait." I steadily held up a finger. "Octopuses? What did they look like?" I didn't slur.

"They had three legs and arms and eyes. It was kinda creepy. I didn't like those aliensss."

They sounded like Quihiri! "I don't like those aliens, either." Since they went to war with us and all. I brushed my hand along the fur on the chief's forearm. "They're not nice and furry, soft, like you."

He brushed his hand/paw along my forearm. "You are sssmooth like a bitty baby or an ancient grandmother. You aren't a baby, are you? Or a grandmother?"

"No," I said, shaking my head and almost falling off my chair. "Tell me more about the aliens."

"They said they wanted to make something they called a treaty," he said. "But it was sssecret. A sssecret treaty."

"What is that?" I didn't sway my words.

"I don't know," he said. "But they gave us a little deliciousss meat. They called it fisssh." He hissed.

I was nodding. "Fisssh is deliciousss."

"And they gave us a sssecret sssomething to hold for them."

"What's a sssecret sssomething?" Was I hissing now, too? I clutched the table so I didn't fall.

"I don't know," he said, clutching the table as he stood. "Do you wanna sssee it?"

"Yesss!" I fumbled for the translator and managed to hang it around my neck.

The two of us made our way carefully down from the dais. The chief was swaying and stumbling. Ha. These cat people really couldn't hold their festival drink, unlike us humans. We put our arms around each other as we walked down a torch-lit path to a large hut.

"S'in here," the chief said. "He pointed at the hut. Do you wanna sssee?"

"Yeah." I nodded and made myself feel a little dizzy for some reason.

We went into the hut; torches lit the inside. In the center stood what looked like three white spheres stuck together.

"What isss it?" the chief asked.

I didn't know. "I don't know."

"Do you want it?" he asked.

"Sssure." I nodded. Oops. Wobbly again.

"You got any fissh you could give uss for it?" he asked.

"*One little fishy swimming in the sea*," I sang. "*Along came another one, and then there were two. Two little fissshies swimming in the sssea*."

"What doess that mean?" he asked.

"Yeah, I got fissshies," I said. "I give you fish. You give me that," I waved at the thing, "that thing, whatever it isss. We do treaty."

He sank down on a pile of pelts. "I knew I liked you." He started snoring.

I stared at him. Then, I turned my head and stared at the thing. What now? I wasn't sure I could carry the thing. It was almost three feet across. And where would I carry it to?

"Is he asleep?" Horvat said from behind me.

I jumped hut-ceiling-high. "Yeah."

I turned around, and Horvat, Patel, and Nguyen stood in black uniforms that made them blend into the shadows. "I need fissshies."

They nodded. "We heard," Horvat said.

I awoke in my small metal box quarters on the *Agincourt*. With a humongous headache. It felt like an icepick was stabbing deep into my temple. I glanced around. Alone. No Max. "Ugh." Wow, that festival drink packed a punch. "Aspirin, I need aspirin…." I moaned.

A shadow in the corner of the ceiling said, "Who's aspirin?"

I jerked back. "Ack!"

The shadow floated down to me, sparkling a little.

"Slid!" I said. "It's so nice to see you!"

"Nice to see you too, Jack!" he said. "Have you seen my mom?"

"Yes," I said. "She's still on Quihiri." At least she had been ...yesterday? Had I seen her only yesterday?

His sparkles turned dark.

"But she's totally fine," I said quickly. "She's great. She said to tell you 'hi,' and she misses you, and she's thinking of you."

His sparkles lightened.

The door to my quarters slid open. Eva stood there, looking as beautiful warrior-princess as ever. She spoke into her comms. "He's up. He looks like shit." She stepped inside, carrying some pills and a large squeeze bulb of liquid.

"He needs aspirin," Slid said. "For the sex, right, Jack?"

Eva shot him a dark look. "What do you know about sex, little one?"

"Nothing," he said.

"Yes, please, I need the aspirin any way I can get it," I said.

She handed me the pills and the squeeze bulb.

I gratefully swallowed the pills, closed my eyes, lay back on the bunk, and sucked the squeeze ball. The cool water felt heavenly in my mouth and going down my throat. "Ahhh..."

"Is that the sex?" Slid asked.

"No, Slid." Eva snickered. "Jack, everyone's waiting for you in the wardroom." She sniffed and grimaced. "But take a shower first." She stepped towards the door. "Come on, Slid. I'll find you some breakfast."

I didn't even feel well enough to ask Eva to join me in the shower. Pity.

The two of them exited. "Jack said my mom said hi...." Slid was saying. The door closed behind them.

I lay back for a couple of minutes, willing my headache to disappear. After a while, the icepick took a breather, and I sat up. I'd slept in my clothes, which wasn't like me. I swung my legs out of bed.

If I was a spare uniform, where would I be?

About ten minutes later, I sauntered towards the wardroom,

my headache feeling significantly better. Last night was a bit fuzzy, …and that was just the cat chief. I snickered.

Last night was fuzzy, but I thought I'd done something pretty awesome. I discovered some secret Quihiri tech and acquired it for the good guys, aka us. I sauntered into the wardroom, a grin on my face.

The business-like conference room was packed, containing all the senior officers from the *Shakespeare* and the senior officers from the *Agincourt* (presumably, I hadn't met all of them), as well as the Color Rangers. There weren't even enough seats. They all immediately quieted and faced me.

I stopped and smiled. Bring on the accolades.

Captain Wright frowned. "What have you gotten us into now, Jones?"

Chapter Eighteen

In the jam-packed *Agincourt*'s wardroom, Captain Wright seemed peeved at me for some reason.

"You started treaty negotiations between TCC and some backwater, never-heard-of civilization?" he asked. "You don't have the authority, Jones!"

Oh, okay, that was the reason.

"It was just some fish," I said in a small voice. "And in return, we get some secret Quihiri tech. Win-win."

"What secret Quihiri tech?" he asked.

"Uh, not sure…." My voice trailed off.

"What?" he asked.

Max (where had he come from?) licked my hand. I glanced down at him, and he gave me an encouraging look. He was right. I was Jack Jones, devastatingly handsome spy extraordinaire and the best singer in the galaxy! My impromptu negotiation last night may have been unconventional, but it was awesome.

"Captain, I think you meant to say, excellent job, Ensign Jones," I said. "You rock! Thanks for saving the day."

The crews were observing us like it was a tennis match, me, then him, then me.

Captain Wright's eyes narrowed. "What?" he said quietly, steel in his voice.

"Yay, Jack!" I said. "Hurray for Ensign Jones!"

The room erupted in energetic discussion. I heard things like "Chain of command! Disobeyed orders!" and, alternately, "Unconventional problem solver. Saved our asses!" It appeared the crew of the *Shakespeare* and the crew of the *Agincourt* had differing opinions of me. Go figure.

The crews were getting quite worked up, flushing, muttering, and shifting from foot to foot. The way things were going, I wouldn't be surprised if it came to blows. And not the good kind.

I started sidling towards the door. Maybe now would be a good time to check in with some folks I hadn't seen in a while. What was my old buddy Ted, the security officer, up to? Maybe I could find him.

"Shut the hell up!" Captain Wright yelled.

I continued to sidle.

The room shut the hell up.

I continued to sidle.

"Freeze, Jones!" he said. "Captain Gomez, Ensign Jones, stay here. Everyone else, out! Get back to work!"

Amongst much muttering, the room cleared out.

Captain Gomez sat at the table next to Captain Wright. Arms crossed in front of her, she looked resigned to her fate, namely, being called on the carpet by another captain.

Once everyone was out, Captain Wright stood to close the door. He spotted Max, still standing behind me. "Him, too."

"Aw," I said. "He's just a dog." I leaned down to pet his back. "He's my buddy. Good boy, Max. Good boy."

Max wagged his tail and barked and acted in a very dog-like manner.

"He won't spill any secrets," I said.

"Fine." Wright frowned but closed the door. "Sit!" he said.

Max and I immediately sat. Me in a chair, Max on the floor.

Wright sat at the table. "So, Gina, I blame you for him." He jerked his head in my direction.

Gina glanced at me, at Max, and then back at Wright. "You're welcome." She smiled as if he'd paid her a huge compliment. Of course, she did. The Gina smile was a rare and beautiful entity. I basked in it for a few moments.

Max smiled.

I smiled.

Wright did not smile. "I cannot make a treaty on behalf of TCC with a bunch of cats," he said.

Max growled softly.

I petted his head. "Easy, boy," I said. "Max, you know they're not truly cats. It's convergent evolution. They only look like cats. You actually have a lot in common. You're both fuzzy, er, furry.

You both like meat. You both like meat a lot. You should make friends with them."

Gina started laughing.

I glanced at her. The Gina laugh was even better than the Gina smile.

"What?" I was feeling a little proud of myself even though I didn't know what for.

"He's right." She pointed at Max. "Max can make a treaty with them." She turned to Wright. "Right?"

Wright started chuckling. Chuckling seemed like a good thing, so I joined in. Gina joined in. Max joined in. Chuckling all around.

Thus, later found me and Max and Gina, the three Color Rangers, and four other *Agincourt* crewmembers flying back down to the never-heard-of planet to trade a bunch of fish for some hopefully awesome Quihiri tech. The four strangers, wearing green camo, huddled in the back of the shuttle, looking very much in cahoots.

The planet looked like a big green fuzzy (appropriate) ball from space.

"What's with the Green Team in the back?" I asked from my seat behind the pilot, Nguyen (Blue).

Horvat (Red), in the co-pilot's seat, said, "You don't need to worry about it."

"They're going to the *Shakespeare*'s escape pods to strip any high-tech stuff from them," Gina said.

"And destroy them," Patel (Yellow) said with restrained glee.

"Is that necessary?" Gina asked.

"Yes," Horvat said. "We don't want to give this crude civilization--"

"Do I have to wear all this stuff?" Max interrupted, strapped into the seat next to me. He had on an elaborate belt with tools--basically, a fancy version of the one the cat chief had worn. In addition, the *Agincourt*'s supposed diplomatic team had fashioned an elaborate vest and a kind of crown for him. He looked miserable.

"Yes," Horvat said.

"I feel stupid and silly," Max said.

I thought he looked a little silly, but I petted him as best I could around his new fashion accessories, nevertheless. “Good boy. Good Max. Hang in there, buddy.”

He seemed to relax a little. “Is it weird that I still like to be petted?”

I grinned. “No way. All hail, King Max, Lord of the pettings, and the entire Canis Familiaris Empire.”

I kept petting him, and his mood improved. There was even some tail wagging.

Nguyen flew the shuttle into a smallish clearing. All I could see through the viewscreen was green: green shrubs, green trees, and other kinds of smaller green plants. Chlorophyll was evidently a very successful pigment in our galaxy.

“This isn’t the right place, is it?” I asked. “Shouldn’t we see some signs of civilization? Huts? Something?” All I saw was jungle.

“No,” Horvat said.

I shrugged and stood.

“Wait, Jack,” Gina said, still seated.

Nguyen landed the shuttle and opened the back door.

The Green Team, laden with equipment, jumped out.

Nguyen closed the door and took off again immediately.

Huh. That had all the makings of a secret mission. I sat back down. *Of thinking too precisely on th’event--a thought which, quarter’d, hath but one part wisdom…*

I turned to Max. “Do you want to go over your mission again?”

“No,” he said. “I know it. I’m the amazing, stupendous King Max, leader of the Canis Familiaris Empire. I’m bestowing our excellent and extremely rare delicacy ‘fish’ on the cat chief as a thank you for him bestowing the useless but minorly interesting spheres of the inconsequential octopus people.”

“Good.” I nodded. “You got it.”

He shook his head a little. “Why did I agree to this?”

“Because I asked you,” I said.

He still looked skeptical.

“Because Jax asked you?” I said. “And the *Shakespeare* agreed to fly you and him anywhere you wanted after we got a working FTL drive?” So far, Jax and I hadn’t really talked. We probably should clear the air, but we hadn't. I didn't know if he was avoiding me or I was avoiding him. At any rate, there was avoiding.

"Oh, right," Max said, nodding. "That was the reason."

Nguyen landed the shuttle again near a large clearing. Through the shuttle's front viewscreen, I could see several huts and firepits in a clearing down a short path.

"This looks more like it." I stood and made sure the translator around my neck was turned on. It wasn't. I turned it on. "This looks more like it." Out of the translator, I heard several hissy meows. "Check." *Mmeows*.

Max jumped out of his seat.

Gina stood. The two of them also wore translators around their necks.

The three of us walked to the back door.

The Color Rangers hung back. Nguyen busied himself with turning off the shuttle. Horvat busied himself with looking important.

"Why aren't you guys coming?" I asked.

"We're gonna hang back; watch your six," Patel said.

"Come on, Jack," Gina said. "Max."

Nguyen opened the door, and humidity swooped into the shuttle on a tide of animal noises.

"*There is special providence in the fall of a sparrow*," Max said.

I nodded. "Nice quote!"

Gina grabbed the large wheeled cart filled with fish and started pushing it. "Come on."

The three of us stepped into the jungle.

Max led the way down the path. Gina followed, having a surprisingly easy time with the cart, considering the unpaved path.

I leaned down and scrutinized the bottom--of the cart, not of Gina (unfortunately). Was it touching the ground? Just barely. There must be an anti-gravity device in it. "Maybe I should get the cart?"

She frowned and said, "Patriarchal society."

It felt wrong to have the *Shakespeare*'s captain doing manual labor, even if it was on a mission, even if it was helped out by antigravity. "Then listen to a man and just stand aside, woman." I marched up and took control of the cart.

"Thanks." She stood aside, wiping a bead of sweat off her forehead.

The three of us entered the village clearing. If the Color Rangers were behind us, I didn't see them.

All the cat people looked at us warily.

As we got closer, I saw their eyes were wide open. Some of the kittens' ears were pointing down. Aw. Scared kitties.

"Never fear, your friend Jack is here!" I boomed out. My translator boomed out something that sounded like, "Meows, meows, meowss!"

More cats came out of the jungle, but they all seemed to relax.

The cat-chief appeared with a smaller cat at his side. They both bared their teeth.

The three of us bared our teeth. The cat people were plainly big on teeth-baring.

The cat chief said something, and my translator said, "Welcome back to our humble village." He looked Max up and down. "I don't think we have met this person. Is he one of your leaders?"

Max said, "Yes, I am the leader of the great Canis Familiaris Empire…."

I tuned him out a little, watching the crowd. The cat children were still adorable; they'd started playing, having decided we weren't a threat.

Several of the smaller adult cats, females (?), seemed very interested in our group, particularly me. I grinned. That was not surprising. These cat people were very discerning.

I smiled at a couple of them. They smiled back.

"Jack." Gina nudged me. "We're ready for the fish. Give him the fish."

With one last sexy grin at the cat ladies, I started unloading the biodegradable boxes of fish. Inside each box, many cans of fish, including tuna, sardines, and the like, resided. I placed the boxes gently at the cat chief's feet.

The crowd watched me, seemingly entranced. Of course! My muscles must be rippling.

Max said, “As you can see, we have held up our side of the bargain.”

“Yes,” the cat chief said. He gestured behind him. Four small cats carried the mysterious spheres on a litter between them.

They approached us.

I smiled and pointed at the now almost empty cart. “Here, please.”

One of the cats holding the litter said quietly, “Aren’t you male?” as she or he walked past me.

“Of course.” I gestured at my bodacious body.

They placed the spheres on the cart.

Max said some more stuff.

The cat I’d been talking to stopped next to me. “In your society, males do manual labor?”

“Yes.” I nodded. “In my society, men and women are equal. They are both valued.” I sidled up next to her. “Which are you? Man or woman?”

“Equal? Both do manual labor?” he or she said. “Who nurtures?”

“Both nurture,” I said. “Why? Do you need some nurturing?”

“I, we,” he or she said, “have a problem.” He or she glanced at the chief. “Maybe you could help.”

“I’d be happy to help in any way I can,” I said.

Suddenly, there was an explosion in the jungle behind us.

Chapter Nineteen

On the cat planet, surrounded by jungle, I heard a boom in the middle of our fish exchange. A gout of flame rose into the air. Everyone at the fish treaty turned around to look at the excitement. Now, there was a considerable plume of smoke. So, explosion: check.

"It is like strong lightning, but there are no storm clouds," the cat chief's friend said.

"What is the meaning of this?" the cat chief said.

What *was* going on here? I had a sneaking suspicion it had something to do with the Green Team's secret mission. Or maybe it wasn't so secret. Hadn't they said they would destroy the *Shakespeare*'s escape pods?

"It must be as your companion said," Max said. "Lightning."

And then it happened again. *Boom!* Ground shook. Ball of flame. Smoke plume. I definitely smelled stuff burning.

And again. *Boom!* Ball of flame. Smoke plume.

I sidled over to Gina and whispered in her ear, "How many escape pods did you land here?"

"All of them," she whispered back.

Some fiercer-looking cat people ran up to the chief, yelling and pointing at the commotion. Many of them wore crude weapons on their tool belts. I thought I saw knives and axes with obsidian or some similar stone. Whatever they were, they looked sharp.

"Perhaps, we should, uh, go inside one of your excellent huts to conclude our treaty," Max said, throwing me a look. Dog faces weren't as expressive as human faces, but I was getting a definite nervous vibe.

The cat-chief held up a paw. "Enough!"

The newcomer cats near him quieted.

The cat chief walked over to me. “Friend, Jack,” he said. “Tell me, what is the meaning of this?”

Gina opened her eyes wide and shook her head a little. I translated that human expression to be: Don’t you dare tell him, Jack. I mean it!

But I knew friends tried to be honest with one another. “Honored chief.” I bowed momentarily and then stood up straight. “We accidentally left some depleted …tools here, and we’re destroying them, so they do not harm your people.”

I wasn’t sure, but the cat chief’s expression seemed to convey thoughtfulness. “What kind of tools?”

On the other hand, I was sure Gina’s expression conveyed anger.

“They conveyed our people here to your lovely planet from space,” I said.

“What is space?” he asked.

“Space.” I pointed up into the sky. “Above us is the sky, and above that is space.”

There was another explosion behind us in the jungle. We all jumped.

“But don’t worry, you are not in danger from the ah, lightning back there,” I said. “It will end quickly, and the fire will not spread.”

“How do you command lightning?” he asked.

Max and I exchanged another look. “Let us discuss it after we conclude our treaty,” Max said. “And celebrate. We brought some of our special festival drink.”

I pointed at the sole remaining item, a bottle we’d brought on the cart. Hopefully, he’d forget all about commanding lightning after the treaty and some celebrating.

“All right, friend Jack,” the cat chief said. “Let us go to my hut.” He turned and pointed back down the path. His cat warriors joined him. Several smaller (female) cats picked up the boxes and followed.

Max followed close behind them, his crown taking on a definite tilt, leaving Gina and me standing alone on the edge of the jungle clearing. In the background, various jungle creatures tweeted, buzzed, or chirped.

"I can't believe you told them all that, Jack," she said.

"You can finish yelling at me later." My headache was starting to come back. "Should I take the device back to the shuttle, or do you want to do it?"

"We'll do it," Horvat said from the jungle behind us.

I jumped again.

Patel snickered. "You're as jumpy as a long-tailed cat in a room full of rocking chairs," he said. I wasn't sure that was the best metaphor under the circumstances.

Nguyen handed me the bottle from the cart and then started pushing it back the way they'd come.

"Come on. Let's get this over with." Gina started walking down the path.

We all signed a plentiful piece of paper and then had a pleasant time drinking our version of festival drink with our new friends in the chief's hut. Circular, it had a dirt floor, thatched roof, and walls made of branches. We sat on big pillows in the center. Off to one side, a sleeping area perched high above the rest. The *Agincourt*'s diplomatic crew had created some wine with an extra high alcohol content. With my headache, I didn't drink much. Neither did Max or Gina, as far as I could tell.

Soon, the chief and his companion were basically falling-down drunk.

"Well, this has been great, Chief," Gina said. "But we have to be going."

"Yes, Chief." I bowed briefly. "It's been an honor getting to know you and your people. We are honored to consider you friends and allies moving forward."

"On behalf of the Canis Empire, thank you, friends," Max said.

"Yeah, yeah, friendsss," the chief said right before he fell off his chair. "Sssafe hunting." He curled up in a ball and started snoring. It was kind of adorable.

"Safe hunting," Max said.

"Time to go," Gina whispered.

The three of us scampered out of the chief's hut. I was anxious to get back to the *Agincourt* and then, hopefully, back to the *Shakespeare*.

We'd just taken a step outside when one of the smaller cat people stepped out of the surrounding jungle. What now?

Gina sighed.

Max said, "Greetings, friend. Can we help you?"

Several more smallish cat people stepped out of the jungle.

The first one said, "We want him." She (?) pointed at me. Of course, they wanted me. Who wouldn't?

I smiled broadly and stepped up to the feline females. "Ladies, I understand that I am enticing, but we have important duties to complete for your lovely chief." It sounded good, right?

"Yes," Max said, following my lead. "We are too big and important to be waylaid."

Gina looked at the two of us, crossed her arms in front of her, and sighed.

"No, you don't understand," the cat lady said. "We only want him."

Another cat lady said, "It's important." That did sound important.

"Gina? Can I go with them?" I asked her.

She peered at me, seemingly considering. "Do *you* think you should?" I knew she thought I was an effective crewmember who accomplished things. Sometimes, she thought I accomplished things by accident, but she was incorrect there.

Glancing at the ladies, I thought my innate charm enabled me to accomplish things on purpose. And, of course, I wanted to get to know the ladies better, and they wanted to know me. "Yes, I do." This seemed like an occasion for said charm.

"Then, go." She relaxed her expression. "Good luck." Possibly, she thought this was an occasion for one of my so-called lucky accidents. "Meet back at the shuttle ASAP."

"Are you sure I shouldn't come, too?" Max asked.

"No chiefs!" the cat lady said.

"Okay," I said. "See you soon, Max, Gina!"

Max dipped his chin, and Gina waved goodbye.

The cat coterie took off into the jungle. I followed. Considering the path was almost nonexistent, they moved quickly.

I was panting by the time we arrived at a falling-down ramshackle hut.

The cat crew gave off a worried vibe, almost standing guard around the small clearing.

"What is it?" I asked. "If I can help, I will. I promise." I wiped the sweat off my face with my sleeve. Rushing through the jungle had done nothing for my hangover.

The leader of the cat clique pointed inside the hut.

I walked inside and sneezed. It smelled musty, full of dust and old hut stuff, and was quite dark.

Something wheezed in the corner. I didn't like the sound of that. I pulled out my fon and shone the light at the thing. I had to suppress an 'Ack' as I beheld what looked like a small melted Quihiri. Unfortunately, this was not the first time I'd seen such a thing.

"We trust you, Jack," the cat covey leader said, "You are a nurturer. We can tell. Can you help her?"

I knelt next to her. "Don't worry, little one," I said softly. "I will help you." I stood. "Can I take her with me?" Judging by her smaller stature, I was guessing she was female.

"Yes," the leader said.

I debated asking what happened. I knew this Quihiri had started her transformation to a higher life form, but I didn't know what triggered it. Could the cat people have been torturing her? Finally, I asked, "Did you hurt her?"

The leader crept right up next to me. "It was the stranger's chief," she said softly. "But our chief went along with it. He doesn't know we still have her, and she's still alive. We've been trying to take care of her, but we don't know what to do. We had to try; we're nurturers. We can't bear to see creatures suffering, even such a strange creature."

"All right," I said. "You did the right thing. I won't reveal your secret. And I will take her with me. My people can help her." I leaned down and picked her up. She was surprisingly light and insubstantial. That did not seem like a fortuitous sign. "Don't worry, little one; you'll soon be healthy."

She stirred and whispered, "Thank you…." Her voice faded. I may have had to blink back a tear. Or sweat. It was probably sweat in my eye.

"Can you lead me to my ship?" I asked.

"Yes." The cats ran off into the jungle, and I followed.

"Slow down!" I said.

My guides stopped on the edge of a small clearing. "It was there." The leader pointed at a now-empty clearing. Was? It did look familiar, aside from the whole emptiness issue.

"Safe hunting, Jack," the leader said right before they all melted back into the jungle.

Still holding the fragile Quihiri, I turned three-hundred-and-sixty degrees, examining the clearing as if the shuttle might magically appear out of nowhere. Maybe it was cloaked?

"Hello? Anyone there?" I walked forward to where I thought the shuttle had been parked. But I made it all the way through to the other side of the clearing without hitting anything. So, not cloaked: check.

I glanced down the wide pathway back towards the cat village. I'd promised the cat coterie I wouldn't reveal what they'd done, i.e., go against their chief, so I couldn't go back there to ask for help or info.

I stepped back to the edge of the clearing and gently set the Quihiri on the ground. I sat down heavily next to her. Head-throbbing, I lay back. It was moist and uneven. The jungle noises were noisier than ever.

I was trying not to freak out. I'd been left alone on a strange cat planet. My friends had ditched me. It didn't make any sense. Sure, Gina thought I was troublesome sometimes, but she basically loved me, right? We were married, after all! And Max cared about me... Of course, he had his 'real' Jack back, Jax, so maybe he didn't need a spare.

I thought I heard a twig break. Maybe the Color Rangers were still here, waiting for me? That made sense. "Horvat?" I asked. "Is that you?" No answer.

"Nguyen? Patel?" No one answered. All my friends were gone.

I was not freaking out. I needed to calm down, to, ah, be even calmer. If only I didn't have this headache. What did I recall about pain relief from the academy? Calm down and relax. I needed to be calm.

I took a deep breath in through my nose and exhaled through my mouth. And again. "I'm calm." In. Out. In. Out.

"Relaxed."

A small voice beside me said, "What are you doing?"

"I'm calming down," I said. "It's supposed to help with pain." As I started to relax, my headache did decrease.

"I have so much pain…" she said. "Kill me. Please, kill me."

And my tension and pain ratcheted right back up again. The horrific experience in the lab on the station came rushing back. I never wanted to do that again. "Please don't say that, little one. As soon as my friends come back, we can help you. Some of my friends are Quihiri. I promise we can help you. Just hold on a little longer."

"I can't stand it anymore," she said. "I can't hold on…." She'd clearly started the transformation to an energy being, but something had stopped her. Maybe *she* was stopping her.

"So, don't," I said gently. "Don't hold on. Let go of your pain. Let go of everything. Just let go." I breathed in and then out. "Let it all go."

And, then, she did.

Chapter Twenty

I was stuck on a cat planet in the jungle with a newly born sldkfjfoisut, an energy cloud floating in the air. She fizzed and scintillated and made a bunch of weird noises--none of which I could understand. I never realized how many different noises sldkfjfoisut could make.

I stood up and held out my hands. "Calm down, little one. You're okay. You're a sldkfjfoisut. It's a wonderful species."

"What?" she said. "What happened to me? Who are you? Are you human? What did you do to me?" She rushed me, and I jerked back, falling onto the moist ground.

"Oof." And now my shirt was as wet as my pants. "I didn't do anything to you. It's a natural process. Many lovely Quihiri turn into lovely sldkfjfoisut."

"I think you did something." She rushed me again, but I couldn't go anywhere since I was on the ground. Her energy buzzed against me. It tickled.

I giggled. I couldn't help it.

"Are you seriously giggling right now?" she said. "This is the worst moment of my life, and you're giggling!" She bobbed there for a moment, colors roiling.

"How do you feel?" I asked. "Do you feel bad? Or do you feel good?"

"I feel good." She started sparkling. "No, I feel great!" She twinkled like she was full of stars and bobbed around the small jungle clearing. "I feel wonderful!"

"Well, there you go. See, being a sldkfjfoisut is wonderful." I sat up. "I'm glad." I watched her bob and sparkle and couldn't help smiling. I also tried to access my comms. "Gina? Max? Horvat? Anyone? I'm at the rendezvous point. Where are you?"

In response, I heard a bunch of cackling and hissing. Nothing more. Gee, that wasn't ominous at all.

I watched the new sldkfjfoisut fly around the clearing. Her joy was infectious. "*Joy, gentle friends! Joy and fresh days of love accompany your hearts*!" I said.

Periodically, I unsuccessfully tried to reach my colleagues.

Eventually, the new sldkfjfoisut calmed down and stayed mostly still, bobbing next to me.

"So, what's your name, little one?" I asked.

"My name's Quibilah," she said.

"Hi, Quibilah," I said. "It's very nice to meet you. Some new sldkfjfoisut keep their Quihiri name, and some pick out an exciting new name to match their exciting new body."

"Hmm, I may need to think on that a bit." She bobbed a little closer. "Aren't you human? What's your name? How do you know so much?"

"I'm Jack Jones, singer extraordinaire, known throughout the galaxy." I paused for applause. It was not forthcoming. Aw. "Anyway, I'm good friends with a few sldkfjfoisut." I paused. How were my good friend sldkfjfoisuts? Were they okay? How long had Addie and Quinta been stuck on Quihiri? How long had Slid been without his mom?

"And I may have helped create a little sldkfjfoisut baby," I said. "I'm essentially the premiere human expert on sldkfjfoisut."

"How do sldkfjfoisut make a baby?" she asked.

I grinned. "Well, when a mommy sldkfjfoisut and a daddy sldkfjfoisut love each other very much, they share a special hug--"

"Ha ha," she said, colors roiling again. "No, really. How do they do it?"

"I'll answer your questions if you answer mine," I said. She must know what the Quihiri had been doing here on this cat planet.

"Okay," she said, colors dulling a little. "What do you want to know?"

"How did you come to be on this planet, Quibilah?"

"I came on a ship with a bunch of other Quihiri," she said. "We were on a secret mission…." She quieted.

"What was your secret mission?" I asked.

"It was a secret," she whispered. "I promised not to reveal it to anyone."

"Okay," I said. "Let's put a pin in that. What happened to you on the mission? Why were you almost dead?" I had my suspicions; namely, the Quihiri she was with had tried to stop her transition.

"The rest of my triple was on the mission with me," she said. "My husbands Quinn and Quaid saw that I was sick, and they tried to help me. They treated me with special medicine, but it didn't work. And then Captain Qadim said I was dying, and we should say our goodbyes--which we did." Her color turned black, and she sank to the ground.

"And what happened, then?" I asked gently.

"Quinn and Quaid were sad; we were all crying." She sounded like she might cry now (which was a good trick since she didn't have tear ducts.) "Captain Qadim said I was not worth saving since I was as good as dead. Captain Qadim left me. My triple left me!"

Harsh. "I'm sorry, Quibilah," I said.

"Then, those lady cats found me. I was too sick to talk to them." She was solidifying into some kind of black goo. "How could my people, my family, just leave me here?"

I thought a significant portion of the Quihiri were bad guys, but I didn't think telling her that would make her feel better. "Maybe they didn't know what was wrong with you…?" Maybe her triple didn't, but probably that Captain Qadim knew. "The important thing is, you're okay now, Quibilah. In fact, you're better than okay. You're awesome! You're a sldkfjfoisut!"

She morphed from goo back into a cloud, albeit a gray one. "Quinn and Quaid will be so glad I'm not dead!" Her colors brightened, and she started sparkling a little again. "I can't wait to see them!"

I was skeptical about how good her husbands were or how happy they'd be to see her in her current form, but maybe she was right. "Personally, I'm delighted you're not dead!" I smiled. "Since I gave you some info, maybe you want to give me some info? Tell me about your secret mission."

"No," she said. "I can't betray Quinn and Quaid like that."

Shoot. I'd been too successful in cheering her up. "Can you

at least tell me what the Quihiri device that you guys left here does?"

"No. I gave my word," she said. "Wait. You found the device? You didn't do anything to it, did you?"

I knew it was petty of me, but it'd been a long day. "Gosh, I can't tell you. It's a secret."

She just bobbed in front of me for a few moments. Finally, she said, "What now? Where's your ship? Can you take me back to Quihiri?"

"Not sure." I accessed comms again. "Gina? Max? Horvat? Anyone? I'm at the rendezvous point. Where are you?"

In response, I again heard a bunch of cackling and hissing.

"Shoot!" I stamped my feet.

Quibilah said, "Why don't you answer them?"

"What now?" I asked. "Answer who?"

"Somebody answered you," she said. "They said the original rendezvous point is compromised, something about aggressive natives approaching and to meet at the backup rendezvous point, the first landing site."

"But I didn't hear that--" I started to say.

And then I heard a stick or something break back from the direction of the cat town. Duh. Aggressive natives. Why were they aggressive? I wasn't going to stick around and ask them, what with those scary claws and those large sharp teeth. "We should go." I stood up. "Come on, quick." I started running along the path away from town.

Soon, I was panting, trying to breathe in the soupy humid air, and sweat poured out of me. Various leaves and branches smacked me as I ran along the increasingly narrow trail.

Quibilah bobbed effortlessly right behind me.

I ran and ran. Eventually, the path petered out, and I had to stop to catch my breath.

"Wow, you're noisy," Quibilah said. "Are you trying to avoid the cat people? You should be quieter."

"Give." Pant. "Me." Pant. "A." Pant. "Minute."

"Oh," she said. "I understand. You can't be quieter. I think I can cancel you out." She bobbed back a few feet and made a weird noise.

Then, I heard a lot of hissing cat-talk. My translator said,

"He must have gone this way." Then another cat said, "But I don't hear anything now. He must have turned off somewhere. Let's backtrack." Then, nothing. If those cat-people backtracked, they did so very quietly.

Quibilah stopped making the weird noise and came over to me. "Are you feeling any better?"

"What happened?" I whispered.

"I blocked your sounds so the cats couldn't hear you." She sparkled a little.

"Wow. That's great. Thanks," I said. "How did you do that?"

"I made sound waves that were equal and opposite to your sound waves, so the net sound wave was zero." She sounded a little smug.

"How'd you know how to do that?" I asked. "Is it a Quihiri thing?"

"No, I think it's a sldkfjfoisut thing. I thought you said you knew about sldkfjfoisut." Definitely smug. But with good reason.

"Sure," I said. "I knew it; I just didn't know you knew it."

My comms crackled.

"Did you understand that?" I asked her.

"Yes," she said. "They're asking why you don't answer them."

I accessed comms. "Jack and Quibilah are on the way." In response, I got crackles.

"Did you get that?" I asked her.

"Yeah," she said. "They said, 'Finally.' And 'Watch out for the natives.'"

"Thanks," I said. "I think we're close to the rendezvous point. Can you scout ahead and see if you can find them? Look for a shuttlecraft or other spaceship."

"Okay." She took off into the sky.

I tried to quietly make my way through the jungle, but with the path gone, it was slow going.

Quibilah floated down to me. "About a hundred meters to your right."

I followed her directions, and soon, I was smelling burnt electronics. I picked my way through the jungle and found myself in a familiar-looking clearing. I saw the burnt-out husk of a *Shakespeare* escape pod.

The Color Rangers stood in the open back door of a shuttle, rifles drawn, pointing in my direction. I'd never been so happy to see energy rifles pointing at me.

"Hi, there!" I smiled brightly and waved. "Is that a rifle in your hand, or are you just happy to see me?"

"Finally, Jones." Horvat lowered his weapon. "What took you so long? And what's with your comms?"

"Hi, there!" Quibilah said, bobbing and sparkling in front of me.

All three of them pointed their rifles at her.

Her color morphed from rainbow to storm cloud. "Uh, oh."

"Relax," I said. "She's a friend. This is Quibilah." I marched into the shuttle. "Seriously. Chill."

After a moment, they lowered their weapons.

Quibilah floated on board.

Horvat said, "Get ready for take-off ASAP."

We all (except Quibilah) strapped in, and soon the shuttle was in the air.

The ship landed in the shuttle bay on the *Agincourt*. Nguyen powered down the engines.

"So, is this a Quihiri ship?" Quibilah asked.

"Ah..." How clueless was she? "No," I said.

The Color Rangers were reaching for their rifles again.

"Are Quinn and Quaid here?" she asked. "Captain Qadim?"

"Is she a Quihiri? I thought you said she was a friend," Patel said in a growly voice.

"A new friend," I said. "We're still, ah, getting to know each other."

"Security to the shuttle bay," Horvat said into his comms.

"Security?" Quibilah said in a high screechy voice and flew up to the ceiling.

"We don't need security," I said. "We're all friends here." I held up my hands in the universal placating gesture. We wanted, no needed, her cooperation to figure out what the strange Quihiri device was.

Plus, she was sldkfjfoisut. It wasn't like they could keep her in the brig. The Color Rangers pointed their guns at her. Shooting her would be bad; shooting would not result in cooperation.

The back door of the shuttle opened. A phalanx of security officers stood there. Their energy rifles swiveled to point at her.

Up near the ceiling, Quibilah made a noise that sounded like, “Eep!”

They shot at her.

Chapter Twenty-One

In the shuttle bay of the Terran warship, the *Agincourt*, a bunch of security officers were shooting at my new friend Quibilah. "Stop it!" I didn't have a weapon, so there wasn't exactly anything I could do about it.

The shots ended. My ears rang; the area filled with smoke.

"That was rude and uncalled for," I said and coughed. The smoke was regular smoke and not sldkfjfoisut, right? I hoped it was regular smoke. It smelled like regular smoke, i.e., burned spaceship. I coughed some more. I leaned over and put my hands on my knees, hacking.

Patel patted me on the back. "You okay there, Jones?"

I stood up, and we all scrutinized the ceiling of the shuttle, which had been scorched black. I examined every corner but didn't see anything unusual. I did see a small vent, and, of course, the shuttle's back door was open. I resisted the urge to call out, "Quibilah, are you okay?" I hoped she'd escaped into that vent or somewhere.

"Did we kill the creature?" the unidentified head security officer said.

Kill? Creature? Didn't he understand Quibilah was sentient? I did not throttle him, even though I wanted to.

His buddies all nodded and said things like, "Yeah, sir." They were a bunch of jerks.

I had my doubts, but wherever Quibilah was, she wasn't here. Poor girl, no one deserved to be shot at like that.

"Jack, we all need to report for a debrief from Captain Wright," Horvat said.

"Nah." I was too angry to spend another second with them. "You guys know more than me, and you're all much more important. You go ahead. In a little while, I'll be in my quarters if you need me."

I hoped Quibilah was okay.

And I hoped we hadn't made a new enemy.

I wanted to at least get a better look at the strange Quihiri artifact we'd recovered from the cat planet. I could be wrong, but I thought it resembled an FTL drive prototype.

In the *Agincourt*'s engineering department, I found my old friend Olivia standing amongst all the electrical equipment and blinking lights. It was curious how engineering departments looked so similar all over the galaxy. If I went to a spaceship of giant dinosaur-like people, engineering'd probably look the same as this. Okay, maybe giant dino-people's engineering department would be giant, but still.

Surprisingly, Olivia did not beam in delight when she saw me coming. "What do you want, Jones?"

"You know what I want," I said and gave her my sexiest smile.

"I'm not having sex with you," she said. Her almond eyes were as beguiling as ever.

"Nice idea, but, er, no." In hindsight, I could see where I'd gone wrong in this conservation. "I want to see that mysterious new Quihiri artifact we recovered from the cat planet."

"Nope, can't do it, Jack," she said, shaking her head vigorously. "It'd be against orders to let you look at it."

I stepped closer to her and gazed into her eyes. "I understand." I filled my voice with sympathy. "You can't disobey your *Agincourt* masters. I get it. You're afraid of them."

"I'm not afraid!" she said immediately, as I knew she would. "Unlike some people, I follow orders."

"I follow orders," I said reasonably.

She snorted.

"What were the orders exactly?" I asked.

"Don't let random people nose around the artifact," she said primly.

I leaned in and said conspiratorially, "But I'm not random people. I'm the one who procured the tech for us, for the good guys, right?" I gazed into her eyes some more. "I'm one of the good guys. I deserve to see it." My gaze was pretty irresistible.

"No," she said, her eyes darting to the back of the room.

"Is it back here?" I strode to the back of the room, flipping on the lights in the darkened space.

"No," she said. "I never said that. Where are you going?"

I picked my way through stacked boxes of spare equipment and the like.

"Stop," she said, following me.

Finally, near the back wall, I saw it and pointed. "There it is. Weird, huh?" I walked right up to it. It looked like three of the Quihiri FTL drives somehow connected together, three smooth white spheres. I nodded. "Huh."

She sighed. "I give up. Between you and me, the *Agincourt* chief engineer has no idea what to make of it," she said. "We've taken tons of scans, too, inside and out."

"Scans?" I asked. "Can I get copies of those?"

"I guess." She shrugged and typed some stuff on her fon. Soon, I got a ping, 'New Data Received.'

"Thanks." I reached out my hands and pressed on the almost invisible dimple near the top of the top sphere. I'd seen the Quihiri technicians open a lot of drives when I was stuck, a prisoner, adjacent to the FTL factory.

The top sphere snicked open.

"Wow," Olivia said. "You're good."

"I know," I said modestly. I recorded the interior with my fon and then closed it back up. I carefully ran my hands over the two other spheres. They were similar. When the other two spheres opened, I also recorded their interiors.

"Can you come tomorrow and show the chief what you just did?" she asked.

I nodded. "Sure." But my calm exterior belied my racing pulse. No doubt, this was important; I was on the verge of discovering something huge!

Trying to calm down, I grabbed some food on my way back to my quarters. What with all the excitement, it was pretty late at night ship-time by now. I was ready for some shut-eye.

I opened the door to my quarters, and the first thing I saw was: me.

"Hi," other-me said, standing in the middle of the room.

"Hi, me," I said.

He grinned. He had an appealing grin. Ahh. Of course. It was Jax. I must have been exhausted since I hadn't figured it out immediately. He stepped aside, and I saw Max, Gina, Carter, Aarav Singh, and Slid. Max sat on the bunk, staring at Jax. Aarav sat next to him, looking from me to Jax and back again. Carter sat next to him, looking annoyed. Gina stood next to the wall opposite the door. Slid floated here and there. They all barely fit in the small space between the metal walls, floor, and ceiling. But they looked great.

I paused for a moment. My family. All together again. "*The wheel is come full circle, I am here*," I whispered.

"Huh?" Carter said.

"Why are you guys all in my cabin?" I said. Somehow, I didn't think they were all here for an orgy. Unfortunately. I might have been able to muster up some energy for an orgy. Dare to dream…

"To plan our next move," Gina said. "What happened? Down on the planet."

"Why are you asking me? What happened with you?" I stepped inside and closed the door behind me. "Why did you abandon me? I went back to the shuttle, and it wasn't there."

"Wright ordered us back to the *Agincourt*," she said. "Sorry." At least she had the grace to look regretful. I'd known it had to be something like that. My buddies wouldn't desert me.

Jax approached the bunk, my bunk. Max jumped down to the floor, and Jax sat in his spot. Max jumped onto Jax's lap, and Jax started petting him--all without a word. I wasn't jealous, nope, not a jot.

"You got back here fine," Carter said. "So, what are you complaining about?"

I didn't think I'd been complaining, but having two awesome me's here had to be intimidating to him, so I cut him some slack. "Uh, so, anyway, the cats had a sick Quihiri with them--"

"Does she know my mom?" Slid interrupted.

"No, sorry," I said. "It was a lovely Quihiri female named Quibilah, and she transformed into a lovely female sldkfjfoisut."

I stared at the little sldkfjfoisut, Slid. Being away from your mom at such a young age must be tough. Poor kid. I hadn't been doing my parental duty. I sat down on the floor, with my back against the door. "Do you want to sit in my lap, Slid?"

He floated over to me and then floated down to my lap. I felt a very slight buzz in my legs. I put my arms around him, and they felt a little tingle as well. "You're okay, buddy."

He nuzzled into me; it felt buzzy and a little tickle-y.

"So, where's Quibilah now?" Aarav asked.

I glanced down at Slid in my arms. "We, uh, got separated in the shuttle bay." Was she dead? How do you kill an energy being? *Could* you kill an energy being?

Gina was staring into my face. "Separated, how?"

I jerked my chin down in Slid's direction. I didn't want to talk about sldkfjfoisuts being shot in front of him. "You know, uh, separated," I said.

Carter snorted.

Gina shot him a look I couldn't see, and he sobered right up.

Maybe I was a little glad I didn't spend more time with my wife, Gina.

"So, what now?" Aarav asked. "Is the *Agincourt* taking me back to TCC headquarters?"

We all looked at him with pity. He was a bureaucrat if he thought a TCC warship would return one man to his desk--during a war.

"I've been trying to get Wright to let us go back to the *Shakespeare*," Gina said. "But he's resistant to part with the supplies."

"Yeah, he says it's pointless since we don't have an FTL drive," Carter said. "But I hate it here, being bossed around by all his minions. I'm a First Officer!"

Now, who was complaining? But I was too generous to say anything. I yawned instead.

I watched Max and Jax interact. Not so long ago, it had been just Max and me alone here, him giving me advice… My mind was percolating with the beginnings of an idea.

"Being under his command does have its, ah, challenges," Gina said. "But we can handle it."

"What if we didn't have to handle it?" I asked. "What if we

had an FTL drive?"

"You don't mean steal the *Agincourt*'s drive?" Aarav said, looking horrified. "Please don't do that."

"No. I would never strand a ship in outer space," I said. "I have something else in mind."

It was zero-dark-thirty, also known as 03:30 ship time. The whole ship was dark, lit only by dim safety lights. Ninety-nine percent of the crew was asleep.

Carter and I stood outside the bridge after stopping at the mess hall. I'd slammed a bunch of espressos. We were currently trying to look unobtrusive and unsuspicious. Considering we were carrying a bunch of beer and a large cake, I'm not sure how successful we were.

Slid flew up to us from inside the bridge. "Yeah, just one guy, and he's definitely sleepy. His eyelids keep closing."

I did feel guilty about involving a child in hijacking a spaceship. "Thanks, Slid. Go back to my quarters, and Jax and Max will take care of you."

He flew off; at least, I thought he did. I couldn't see a dim cloud in a dark hallway.

"You ready?" I asked Carter.

"You realize if this harebrained scheme lands me in the brig, I'll have to kill you," he said, shifting the bottles of beer in his hands.

It wasn't harebrained. "It's not harebrained!" What did that mean, anyway? Thinking like a rabbit? I shook my head. "Come on." I proudly held the chocolate cake in my hands and stepped onto the bridge.

Our not-harebrained scheme involved me distracting the bridge officer--one way or another--long enough for Carter to input a one-inch FTL jump and execute it. At which time, I'd wish for an FTL drive for the *Shakespeare.* A functional FTL drive. I'd remembered that virtually all the FTL drives in the galaxy weren't working--thanks to the evil Quihiri.

"Happy Birthday!" I said loudly, walking towards the captain's chair and checking everything out. Our prey was the only crew member on the bridge.

Then, I spied my fon on the console next to the captain's

chair.

Carter walked behind me and said, "Happy Birthday," half-heartedly.

"Who are you?" the bridge officer said, jerking up and rubbing his eyes. "I wasn't asleep."

He must have fallen asleep. "I know you weren't asleep," I said. "You wouldn't do that on your birthday." I threw my most dazzling sexy smile his way.

He seemed a little dazed and smiled back. "Uh, my birthday?"

Carter put down the beers and started edging towards the FTL controls.

I got closer to our prey, smiling. "Yes. A sexy man like you deserves some delicious chocolate cake," I raised and lowered the cake a few times," on your birthday." I tried to make my eyes twinkle.

He stared into my eyes. I gazed back. His eyes were the most delicious hazel color, with brown flecks near the iris and greenish on the outside. I may have lost track of time for a short, slight period.

However, while my brain was engaged with my mark, the rest of my body was not--if you know what I mean.

"Now, Jack!" Carter yelled.

I was tempted to wish Quibilah was okay for a second, but I squelched it down. That was not the mission.

I closed my eyes and concentrated. *The Shakespeare has a new functional FTL drive installed in engineering. The Shakespeare has a new functional FTL drive installed in engineering. The Shakespeare has a new functional FTL drive installed in engineering.*

"Hey, wait a minute," the bridge officer said. "What are you doing?"

The minuscule FTL shift would be over by now. I opened my eyes. The officer was staring at Carter.

Carter pointed at the bottles of beer. "I brought the beer. Would you like a beer?"

While they were focused on the beer, I slipped my fon into my pocket.

The officer threw me a glance.

I smiled at him.

"Who said it was my birthday?" he asked. Uh oh. The jig was up.

My brain raced. "Patel." He was the perfect annoying guy to throw under the bus. "Wait. Are you saying it's not your birthday?"

"No," he said. "And I'm not allowed to drink on duty. And I don't think you're supposed to be here. Who are you?"

"I think Patel tried to trick us," I said to Carter. "A prank? Some kind of hazing?"

"Oh no," Carter said, shaking his head. "That Patel." He took a couple of steps towards the door. "He's a real scamp."

"Take the beer!" the officer said, pointing.

Carter scooped it up. "A scoundrel."

I smiled. "Should I leave the cake?"

The officer nodded.

I set it down and followed Carter out.

Back in the hallway, I whispered, "Scamp? Scoundrel? What are you living in the 1920s or something?"

"Okay, I panicked," he whispered back. "I'm not as used to playing the temptress as you apparently are." Fair point.

We walked quickly but unobtrusively down the hall back to my quarters. I put my hand in my pocket and stroked my fon. Yay, fon!

We entered and closed the door behind us. Inside I saw Gina, Jax, and Max. We'd decided to exclude Aarav; charming as he was, he wasn't a spy like us. Presumably, he was currently safe and sound, sleeping in his own quarters.

"Well!" Gina said. "Did it work? Does the *Shakespeare* have a functional FTL drive?" We'd decided she was too high-profile to participate in the caper.

"I think so," I said. "But we won't know until we go check."

"I still don't understand why you made such a crazy wish," Jax said. "Why not something more reasonable?" He and Max sat on my bunk again. These two were not spies, so they were only observers.

"It's a long story," I said. "But the bottom line is more unlikely things seem easier to instantiate."

Jax shook his head. "I guess I'll have to take your word for it."

"Makes sense to me," Max said. "Quantum Field Theory." I decided not to dwell on the idea that a dog might be smarter than me. Or the other me. Or, the other-other-me back on Earth.

I looked around the cabin. "Did Slid come back?"

"I don't know," Gina said. "Did he?"

"Slid?" I asked.

No answer. I was starting to get worried about him.

"Slid?"

The next morning was the first morning in a long time I felt like myself. I completed all my morning ablutions, including recording my memories of all the crazy events of the last days. I headed off for breakfast, stomach growling. Late-night capers apparently made a person hungry.

I ran into my partners-in-crime in the mess hall. It was a large room filled with long rectangular tables and attached benches, and there were at least a couple dozen other people in there, eating.

Gina sat down next to me. "I finally convinced Wright to let the three of us go back to the *Shakespeare* one last time."

"How'd you managed that?" Carter said.

"We're coming with you when you take off, right?" Jax interrupted. "You said you'd take Max and me where we wanted. And Max said something about puppies."

"You said you'd take me back to Earth," Aarav said.

We also said we'd reunite Slid with his mom. "Slid?" I looked around the mess hall but didn't see him. I was worried about him. And I was worried about Addie and Quinta left on Quihiri. And Quibilah.

"I told Wright we needed to take a final inspection before we leave the system," Gina said quietly. "He doesn't know it yet, but the *Shakespeare* and all her crew will be leaving the *Agincourt* soon."

"Sounds good to me," I said quietly. "So, we should pack our stuff up in case we have to leave quickly?"

"We abandoned ship," Carter said. "Our lives were in danger. We don't have any stuff to pack up."

"Right." I touched my fon in my pocket. "I knew that." Of

course, that wasn't the case for me; my quarters were filled with new provisions I'd gotten the last time I was on Earth, but it was all replaceable.

An hour later, the *Agincourt* flew up to the scorch-marked *Shakespeare*, still floating listlessly in outer space.

I'd spent that hour running around the *Agincourt* whispering, "Slid, I need to talk to you. Where are you?" and staring up at the ceiling and peering in various corners. I couldn't find him. And I couldn't find Quibilah. My worry had morphed into fear. Where was he? What happened to him? What happened to her? Was she dead? Or could missing-Quibilah have something to do with missing-Slid?

Me and the Color Rangers, along with Gina and Carter, were suited up in a shuttle. If anything, this vanilla loaner spacesuit was more uncomfortable than the other one I'd worn. I shifted in my seat, trying to get comfortable.

Patel/Yellow was with us. Clearly, the fertilizer from our caper hadn't hit the fan yet.

The shuttle flew out of the *Agincourt*'s bay, into the Shakespeare's shuttle bay, and parked.

"This is a waste of time," Horvat said, wearing his bright red suit. "I checked the FTL drive. It was gone." We turned on our suit lights, exited the shuttle and clicked across the bay (magnetic boots) to the door of the *Shakespeare*.

"Aw, Horvat," I said. "It's not so easy to just leave our ship forever. She's a good ship. We love her." I had a clammy feeling on my back. I guessed I'd underestimated my feelings for the *Shakespeare*.

"You guys can stay in the shuttle if you want," Carter said.

"Okay," Horvat/Red said.

"Fine," Patel/Yellow said. "I'm staying." The two men turned and marched back to the shuttle.

Nguyen/Blue shrugged and followed them.

In a generic white suit with a clear faceplate, Gina opened the door and stepped inside the *Shakespeare*. Carter and I, also in generic white, followed her.

She closed the door behind us and held up three fingers.

Oh, channel three. We all switched frequencies.

"Good. It'll be easier to find the 'spare' FTL drive without them." She made the air quotes.

I appreciated her faith in my power. I smiled at her.

She smiled back.

Looking at the two of us, Carter frowned. "Let's get this over with." He took off for engineering.

The Shakespeare's murals felt like old friends even in the dim light. I spied the spooky Hamlet mural. "Hello, Hamlet. Hello, Hamlet's father's ghost."

Soon we were in engineering.

Soon we saw a big beautiful FTL drive right where it was supposed to be.

"Woo hoo!" I jumped up. "Woo hoo!" My helmeted head hit the ceiling, and then I bounced off, going back down. "Woo hoo!" My magnetic books smacked into the floor, and I stuck.

"Yes!" Gina smiled.

"Okay, I'll admit it," Carter said. "That's pretty sweet."

Gina switched back to frequency one. "Great news, Horvat. We, ah, still have an extra FTL drive. We're placing it in position now."

"What?" Horvat said over comms. "An extra FTL drive? No one has an extra FTL drive."

"That doesn't make sense," Patel said. "We need to investigate--"

He was interrupted by another voice over comms. "Patel, report to Security ASAP."

Chapter Twenty-Two

"Comms off," Gina said. I don't know what she did, but I couldn't hear the Color Rangers anymore. She touched her helmet to mine and grabbed Carter to pull him close, too. I was enjoying the closeness, but what was the point with us all wearing spacesuits?

With all three helmets touching, Gina said, "Did you guys somehow blame Patel for your caper last night?"

I could hear her without using comms. Neat! Communication was the point of this closeness. "Uh, golly gosh," I said. "Why would you say that?"

Carter said, "Yes."

"Okay," she said. "I think you guys should stay here and bring the *Shakespeare* back online. Hopefully, I can convince Wright to give us fuel and air, etc."

"He should," Carter said. "It helps the TCC to have the *Shakespeare* back in operation."

"He should," Gina said. "But it depends on how pissed he is." She threw me a very annoyed look. I found myself wishing she had one of those fancy mirrored faceplates so that I couldn't see her expression.

"Comms on," she said.

"…repeat, come in, Gomez," Horvat was saying.

"I copy, Horvat," Gina said. "I'm on my way back to the shuttle." She waved to Carter and me before she started walking back to the shuttle bay.

Carter took a step away from me and held up three fingers.

I switched comms frequency. "How do we bring the ship back online with no fuel?" I asked.

"The pirates stole most of the fuel, but there should be

some dregs left," he said. "Enough to get her operational, at least ready to accept supplies from the *Agincourt*."

Now my neck felt hot. "What about air?" I asked. "I need to get out of this suit."

"Maybe we can pressurize a room or two, but that's probably it," he said. "Let's get to the bridge."

On the bridge, I helped Carter power the ship up. He was right; there was enough power to operate minimal ship systems, including the computers on the bridge.

"Powering up fuel and air sensors and pumps," he said and then leaned back in the captain's chair. Even through his faceplate, I could tell he looked pleased.

"Come in, *Shakespeare*," a familiar voice said over comms. "This is Captain Wright. Am I to understand you have an FTL drive?"

"Affirmative, Captain," I said over comms. "We await delivery of fuel and other supplies."

I glanced at Carter, but he still seemed to be happy and chilling--at least as much as you could in a spacesuit.

"Not so fast," Wright said. "I'm sending over Horvat and Nguyen to verify." If he could get the *Shakespeare* crew out of his hair, he would. But the *Shakespeare* would need to be operational for that to happen.

I noticed he didn't mention Patel. I had to tamp down a sudden giggle fit.

Wright continued, "In the meantime, Jones, Nillion, come back to the *Agincourt* ASAP. I have some questions for you."

And then, I felt a tickle in my torso area. I couldn't help giggling.

"Jack!" Carter said.

I tried not to laugh. "Eggative. Omms Roken." *Garble*. "Out." I turned off my comms system and fell to the floor, laughing. Since the artificial gravity was still off, I was soon bouncing and floating around the room. "Stop, stop," I said between laughs. "Please stop. Stop the tickling. It's killing me. I can't take any more."

"What is this tickling?" a female voice said. "How is it fatal?"

"Maybe move away from him more," Slid said. I recognized

his voice coming from the direction of my torso.

"But there's nowhere to move," the female said, also from the direction of my torso.

And then my helmet filled with smoke. However, the tickling stopped. Thank goodness. I tried not to breathe in the smoke because I'd finally figured out what was happening. Quibilah and Slid had hitchhiked over to the *Shakespeare* in my spacesuit. Yay! They were both okay!

Someone grabbed me from the middle of the room and banged his helmet against mine. "What's wrong with you, Jack?" Carter asked, holding his helmet against mine.

The smoke parted in front of my eyes.

"Quibilah and Slid are in my suit with me, and it started to tickle," I said.

He exhaled loudly. "I thought something was seriously wrong with you this time."

I stared into his faceplate. Our faces were only inches apart. He looked genuinely upset. "Aw. I care about you too, Carter."

"Oh, good grief." He let go of me, and I floated in the opposite direction.

"Are you okay, Jack?" Slid asked.

"I'm sorry if I unintentionally injured you," Quibilah said. "I did not mean to kill you."

"No worries," I said. "No injuries. I'm okay."

"I cannot go back to that ship," she said.

Now that I was back home on the *Shakespeare,* there was no way I wanted to leave again. "I can't go back, either," I said. "We won't."

I suddenly moved in a different direction. Carter grabbed me again and put his helmet next to mine. "Put your comms back on. Wright's demanding we go back to the *Agincourt* for questioning."

"No," I said. "I'm not going back."

"Horvat and Nguyen are already on their way," he said. "They'll be here in minutes. How do you propose we avoid it? Shoot them?"

My brain was racing. "No, that would just make things worse," I said. "But what if you were right? What if there is something wrong with me?"

"What the hell are you talking about now, Jack?" he asked.

"What if I'm sick?" I asked.

"But you're not sick," he said. "And you're in a spacesuit, so you're not exactly contagious."

"What if I was sick?" I asked again. "And what if I wasn't in a spacesuit? Gosh, you might be contaminated, too."

He froze for a moment. Then, he said, "That's a little bit brilliant. The last thing Wright wants is a contagion on a closed environment like a spaceship."

"Gosh, I must have caught it from those cat people," I said, grinning. I knew enough about sldkfjfoisut to know they could simulate some horrible skin conditions.

"Uh, oh," Carter said. "Horvat and Nguyen are down the corridor."

"Quick, pressurize the bridge!" I said.

Carter ran back to the captain's station and started inputting commands.

As soon as the bridge door closed, I started releasing air from my suit.

He worked fast and furious, muttering, but I couldn't hear him.

As soon as my suit indicators said the bridge had enough air, I took off my helmet. It smelled like …home.

Quibilah and Slid flew out, whooshing by my face. It felt like a strong wind for a couple of seconds there. They both looked like white-gray clouds.

"Ahhh," Slid said, darting all over, starting to sparkle a little.

"Much better," Quibilah said, starting to show some colors in the blue end of the spectrum.

Carter finished his command system tasks and quickly took off his helmet.

And it was just in time because someone pounded on the door to the bridge.

"Quick, Slid, get on my face and look like pustules or something!" I said.

I felt Slid touch and then cover most of my face. "How's it look?" I asked Quibilah.

She conveyed the impression of a shrug. "Pustule-y?"

Carter was doing something with the controls.

"Open the door!" Horvat said. Ah, Carter had been working on communications.

"Sorry," I said. "I'm sick. So, sick." I approached the tiny window in the closed door.

As I passed Carter, he took one look at my face and blanched. "Maybe dial it back a notch," he whispered.

"Smaller pustules, Slid?" I whispered and stopped in front of the window, pointing at my face. "My face feels funny. Does it look okay? Gosh, I hope I'm not contagious. Maybe I caught something on the cat planet?"

Horvat jerked back and said something that sounded like, "Ack."

Nguyen took a step back.

"But give us a minute to get suited up," I said. "We'd be happy to come back to the *Agincourt*. How are you feeling, Carter? You don't feel feverish, do you?"

He pretended to stumble. "Only a little. It's probably not contagious. Probably." He wiped his brow like he was wiping off sweat. "Is it hot in here?"

Out in the corridor, both Horvat and Nguyen had taken another step back from the door.

"Hey, you guys were down on the planet, too," I said. "How do you feel? You don't feel sick, do you? Or hot? Sweaty?" I knew from experience it was common to feel hot and sweaty in a spacesuit.

"Uh…" Horvat said, taking another step back.

"I'm ready to give my life for TCC if need be," I said. "*Ah, Warwick, Montague hath breath'd his last, and to the latest gasp cried out for Warwick, and said--*"

Carter interrupted, "*Commend me to my valiant brother.*"

I turned around, nodding. "Nice."

In the hall, Horvat and Nguyen turned around and ran away.

After a few moments, Gina said over comms, "Jack, Carter, what's this I hear about you two being infected by cat leprosy?"

"Hi, honey," Carter said. "Please don't worry about us."

"Gina!" I said. "It's so good to hear your voice during this difficult time. Fuel for the *Shakespeare* might make us feel a little bit better…."

She didn't answer right away. After a few minutes, she said,

"Fuel transfer initiation on my mark, in three, two, one, mark. Fuel transfer initiated."

Carter and I crowded around the console, monitoring fuel. The volume started increasing.

"Yay!" I said.

"Yes!" Carter said.

Over comms, Gina said, "Air transfer initiation on my mark, in three, two, one, mark. Air transfer initiated."

The amount of air pressure on the ship started going up.

"Yay! Woo hoo!" I yelled.

Carter smiled.

Over comms, Gina said, "All *Shakespeare* personnel prepare to disembark the *Agincourt*."

"Woo hoo!" I yelled.

"See you soon, hon," Carter said.

"Doctor Sharma, report to the *Shakespeare* bridge ASAP," Gina said.

"Yes, ma'am," Dr. Sharma said.

I grabbed the comms. "Thank you, Captain Wright, for helping me save the *Shakespeare* crew."

But he said only, "Long live the TCC. Wright out."

Soon, Carter and I had gotten all ship systems operational. Artificial gravity was on. All the lights were on.

Sensors showed the crew was streaming on board from the *Agincourt*. Using the ship's communications system, I did a little eavesdropping. Everyone was smiling and hugging each other as they stepped aboard. I heard a lot of laughing, ' Welcome home!' and 'It's great to be home!'

My heart felt full. I may, or may not, have had to blink back a couple of tears.

Someone pounded on the still-closed door of the bridge. "It's Dr. Sharma." Correction, Dr. Sharma pounded on the still-closed door of the bridge.

I went over and looked at him through the tiny window.

"What's going on in there?" he asked. "Are you sick? Or is it some blue flu thing?"

Blue? I looked at my hands. They didn't look blue. Why would I be blue?

Gina stepped around him. "Just open the door."

Without me doing anything, the door whooshed open.

Carter stepped around me and ran out into the hall to hug Gina. She hugged him back. I wasn't jealous watching them embrace. Okay, I was slightly jealous. Okay, I was pretty jealous.

"So, you're not sick?" Dr. Sharma asked me.

"No," I said, still watching the longest hug ever.

"Do you need a hug?" he asked.

"Yeah," I said, and he wrapped me in his arms. Ahhh. "What's blue flu?" I said into his shoulder.

"It's an old Terran idea," he said into my shoulder. "Law enforcement couldn't go on strike, so they might say they were sick and couldn't work." He released me. "For a good cause. It was like a protest."

"Thanks," I said and smiled at him. "I guess it was a blue flu thing."

Gina and Carter finally separated. She walked onto the bridge. When we didn't immediately follow, she turned around and said, "Well, come on."

We joined her on the bridge.

"Status report," she said.

Carter said, "Crew is all aboard. Wright gave us one shuttle."

"Yay!" I gave a little cheer, throwing my fists in the air.

"Fuel and air are sufficient," he said. "What about food and water?"

Gina shook her head. "That's a no-go." That sounded like a problem.

How could we get food and water? My mind was racing. "What about the mysterious Quihiri artifact? Did we get it?"

Gina shook her head again. "That's a no. Wright wouldn't give it up."

"Shoot!" I said. We needed to act quickly before the *Agincourt* left the system. "But I know how we can get it…."

A little later, the entire *Shakespeare* crew was wearing their appropriate uniforms. The *Shakespeare*'s bridge crew was once again on the bridge where it belonged. It was awesome. I glanced from one face to another. I wanted to hug them all.

Sitting in the center of the room, Gina cleared her throat. "When you're ready, Carter, Jack."

"I'm ready," I said.

"One-inch FTL jump initiating now," Carter said at the FTL controls.

Standing near him, I closed my eyes and concentrated. *We have the mysterious Quihiri artifact here on the Shakespeare bridge. We have the mysterious Quihiri artifact here on the Shakespeare bridge. We have the mysterious Quihiri artifact here on the Shakespeare bridge.*

"FTL jump concluded," Carter said.

I opened my eyes. "Did it work?" I looked all around the bridge. It looked exactly the same as it had a moment ago. I didn't see any artifacts, mysterious or otherwise.

"It does not appear to have worked," Gina said.

"What happened?" Carter asked.

"Usually, my power kicks in when I'm making out with someone," I said. "Let's try it again, but this time, kiss me."

"No!" he said, scowling.

"Oh, come on," I said, grinning. "I'm a good kisser."

"Absolutely not," he said.

"Well, somebody needs to kiss me," I said. "For the war effort."

"I'll do it," Gina said and stood up from her fancy captain's chair and started walking towards us.

Carter looked like he really, really, really wanted to say 'No!' But he didn't.

"When you're ready, gentlemen," she said.

"I'm ready," I said and reached for her.

She smiled as I held her face gently in my hands. We kissed. Mmm. It was lovely, warm, and so sexy... All of me started enjoying it.

"One-inch FTL jump initiating now," Carter said.

I closed my eyes and concentrated. *We have the mysterious Quihiri artifact here on the Shakespeare bridge. We have the mysterious Quihiri artifact here on the Shakespeare bridge. We have the mysterious Quihiri artifact here on the Shakespeare bridge.* But my enjoyment was continuing.

"FTL jump concluded," Carter said.

I opened my eyes and looked into Gina's beautiful browns.
I knew it hadn't worked. Because I still felt sexy.
She knew it hadn't worked.
Why hadn't it worked?

Chapter Twenty-Three

The *Shakespeare* was all fueled up, and her crew was home--all of which was yay-worthy. However, my special skill did not seem to work anymore. This was not yay-worthy.

On the bridge, Carter said, "What's going on? Why didn't it work? "

I just looked at him. Why hadn't it worked? If I recalled correctly, it did not always work. Unfortunately, I could not recall exactly when it didn't work. I should review my recorded memories and see if there was a pattern.

Gina walked back to the captain's chair in the middle of the room. "Put us in orbit around the cat planet. Scan for uninhabited areas with fresh water and plenty of non-sentient plants and animals."

The bridge officers started implementing her orders.

I still stood in the middle of the room and whispered, "*I have no spur to prick the sides of my intent, but only vaulting ambition, which o'erleaps itself, and falls on th'other.*"

"Jack," Gina said. "Quit mumbling. Do what you need to do to rest and relax. We'll try it again later, and I need you to be at one hundred percent."

"Uh, okay," I said, a little dazed and confused.

I walked off the bridge and back to my quarters. When I opened my door, however, I was already there. With Max. And Slid. And Quibilah. And Aarav. Slid and Quibilah floated around, flashing rainbow colors periodically. Max, Jax, and Aarav sat on my bunk. "What are all of you doing here?"

"Waiting for you, of course," Aarav said.

"Thank you for rescuing me from the cat planet," Jax said with a smile.

"I can't thank you enough for saving my family," Max said with his doggy smile, tail wagging furiously.

"Yeah, thanks for rescuing me from that backwater planet," Slid said.

"And thank you for helping me transition to this," Quibilah said and sparkled. "And thanks for getting me away from those horrible *Agincourt* people. They could have killed me."

I sat down in my desk chair and stared at my wonderful friends. I was getting emotional whiplash. When I'd walked in the door, I'd felt like a failure--which was a new experience for me. But now, I remembered I was a hero. I was awesome!

So, what would help me rest and relax the most?

"What's happening next?" Aarav asked. "Are we going to Earth?" He was an attractive man...

"Are we going to Quihiri?" Slid asked. He put thoughts of attractiveness right out of my head.

"Are we going to the station?" Jax asked.

Max barked once and then said, "Ugh, why would we go there?"

"It's the best place to get a lead on the *Whydah* crew," Jax said. "Until we catch them, they're a threat to all of us."

These were all valid questions and suggestions, but my head was spinning. "Yes," I said.

"Yes, what?" Jax said.

"Yes. We are going all those places after we take on supplies from the cat planet," I said.

Then, I was peppered with questions and comments. "But where first?"

"We don't have to go down to the surface of the cat planet, do we?"

"I want to go to Earth first."

"No, Quihiri first."

"No, the station."

I couldn't even keep track of who said what.

I held up my hand, and they quieted. "The first place all of you are going is away from here." I pointed at them all in turn. "I have to rest. I have to think. I have to review my memories."

"But..." Slid said.

"Hush, little one," Quibilah said. "You can hang out with me."

They both started bobbing for the door.

Everyone else stood up.

"Are you sure?" Aarav asked, looking particularly disappointed.

"Yes," I said. "I'll catch up with you guys later. For now, I need some alone time."

They sighed and dejectedly walked or floated out the door. The door swished closed behind them.

I was enveloped in exquisite silence. I took in my small cabin with its desk, chair, bunk, and small bathroom. I put the various pictures of Old Jack back on the wall. "Ah…" I sighed in relief. "Home, sweet home." It felt like forever since I'd been here. After a few moments of appreciation, I grabbed my memory rig from the bathroom and uploaded all my recent memories from my fon.

Standing right there next to my very own shower, I decided to take advantage of it and shucked my uniform. The warm water felt wonderful on my skin. I luxuriated in my own shower in my own bathroom, with my own soap, my own shampoo.

After a few moments, I ended the shower, toweled off, grabbed my memory rig, and lay down on my bunk. "Okay, special skill, exactly when did you work?"

The door to my quarters slid open. Warrior-princess Eva stood there. I got déjà vu. "You're napping? You know there's a war on, right?"

So much had happened, it had slipped my mind for a few moments. But I had enough sense not to say it.

"No." I cleared my throat and sat up. "I've been reviewing my memories, trying to figure out when my special skill works." I'd even finally read the TCC briefing on Quihiri. And, okay, sure, I'd done some napping, too.

She came inside, closing the door behind her. She smiled and sat next to me on the bed. "So, what'd you figure out?"

The smile that had automatically answered hers faded. "It doesn't always work."

"Not exactly a huge revelation," she said, putting her hand on my bare knee. "Anything else?"

I was starting to get distracted. "Uh, no, I did figure

something out." She moved her hand up my leg a skosh. "Uh… what was it?"

"I don't know," she said in a sexy voice right in my ear. "What?"

I tried to focus. "When I was stuck in the Quihiri jail next to the FTL drive factory, I tried to use it to escape, but it only worked infrequently. I think the particular FTL drive has to be broken, leaking quantum probabilities somehow."

"Interesting hypothesis." She leaned in and kissed me.

I kissed back. Mmmm. It was lovely. For a few moments, I lost myself in her luscious lips, her exploring hands…

She leaned back.

"Aw." I reached for her. "Come back."

Leaning away, she smiled and activated her fon. "Hi Gina, this is Eva. He can't do it."

I pointed down. "I can do it. I can do all of it. Let me do it." I was so ready to do it.

She covered her fon and laughed a little. She listened and nodded. "Yes, ma'am." She ended the call.

"I can do whatever you want, Eva," I said and grinned.

"We finished taking on supplies from the cat planet, and we've been in FTL space for an hour," she said and pointed at me. "Obviously, your special skill isn't working."

I wrapped my arms around her. "Oh, I've got a special skill for you."

She laughed and leaned in.

When I woke, holding Eva in my arms, I was happy. "*Is this love…*" I sang quietly.

She opened her eyes. "What?"

"*…that I'm feeling*?" I sang.

"That's not Shakespeare." She laughed. "What is that?" She sat up. "Never mind. We should be close to Quihiri by now." She looked at her fon. "Yeah." She started pulling on her clothes.

When I didn't immediately dress, she said, "Aren't you coming? We're rescuing Addie and Quinta. I thought you'd be all over this."

I jumped out of bed. "*Once more unto the breach, dear friends, once more--*"

She interrupted me. "Yeah, yeah. We're due in the shuttle bay."

A little later, me (wearing my own actual uniform!), Eva, Carter, security officer Ted and his boss Commander Lu were buckling into seats on the *Shakespeare*'s shuttle. Slid and Quibilah bobbed around, sparkling and fizzing.

"Mommy, I'm going to see my mommy!" Slid kept saying.

"My triple, my triple, I'm going to see my triple," Quibilah kept saying. I had my doubts about how well that would work out.

Carter flew us out of the *Shakespeare*'s shuttle bay. Cloaked, we flew around the largest Quihiri moon (where the ship had been hiding), finally seeing the planet Quihiri itself. It was a beautiful blue and white marble, all oceans and white clouds. From this far out, it looked surprisingly like Earth. I guessed it was pretty similar to Earth; it just had fewer landmasses. Blue and white marble planets were my favorite.

"I'm the security chief of this mission," Commander Lu said, face grim. "You'll see your triple if I deem it safe, uh, Ms. Quibilah."

Quibilah turned red and black and spit sparks. That couldn't be good.

I glanced at Ted, sitting next to Lu, and sighed. Ted and I used to be very close, but he didn't remember. The Quihiri had whammied us with a weird memory-erasing drug. "Everyone should backup their memories if they haven't recently," I said. "Come here, Slid."

He came and buzzed in my lap.

Soon we were landing, still cloaked, on the Quihiri planet in a deserted land area near the giant capital/embassy complex. Apparently, the Quihiri didn't enjoy the outdoors much if it was dry land.

I stood up and peered out the front viewscreen. It was overcast. I couldn't see anything but wet gray rocks and wet gray ground. I hoped Addie and Quinta were here and both okay.

Carter powered down the shuttle and opened the door. Humidity rolled inside the shuttle.

Quibilah quickly flew out. "I'm coming, Quinn and Quaid!"

"No!" Commander Lu said.

"Come back, Quibilah," I said. "It's not safe. Quibilah!"

But she was gone.

Crap. What if the Quihiri found her? Scratch that. They would find her; she wasn't trying to remain secret. Since she was seeking the loves of her life, I couldn't exactly blame her.

Ted and Commander Lu ran after her, drawing their weapons.

"Quibilah!" I yelled.

Still inside, Carter, Eva, and I exchanged knowing looks that said, 'Well, that's hopeless.'

"Is my mommy here?" Slid asked.

"I think so, buddy," I said. "Let's go find out."

Carter and Eva drew their weapons as they stepped out of the shuttle.

I just held Slid, hoping Addie was okay, hoping Quinta was okay. Outside, it was so humid it felt like the air was liquid. The heavy gray clouds above, gray rocks, and gray ground surrounded us in a gloomy blah.

We picked our way through the rocks to the spot where we'd met Addie and Quinta before.

I started scrutinizing each rock. "Addie?" I whispered. "Quinta? Hello?"

None of the rocks answered me.

Carter and Eva didn't seem to know what to make of my behavior.

Finally, Carter sighed and said, "So, that's it? You've finally lost it, Jones?"

Eva holstered her weapon. "*Though this be madness, yet there is method in 't.*"

I straightened and smiled at her. I appreciated her faith in me even if she didn't know exactly what I was up to. "Yes! Thanks, babe. The last time I was here on the surface, Addie and Quinta were here, pretending to be big rocks."

"Where's my mommy?" Slid asked.

"I don't know, little one," I said. "She doesn't seem to be here." My skin started feeling clammy, and I didn't think it was because of the humidity. Where were my friends? Had they been discovered? Were they arrested? In prison? Worse?

"Let's go back to the shuttle and regroup," Eva said.

"Give me a second. There are a few rocks I haven't talked to yet." I started patting all the biggest rocks. "Addie? Quinta?"

But they were not here.

The three of us humans trudged back to the shuttle.

I still held Slid. He resembled a soggy gray cloud.

Once Carter closed the door and powered up the environmental controls inside the shuttle, we left the soup behind.

"Now what?" Carter asked.

"Can you monitor Quihiri communications?" I asked. "See if anything weird is going on?"

"Good idea, Jack," Eva said and swiveled in the co-pilot's chair. "Implement it, Carter."

Soon, we heard a lot of weird noises, including hissing and fizzing and grunts. I started looking around for one of our translation machines.

"What is that?" Carter asked. "Language or technical difficulties?"

Slid brightened a little and floated up towards a speaker. "Oh, no!"

"You can understand that, Slid?" I asked.

"It's a security alert!" Slid yelled. "They're saying something about an invasion of enemy combatants. What's that?"

Trouble.

Chapter Twenty-Four

On Quihiri, I was stuck in a shuttle with some friends in the middle of an invasion. Granted, my other friends were the ones doing the invading, but that didn't mean the rest of us weren't in some trouble.

"Where's my mommy?" Slid asked, quivering up near the ceiling.

I found a translator and switched it on. Faintly, we heard things like, 'Red alert, red alert,' coming from the Quihiri communications channel.

"Come here, Slid." I held out my arms, and he floated down. I nuzzled him against my chest. "We'll find your mommy. I promise."

Eva frowned at me. I parsed her expression to say, 'You shouldn't make promises you may not be able to keep.'

"What's the plan, then, Jack?" Carter asked. "It's three, er, three-and-a-half of us versus a whole planet." He waved his hands at the three-and-a-half of us in turn.

Now, Eva was frowning out the front viewscreen, possibly looking for some sign of Ted and Commander Lu. Or, perhaps, Quihiri soldiers. Suddenly, she pointed out the front. "Look! Someone's coming!"

I held Slid tighter. We all stepped up to the front window and peered out. I could just barely make out some shadowy figures approaching. Were they good guys or bad guys?

Carter cleared his throat. "The cloak's still working, isn't it?"

"Yes," she said.

The figures came into focus. It was Ted and Commander Lu! Yay!

"Stand by to open the shuttle door," Carter said.

Eva's expression said, 'Duh.' Her finger was poised over the door control.

Ted and Lu passed out of view of the front window; then, we heard knocking at the back door. How had they found the back of the shuttle since it was cloaked? Lu must have some special equipment. Or he remembered where we were.

Eva pressed the button, and the door whooshed open. The two men stepped in, along with a lot of water vapor.

"I'm glad you're okay," I said. The door whooshed closed.

Commander Lu, frowning mightily, said, "We lost her."

Ted nodded at me and wiped the moisture off his face with his sleeve. "Yeah, those sldkfjfoisut are quick. Who knew they could move so fast?"

Slid and I looked at each other. We knew they could move so fast.

"Where's my mommy?" he asked again. "I want my mommy."

The crackles over the communications system increased in number and volume.

"Human Jack Jones," the translator said, "part of the Terran Command triple, this is the Quihiri Primary Tertian. We know you're out there. We've captured your evil, deformed spy Quibilah. Turn yourself and your team in immediately, or we will execute her."

Slid started shivering in my arms. I looked over my compatriots. Of this group, Ted was probably the most maternal. I held out my arms. "Ted, will you take care of Slid?"

Ted took a step towards me.

"You're turning yourself in?" Eva said. "That's crazy!"

"We're still cloaked," Commander Lu said. "We can probably fly away without detection."

"But they're going to execute her!" I said. I didn't even know how to execute a sldkfjfoisut, but I had no doubt the Quihiri did.

"Yeah." Ted held out his arms. "I'll take care of Slid."

Eva looked at me with her eyelids drooping and her brow furrowed. The corners of her lips turned down. That was her sad look. I had to stop myself from going over and hugging her.

"As *Shakespeare* First Officer, I'm the commander of this mission, and I forbid it," Carter said. Everyone turned to him. He forbade it?

"Don't worry, I'll tell them I'm here on my own," I said. "I won't give you guys up."

There were a lot of crackles over comms. "Okay, we're about to execute the horrible traitor Quibilah. Here we go."

I lurched for the comms. "Don't do it!" I said. "I'm turning myself in!"

"I formally object," Lu said.

Ted looked confused. In his arms, Slid was the color of blackest night.

"I'll do it on one condition," I said into comms. "I demand a Planetary Public Tribunal!" It turned out that reading the planetary briefing can be pretty helpful. Among other things, here, they were sticklers for rules and regulations.

"You're in no position to make demands," the Quihiri on the other end said.

"It's part of the Galactic Treaty!" I said. "I demand you uphold the treaty. *According to the fair play of the world, let me have audience.*"

"Just a minute," the Quihiri said. The comms quieted. A few moments later, he said, "Okay. If you turn yourself in, we'll convene a Planetary Public Tribunal."

"Good," I said over comms and then flicked them off. "Who wants to be my legate? I'm allowed one according to tradition." I eagerly glanced from one compatriot to the other. No doubt, they'd be clamoring to help me with my virtuous quest.

"As commanding officer, I forbid this," Carter said.

No one else spoke up.

"Orders," Ted said. "And I, uh, have to take care of Slid," he said, gesturing to the child in his arms.

"I can't disobey a direct order. I need to cover TCC security interests," Lu said.

"Orders," Eva said, arms crossed, clearly unhappy to obey said orders.

"I'll help!" Slid said.

"No, little one," I said. "It's too dangerous. Are you sure, Carter?"

Everyone turned to look at him.

"I'm sure," he said. "I'm not going to be Jack's legume or

whatever. It's stupid. I don't get why you're turning yourself in, Jack. You're just going to end up in jail. Or worse. I order you to stand down."

Talk about a negative attitude! "Well, if that's your attitude, I don't want you for my legume, I mean legate." I started getting some stuff together, including water, a snack, my fon, and a translator.

As I stomped around the shuttle, accessing various hatches, I realized they might have a point. I might be going to my death. And for what?

For Quibilah. I had helped her transition, and I brought her here to Quihiri. She was my responsibility. I didn't abandon my friends.

Finally, I walked to the shuttle's door. I stopped and glanced back at my other friends, holding my head up high. "I guess I understand. We are at war. We need to find Addie and Quinta and see if they've had any success finding Quihiri who are sympathetic to our cause, namely, freedom throughout the galaxy. You all do that." I pointed at them. "I'll change hearts and minds on my mission, the Tribunal."

"Sure, you will, Jack." Ted smiled weakly at me.

Eva darted forward and gave me a little hug. My warrior princess was not a big fan of public displays of affection, so I tried not to worry that that meant she thought I was going to die.

"Fear not, I will not die. *To die is to be a counterfeit, for he is but the counterfeit of a man who hath not the life of a man. But to counterfeit dying, when a man thereby liveth, is to be no counterfeit, but the true and perfect image of life indeed.*" I saluted them all. "Door."

Ted said, "Huh?"

Carter, muttering and shaking his head, opened the back door.

Moisture roiled in. I roiled out and started walking away.

Within moments, sounds told me the shuttle powered up and flew away. Where were they going? It was probably best I didn't know.

I started walking to the secret entrance of the Quihiri capital city complex that I had used previously. Moisture rolled down my face, down my back, down my legs, basically, down everything.

My uniform was quite damp.

When I tried to access the building's exterior door, some Quihiri security officers barreled out, pointing weapons at me. One said, "Who are you?"

"Jack Jones," I said. "You're expecting me."

Surprisingly quickly, I found myself on stage at the bottom of a ginormous auditorium, near three small pools (also on stage), surrounded by octopus people. Although the stage was dry (except for the pools), the humidity theme continued. The lighting had a distinctive orange hue. The people seemed to be chatting quietly amongst themselves in the audience, but I couldn't make anything out. They were all shades of gray, black, and dark blue.

A large Quihiri made his way to the center pool and slipped in, standing in the shallow water. A smaller male Quihiri stood behind him. They were both a sort of dark blue-gray color. They did look familiar. I wasn't great at telling the octopus people apart, but I was guessing they were the Quihiri Ambassador and his husband, both Quinta's former husbands. They blamed me for their wife transforming into a sldkfjfoisut and leaving them. Quinta was the first Quihiri I'd seen transform.

Technically, Quinta and I spent the night together a while ago, so I was not totally without fault. Consequently, their involvement was not a great development for me.

The Ambassador made a sound like throat-clearing. Immediately, all the chatter stopped. "You all know why we're here. This evil creature, Jack Jones," he pointed a tentacle at me, "from Terra has deformed and violated our sister Quibilah." I didn't see a microphone or speakers, but everyone could hear him perfectly. Including me; he was speaking English. It was one of the rules of the Tribunal: speak in the accused's language.

I looked around for Quibilah and saw her off to the side, in some kind of energy prison. I took a small step in her direction.

He continued, "He perverted and murdered my dear wife, Quinta. This Jack creature utterly destroyed my triple. He is the one and only reason war has broken out in the galaxy." Well, that wasn't true at all. *He* was the reason we were at war.

The octopus crowd glared at me. If looks could kill, I would have been dead several dozen times. I took another step.

For the first time, I started to get a little prickle of fear. They were required to let me speak uninterrupted, but that was about it. What if doing the right thing for Quibilah ended up ending me? I took yet another step towards her.

"Quibilah's husbands, the heart of her triple, Quaid and Quinn, will now testify against him."

Two average-looking Quihiri slid up from behind us and slithered into the other two pools.

One said, "Quibilah was a wonderful sweet wife. She completed our triple...."

I tuned him out. I needed to focus on saving Quibilah. I needed to focus on my plan. Among other things, I needed to find out if Quibilah was okay. No one on stage seemed to care that I was extremely slowly shuffling my way over to Quibilah.

Finally, I was close enough to whisper, "Quibilah, are you okay?"

"No," she said, sounding as if she'd been crying. She looked like a black storm cloud, complete with lightning bolts inside.

"What happened?" I asked. "Did they hurt you? They didn't torture you, did they?"

"I found Quinn and Quaid, and they rejected me!" she cried. "We were a family, a triple, and they said they didn't want me anymore. They said I was deformed. A monster. They said they didn't love me anymore." A lightning bolt escaped her and sizzled against the energy field containing her.

"Oh, honey, you're not a monster," I said. "If they don't love you just because you're a little different, they're the monsters."

Then, a tentacle touched my arm, and I jumped.

When I turned around, one of the Quihiri security team stood next to me. "Are you gonna talk, then, or should we just go ahead and kill you now?"

I glanced around the auditorium. No one on stage was speaking any longer. The audience was all staring at me.

The security squids parted, seemingly directing me to the center pond.

I marched my way to the pond and bravely stepped in. The water came up to my ankles, filling my boots. It smelled of seaweed and fish, but I smiled broadly. I knew some things first-hand about the Quihiri. One of them was: they loved Earth culture. That was the whole reason we'd interacted with them in the first place.

"Listen closely, lords and ladies," I said. "*I will a round unvarnish'd tale deliver.*" This was going to be the performance of my life. It would have to be, or it'd be the last performance of my life.

"I'm very sorry to say, fellows and females, your leaders have been deceiving you." I pointed at the ambassador.

He turned dark black.

"I have not murdered anyone. Quinta is alive and well. I have not deformed or perverted anyone. Quibilah is alive and well." I pointed at her. "She desired nothing more than to be reunited with her beloved triple. I do not want war. I want peace between our great peoples." I started singing, "*Would I lie to you?...*"

Some of the audience's colors were lightening as I sang.

Then, I said, "Guys and gals, your government has suppressed and lied about a completely natural process for years, maybe decades, maybe centuries. The transformation from Quihiri to sldkfjfoisut is a normal, natural part of your race's evolutionary process--"

Someone yelled, "How dare you!"

"Look out, Jack!" Quibilah called out.

I jumped out of the pond, landing prone on the stage.

An energy weapon sizzled into the pond, crackling and popping. *Phew.* That was a close one.

It gave me an idea. Still prone, I splashed water along the stage to Quibilah. It hit her force field prison with a loud crack. It was as if a bolt of lightning erupted inside the auditorium.

With another *crack!* the lights went out in the auditorium.

As my eyes adjusted to the low light, I realized there were sldkfjfoisut scattered throughout the auditorium, sparkling dimly.

I sang, "*Why don't you show yourself?...*"

And, then, it was as if we were surrounded by hundreds of stars, as bright lights appeared all around the room.

They brought light to the darkness, sparkling with hope.

Chapter Twenty-Five

I scrambled to my feet on the Quihiri stage at the bottom of the spacious auditorium. An adult Quihiri with a weapon lay unmoving near Quibilah.

After a moment of stunned silence, the crowd started screaming in terror at the sldkfjfoisut surrounding them.

"Don't be afraid!" I yelled. "These are your brothers and sisters." I started singing. "*Don't be afraid to love and get love returned...*" Were their screams getting slightly less frantic? I kept singing.

I looked around for Quibilah. She was still on stage. "Quibilah!" I whispered.

She floated towards me. "I had no idea there were so many sldkfjfoisut here."

"Do you know this song?"

"The Carpenters of Terra are very popular here," she said.

"So, sing!" I said. "Let's get people singing rather than screaming. Or fighting." I took a deep breath. "*Love is a groovy thing*."

Quibilah sang with me. Other sldkfjfoisut in the room joined in. Soon, the melody spread around the space.

The screaming decreased. The Quihiri seemed quite confused; some of them even started singing.

And, then, some Quihiri security officers rushed in a door halfway up the auditorium, weapons pointing this way and that, making a lot of noise. My translator said, "Freeze evil sldkfjfoisut!"

We sang louder, and the harmonies started overcoming the hostilities. The softly glowing sldkfjfoisut provided the only illumination.

Security was confused. They didn't know where to direct their weapons.

And then, Commander Lu and the rest of my TCC friends rushed in through another door halfway up the auditorium. They had their weapons out, looking for people to point them at.

"Jack!" Ted called out. "Come on!"

"*So, come on and live and be happy, live and be happy*," I sang.

I don't know who did it, but someone fired a shot, and then we were back to screaming as everyone stopped singing.

Energy rays flew back and forth through the space. *Pew, pew*. Everyone ducked down. *Pew, pew.*

"Jack!" Ted yelled.

The room got darker as all the sldkfjfoisut dimmed significantly. People streamed towards the exits.

"Follow me, Jack!" Quibilah said and started up the stairs towards our friends. I followed her dim glow as we raced up. And up. And up. I was panting by the time I reached Ted and the others. They were all crouched down behind seats.

Pew, pew.

"We came to rescue you, Jack!" Ted said.

The others were too busy firing their weapons to greet me.

Many, many thoughts went through my mind as I looked at Ted's eager smile in the dim light. Most were along the lines of 'Your unnecessary rescue seems to have made matters much worse.' But after a few moments, I merely smiled, clasped him on the shoulder, and said, "Thanks, Ted. I appreciate it."

Pew, pew.

He smiled back.

The auditorium was quickly emptying. Talk about bringing down the house--but not in a good way.

"Let's go!" I said and pointed at the exit behind us.

We all darted out the door into the relative calm of the corridor.

Quinta and Addie were in the hallway. Yay! Slid was cradled in his mom, and he was emitting bright, happy sparks. "Quinta! Addie!" I darted towards them. "It's wonderful to see you! Are you all right?" I wanted to hug them but couldn't quite figure out how.

"Yes," Addie said. "We have news--"

"This isn't the time or place to talk," Commander Lu said. "And, kid, tone down the sparkles." They did make us an obvious target. Thankfully, there was no Quihiri security in sight. For now.

Slid dimmed.

"Let's go!" Quinta started bobbing down the hall outside the auditorium.

We followed. The sldkfjfoisut (the good guys) soon flew to the front of the group.

We were closely pursued by Quihiri security forces, shooting their energy weapons at us. It's hard to run and duck down simultaneously, let me tell you.

Bringing up the rear of our group Ted, Eva, Carter, and Commander Lu did their best, shooting their weapons while also trying to duck and run.

We inadvertently approached a group of Quihiri soldiers shooting at someone else. Luckily, we heard the firefight before we were in danger of being hit by it. We ducked into an empty office filled with desks and chairs clustered in groups of three. All the sldkfjfoisut bobbed around, showing off gray and black swirls. We seemed to have collected quite a conglomeration of them.

I peeked into the hall back in the direction we'd come. The soldiers were almost on top of us. "Hide!" I whisper-shouted. We all ducked down behind furniture.

A contingent of octopus soldiers oozed past us. Almost immediately, I heard the soldiers following us greet the soldiers in front of us. Then, the shooting began in earnest again.

I crawled over to Commander Lu. "Who are they shooting at?" I asked him.

"I'm not sure." He pulled his fon out of his pocket and looked at it. Then, he grunted.

"What?" I asked.

"It's above your pay grade," he said, typing something into his fon.

I pointed in the direction of the firefight. "Seriously?"

He glanced that way and then shrugged. "Okay. I guess the cat's out of the bag now. We, and especially you, were the diversion. Terran forces, the Agincourt crew, the Shakespeare crew, and whoever else was available landed on Quihiri. We're trying to take the Quihiri command center and force them to surrender."

My first instinct was to scream, 'What? Did you put me in danger as a diversion? Did you put the sldkfjfoisut in danger as a diversion!' But screaming was contra-indicated for people hiding in a random office right near a major battle, from the sound of it.

While I was staring at him, trying to get my emotions under control, his fon pinged, and he grunted again.

"What?" I asked.

"We have orders to join the battle," he said.

I held up my empty hands. "With what?"

"Not you," he said. "Eva, Carter, Ted, and me. You're supposed to evacuate the sldkfjfoisut."

'What!' My emotions were getting the better of me again. "Let me get this straight; the orders are for all the people with weapons to abandon the people without weapons?"

"Yes." His face like granite, he nodded.

"Ready to fall out, Commander," Eva said. Where'd she come from? "Sorry, Jack."

"Me too," Carter said.

"That doesn't seem quite fair," Ted said. "Permission to accompany Jack and the others, sir?"

Commander Lu looked at him for a moment before he finally said, "Okay, Ted." For some reason, I'd thought he would say, 'Your funeral, Ted.' But he didn't.

Within moments, the armed crew stealthily crept out of the office.

I stealthily crept to the doorway and peeked through. My three brave friends chased a group of Quihiri down the hall, around a corner. *He that outlives this day, and comes safe home, will stand a' tiptoe when this day is named…*

I crept back to Ted and the sldkfjfoisut. "We should go while the coast is clear." I put on my lean and hungry look.

We backtracked. The Quihiri embassy complex was immense. I got utterly lost, following the sldkfjfoisut down hallways through passages and offices.

Every once in a while, I heard the sounds of battle in the distance, energy weapon discharges, and screams.

Eventually, we found ourselves next to a familiar hole in

the wall in the Quihiri embassy complex. Quinta, Addie, Slid, Quibilah, and most of the other sldkfjfoisut squeezed through the six-inch-diameter opening that stood about three feet off the floor. The rest of us (humans) stood there, gaping.

"What is this?" Ted asked.

Slid poked part of himself back through. "Come on!" He sparkled a little. That young fellow was happy to be reunited with his mom.

"Surely, you're joking," Ted said.

"Relax," I said. "I've been on the other side." I leaned down and looked through it. The cavernous space on the other side of the wall was dimly lit by a warm orange light. "Are you guys sure?" I asked the sldkfjfoisut.

Addie floated into view. "Yes. Come on." Her color was brightening.

"Okay. I trust you." I straightened up.

"I've heard you're flexible, Jack," Ted said. "But there's no way you fit through that hole."

I smiled and patted him on the back. Interesting. Who told him I was flexible? "I didn't go through that specific opening." I pointed. "The FTL drive factory is through there next to the dungeon. I know another way. Come on!" I rushed off, and they followed. Some of the sldkfjfoisut stayed with us.

We approached the Quihiri dungeon. A dungeon would be a great place to hide; the authorities would never expect to find us here. Assuming we didn't run into any guards. "Stay frosty, people." I very carefully pushed open the battered wooden dungeon door. I looked both ways. The coast seemed clear, so I stepped inside.

Ted was right behind me. "Wait." He stopped abruptly. "Is this the prison?"

I glanced around at the various prison cells, most in pools of water. "Yeah."

Everyone stopped now.

Ted shook his head, muttering, "Jack, are you putting *yourself* in jail now?"

"Jack has a plan," one of the sldkfjfoisut said. "Don't you, Jack?" She(?) leaned in towards me and said quietly, "Please tell me you have a plan."

"My initial plan is to do what Addie says," I said. "She said to come here. I trust her." I marched resolutely forward. "*I will here shroud till the dregs of the storm be past.*"

Ted was right behind me. He shrugged. "Makes sense to me. The prison is the last place the Quihiri security forces would look for us."

We crept through the dungeon. Up ahead, the light seemed brighter. "Is it brighter up there?"

"Yeah," Ted said.

We continued to creep until we ducked through a low doorway into the spacious FTL drive factory. The warehouse-sized room was chock full of faintly glowing sldkfjfoisut.

Addie floated up to me. "We found the Resistance against the Quihiri, Jack. Look."

The sldkfjfoisut turned up their luminosity.

Quinta said, "There are so many new sldkfjfoisut on Quihiri! The evolutionary process is accelerating. More and more Quihiri are transforming all the time."

Slid fizzed, and sparkled. "Resistance! Resistance! Neat-o resistance." He bobbed over next to his mom. "What's resistance?"

"I'm glad for all of you," I said, glancing at the factory in front of us. There were answers here, many answers. If I couldn't figure out how to turn the FTL drives back on from here, I never would.

"Is anyone here former Quihiri security?" Ted called out.

Someone in the crowd replied, "Yeah!"

"Can we talk?" Ted asked.

"Yeah," the person answered.

The crowd of sldkfjfoisut surged forward.

I stared at the computers. "Can I investigate the FTL drives?"

Addie said, "Only if you're trying to turn them back on throughout the galaxy."

"You know me so well," I said, grinning.

"Well, we were lovers," she said. Somebody gasped, but I didn't see who.

"Is anyone here a former FTL drive factory worker?" I called out.

"Yeah," someone answered.

"Will you please help me?" I pointed at the computers.

"Okay," they said. A sldkfjfoisut started bobbing towards me through the crowd.

I jogged to the computer system, and he or she followed me. When I got there, I leaned down, squinting at the main machine. Initially, I didn't even see how to turn it on--if it wasn't on.

I glanced over at my new compatriot. "Hi, there, friend. My name's Jack." I shrugged and held out my hand as if to shake hands.

He/she engulfed my hand with their body. It tickled in a buzzy kind of way. "Nice to meet you, Jack. My name's Love."

"Wow! Great name," I blurted out.

"I've, we've, all heard a lot about you." I decided his voice sounded male. He withdrew, giving me back my hand. "You're a good singer. The Terran Carpenters. Wow."

"I know, Love." I smiled. "So, anyway, can we turn the FTL drives back on from here?"

"Yeah," he said.

"We can? Awesome!" I was totally awesome. "Point me to it!" I may have jumped up and down a few times. Yay, me!

"We *could*," he continued. "If we knew the password that unlocks the whole system."

I quit jumping around. "So, we don't have the password?"

"No." Love's color darkened.

"And we definitely need the password?" I asked.

"Yes," he said. "To do anything other than the most basic tasks."

No doubt, at this point, my color darkened. "So, how do we get the password?"

"Only the Quihiri Primary Tertian has the password."

"Is anyone here the Quihiri Primary Tertian?" I called out.

No one replied in the affirmative, but it was worth a try.

"Does anyone know the Primary Tertian?" I asked.

"Yes!" basically all the sldkfjfoisut said.

"Does anyone know the Primary Tertian's password?" I asked.

All I got back was a lot of muttering.

Love said, “He’s old and overly self-important. Maybe his password is ‘password.’”

“It’s worth a try,” I said. “Input it.” I didn’t want to reveal that I had no idea how to work the Quihiri computer.

Love did something, and we got the *bzzzz* of an incorrect password. It was a good thing, unifying, that sentients throughout the galaxy all had similar experiences when they forgot their passwords. Right?

Unfortunately, right this second, it didn’t feel like a good thing. I sat on one of the three stools at the central console.

Ted came over. “We’re getting some great intel about the whole Quihiri military.”

“What?” I asked.

“It’s so good, perhaps we should get back to the *Shakespeare* ASAP,” he said.

“You can’t just leave us, Jack!” Love cried.

I was inundated with, “Don’t leave!” and “You can’t leave!” and “We need you.” Sometimes, being awesome was a bit of a burden.

Addie and Slid bobbed over. “We have to free the sldkfjfoisut from the Quihiri,” she said.

“Yeah,” Quinta said.

“Yeah,” Slid said.

“What about the mission?” Ted asked.

“I’m going to stay,” I said. “I think figuring out the FTL drive is the mission.”

“I’ll help!” Slid said.

“Thank you, Slid,” I said. “I appreciate it. Of course, maybe you sldkfjfoisut should try to get back to the *Shakespeare*. It would be safer.”

“No,” Addie said. “We should all stick together.”

Ted looked at me. Finally, he said, “I’m up for whatever you think.”

I put my arm around his shoulder. “Don’t worry, Ted. I have a feeling we’ll get along pretty well.”

He blushed. “What now?”

I pointed at Love. “We’re going to fire up some FTL drives.” I knew once-in-a-while FTL drives were defective…

"We should be able to do that," Love said.

I recalled the FTL drive quality control involved turning on the drive. If it worked, a portal to another world whooshed open. Occasionally, a drive was turned on, and nothing happened. Thus, that drive must be faulty. My hypothesis was: I needed one of *those* drives to make my special power work. I needed a defective drive to leak improbabilities so I could take advantage of them.

So, some hours later, I was quite sick of turning on FTL drives. I was sick of portals to other planetary systems whooshing on. I was sick of different-colored sunlight filling the space and then being replaced with Quihiri's orange light. So far, none of the FTL drives were defective.

So far, my special skill refused to work.

I sagged on a stool near the portal place. Yellow starlight bathed us in its glow.

"Do you want me to kiss you some more, Jack?" Ted asked.

My lips were swollen and sore. I couldn't believe it, but I was almost sick of kissing. I held up my hand. "Give me a minute." A breeze from the portal ruffled my hair.

It must be stress. How had I become responsible for most of a race of people, namely, the sldkfjfoisut people? What had I been thinking?

Addie zoomed up to me. "Our sentries say an armed force of Quihiri is coming this way!"

We had sentries? What an excellent idea.

"Jack!" she said, turning black and stormy.

I peered at her. "We have a lot of sldkfjfoisut here. Can we fight?"

"We don't have any weapons," she said. "And I'm sure the Quihiri have weapons that are specially designed against us."

I heard some weird noises. Weapon noises?

"Oh, no!" she said. "They're almost here!"

"Oh, no!" Slid had floated up to us. "Who's almost here?"

I glanced at him. There was no way I would let little Slid get injured or killed in some firefight. There was no way I wanted Slid to even be in a firefight.

I smelled something; maybe freshly mown hay? Was it coming from the portal? "Love, do Quihiri ever travel via these portals?" I pointed behind us.

"No," he said. "It's too dangerous. You have no idea where you'll end up. It could be vacuum on the other end."

I squinted into the portal, seeing a blue sky and some grassy-looking golden plants. "Looks like grass to me." I sniffed. It smelled like a summer day on Earth. In a hay field.

"And how would you get back?" Love turned black. "No. It is strictly forbidden. Too dangerous. Expressly forbidden."

The sounds of energy weapons being discharged approached us, getting louder and louder.

"I'm not sure we have a choice," I said. "What do you think, Addie?"

Pew, pew. An energy beam shot into the room, traveled over our heads and hit the far wall with a sizzle.

Addie didn't answer me immediately, no doubt worried about Slid. Finally, she said, "I don't want Slid to get shot."

Pew, pew.

I didn't point out that staying here might very well result in being shot. "*Be not afraid of greatness*!" I ran to the portal. "Come on, everyone!"

I jumped.

Chapter Twenty-Six

I landed gracefully on my derrière in the middle of a massive field of hay, or, rather, convergent-evolution plants that looked a lot like Terran hay. And smelled a lot like Terran hay. I sneezed. Rolling golden hay-ish covered hills stretched out in every direction.

My friends floated through the portal after me, first Addie and Slid, then Love and the other members of the sldkfjfoisut Resistance. Ted brought up the rear, tumbling through, not landing nearly as gracefully as I. I grinned.

"What's this?" Ted pointed at a scorched, blackened area in the field as he scrambled up.

"Must be weapons fire from the Quihiri security forces?" I said.

Pew, pew. An energy bolt flew through the portal, hitting the ground near us--right where Ted had been mere moments ago.

"Focus, Terrans!" Addie said. "How do we close the portal behind us?"

"Are you s-sure that's a good idea?" Love said, stuttering. He was clearly nervous.

Pew, pew. I ducked out of the way just in time. "Close it!" I said. "Close it!"

"I guess I could shoot the controls through the portal?" Ted said, holding up his energy weapon.

"I don't think--" Love said.

Pew, pew.

"Do it!" I said.

Ted shrugged and shot at something on the other side of the portal.

It closed very calmly and quietly, disappearing with a small final *pop!*

We appeared to be in the middle of extensive farmlands, filled with some grassy crop. We seemed to be in the middle of nowhere.

"What now, sir?" Ted asked, staring at me.

Sir? Nice. I was going to like being the senior Terran officer on this op.

"We need to figure out where in the galaxy we are ASAP," Addie said. "And try to meet up with any other sldkfjfoisut or other allies in the area."

Ted gazed around, taking in the blue sky with a few wispy white clouds. "Looks like Earth."

I sneezed again.

"Smells like Earth," he said.

But I wasn't allergic to Terran hay, so it couldn't be Earth.

Love bobbed over above the burnt area. "This burn worries me. It's so big. What caused this?" I was beginning to realize Love was a pretty effective worrier.

I pulled my fon out of my pocket. "I'll check the Galactic Positioning System, and we'll know where we are in a jiff. And then I should call Gina."

The other sldkfjfoisut floated around us. It was a little reminiscent of a loose football huddle before game time.

"If you can get a signal here, in the middle of a field, in the middle of nowhere," Love said, sounding extremely downtrodden and depressed.

I pointed at him. "You remind me of someone, someone fictional. From my childhood." I found the GPS app. "Ha. I do have a signal." I started to access the app.

Suddenly, it became overcast.

We all looked up to spy a whopping winged beast, some kind of reptile, flying over us. It was an iridescent blue, at least thirty feet long, with four legs, huge wings, a lengthy tail, and a long neck. It was beautiful, in a terrifying way, but where had it come from?

"Is that a …" Love halted, seemingly petrified.

Directly above us now, the creature opened its mouth. I smelled sulfur. I whispered, "*Our ancient word of courage, fair Saint George, inspire us with spleen of fiery dragons.*"

"Dinosaur?" Ted said and started raising his weapon.

"Is that a dragon, Mommy?" Slid asked very quietly. Wow. Now the burnt area made much more sense.

And, definitely, positively, not Earth.

If it was a dragon, an angry, defensive dragon, we didn't stand a chance. There was no cover anywhere.

I pushed Ted's weapon arm down. "Hello, up there, sir!" I called up to it. "Are we trespassing?" I glanced around. Could all these plants be the result of agriculture? Maybe. "If so, we sincerely apologize, sir. Lovely farm. Lovely spot you have here."

The creature exhaled, and I got a strong whiff of sulfur again. Then, it inhaled, drawing in a huge breath.

"We have juveniles here, sir," I said. "They don't deserve to be hurt."

Addie had pushed Slid down towards the ground and spread her body out above him.

The creature flapped its wings, held them up, and landed heavily on four legs next to us. Then it folded its wings neatly onto its back.

The huddle of sldkfjfoisut scooted behind me. It was as if I was a comet with an elongated sldkfjfoisut tail.

I smiled broadly and bowed deeply. "Jack Jones at your service, sire."

"This portal is tiresome," she said with a voice as deep as time itself. A female! "Are you from Quihiri? You're lucky I haven't burnt you to a crisp already." Her words smelled of wildfires decimating the entire countryside.

I bowed again. "*She had all the royal makings of a queen, as holy oil, Edward Confessor's crown, the rod, and bird of peace, and all such emblems laid nobly on her.*" I stood up straight and gave her my sexiest smile. "Then, we have a common enemy, Your Highness. We hate the Quihiri." I gave a flourish with my arms. "We are all at your service, oh, Exalted One. We stand at the ready."

"What are all the creatures cowering behind you?" she asked. "Are they made of smoke?"

"These sldkfjfoisut are also at your service, Your Majesty," I said, flashing her my sexy smile again.

"Sldkfjfoisut?" She peered over my head. I tried not to flinch as the odor of fire increased. "I have heard of such creatures but never met one. I understood them to be rare, yet, here, there are many."

"Yes." I nodded solemnly. "And they are here under my protection."

She withdrew a little and examined my face. "What was your name, Terran?"

"Jack Jones, Your Eminence," I said with another flourish.

Near my ear, Slid said, "Is she a dragon? Is she going to burn us?"

"No, little one," Addie said. Then she slipped around to float next to me. "Your Ladyship, we apologize for this inconvenience." Her gray cloudiness took on some bright blue sparkles. "We are indeed a large cohort of sldkfjfoisut and are at your service, as Jack says. We did arrive here via the Quihiri portal. They were trying to execute us, and we needed to escape with some haste. You may call me Addie; I speak for the sldkfjfoisut. Our circumstances seem to be changing. More and more sldkfjfoisut are being created." She sparkled more brightly. "Possibly, as a result of this Terran." That was the first I'd heard of it. She bobbed closer to me. "Whatever the reason, the Quihiri have declared war on us."

Our new, very large friend looked thoughtful.

"May we have safe passage until we can meet up with our allies?" I asked.

I felt something touch my back, and I whirled around. It was Ted.

"What about some water?" he whispered. "And food? And beds?"

I sneezed. "I wouldn't mind leaving this, uh, beautiful pasture," I said to the creature. "Possibly there's a town near here? Where we could rest?"

"Nonsense!" The dragon stood up straight and flexed her wings. "You shall come to my home. I would like to get to know some of the rare sldkfjfoisut. And I'm intrigued to hear how a Terran can increase fertility. The numbers of my great people have been in decline."

I had the alarming thought that she might expect me to help with dragon fertility somehow. That was asking a lot. My blood pressure started to go up.

"I can give the Terrans a ride," she said. "Can the rest of you fly alongside?"

"Yes," Addie said.

"No," Love said dejectedly from somewhere behind me. Eeyore! That's who he reminded me of.

Addie, quite sparkly now, made a laughing sound. "Certainly, you can, Love.

Now, I was recalling more literature from my childhood. Little boy Jack would have loved to ride a dragon like Ramoth or Ruth. It would have been a dream come true.

Our hostess bent her head down low to the ground. "Step aboard, Terrans. Carefully."

If little-boy Jack could do it, surely, I could do it. I clambered onto her neck and shimmied down to her violaceous torso. "Come on up, Ted!"

Looking worried, he clambered after me.

"Mind the wings," our conveyance said. Then she flapped her wings, took a few running steps, and jumped into the air. I wrapped my legs around the base of her neck like a vice.

"Oh, my God!" Ted said. "Oh, my God!"

I folded my arms around his waist. "You're okay, Ted. I've got you."

He whimpered in reply.

We rose into the air like, well, a dragon or maybe, a really big bird. The wind whipped through my hair. "Woo hoo!" I yelled.

I felt a small buzzing sensation on my back and twisted around to see Slid pressed against me. Many other sldkfjfoisut balanced behind him, between the massive wings.

"Woo hoo!" I yelled again, grinning. This was the best thing that had ever happened to me. Little boy Jack would consider this to be an excellent lifetime achievement.

We flew on.

And on.

The wind whipping past began to cause a chill.

I pressed my chest against Ted's back to borrow some of his body heat. He was still whimpering softly.

After I don't know how long, we started to fly downwards. I turned my attention to the land ahead of us and spied a magnificent gray stone square castle with a gatehouse, battlements, three towers and a keep on the four corners. Wow. I loved this planet!

We slowed down. Our ride spread her wings wide and glided to land in a stone courtyard. From the air, you could tell how colossal it was, but now I felt like an ant in the mammoth courtyard. The portcullis alone must be at least fifty feet squared.

I immediately scooted off our hostess. "Wow, Your Highness. That was wonderful! Thank you!"

The sldkfjfoisut floated all around me.

"Get off, Terran." The dragon-like creature twitched her back.

I held out a hand to Ted. "I got you, buddy."

He clasped it and sort of fell off, landing with an 'oof' on the pavement.

"Are you afraid of heights?" I asked him.

"Yeah-huh," he said from the ground.

"Kind of a weird phobia for an astronaut, don't you think?" I reached another hand out to him, down this time.

"No," he said. "There's no up or down in outer space." He stood up.

"That's a good point," I said.

"This way, if you please," the dragon said and strode for the keep's entrance. Please was a good sign, wasn't it?

I had to run after her to catch up, and once I did, I had to jog to keep up. The others ran or floated behind me.

She pushed open a grandiose door. "I'm home!" she called out, her voice almost cheerful. "It was the Quihiri portal. We have company, a bunch of sldkfjfoisut, and a couple of Terrans. Honey?"

Coming from the depths of the vast, seemingly empty gray-stone room, I heard a deep-throated growl and smelled sulfur.

"Duck!" I yelled and ducked down. Ted and the others ducked down behind my back.

A gout of orange-yellow flame flicked our hostess's nose.

It sounded as if she laughed in response. Then, she said, "Don't be rude. It's bad manners to burn guests."

For our part, said 'guests' all froze in place.

Ted whispered, "Did I ever tell you I'm afraid of burning to death?"

"Me, too," Love muttered.

"Maybe we should just turn around and leave," Ted said. "Very quietly." He turned around.

"We can try to leave," Love said. "She might not let us."

Ted took a step back. "Shh! Maybe if we're quiet, she'll forget about us."

Love floated back.

Then, I sneezed. The sound echoed back and forth, bouncing around the immense chamber. Oops. "Pardon me."

Our hostess turned around. "Come this way, Terrans, sldkfjfoisut."

"We're in for it now," Love said.

Little boy Jack would love this, meeting a dragon family in their humongous castle. I threw out my chest and stepped forward.

Chapter Twenty-Seven

My new dragon friend led us into a kind of sitting room, at least the size of a world-class auditorium, with stone walls, floor, and ceiling. It contained a couple of gigantic couches and similarly-sized side tables with lamps. In a substantial fireplace, a wood fire crackled and popped. The wood smoke smelled comforting. I'd been around the galaxy a few times, but I couldn't help oohing and ahhing at it all.

Her mate, an iridescent sparkly green, at least thirty feet long, with four legs, huge wings, a long tail, and a lengthy neck, lounged on a ginormous couch. He looked our way. "What are those sparkly creatures?" His voice was as deep as the ocean. "They remind me of smoke. Come closer, friends."

"These are sldkfjfoisut, honey," our hostess said.

The sldkfjfoisut floated closer to the male dragon, amping up the light show. It was as if he were enveloped in gentle fireworks. Now, I smelled sulfur.

He laughed. "It tickles a little. I like them! It's as if my smoke has come to life."

"They came through the Quihiri portal," the female said, her voice not pleased.

"That damn portal," he said.

O, courage, courage, courage, Prince! I stepped forward. "Excuse me, Excellencies. There's a civil war raging on Quihiri right now, and we came through the portal to avoid getting shot."

"Whose side are you on?" the male asked.

"On the side of freedom and liberty, of course!" I flourished dramatically with my hands.

"That's pretty vague," the female said.

"Perhaps I can be of some assistance," Addie said.

"Sldkfjfoisut like myself can breed amongst ourselves, or we can be made by Quihiri evolving into us."

"What's this?" the male said. "I've never heard of this."

"Neither have I," the female said.

"The war is between the evil Quihiri suppressing this evolutionary process, trying to prop up the status quo, and those virtuous Quihiri who want the freedom to evolve," I said, with more flourishes.

"Virtuous Quihiri?" the male dragon muttered.

Next to me, Ted said quietly, "And the evil Quihiri turned off the FTL drives and attacked a bunch of other planets."

Right. "The evil Quihiri turned off the FTL drives and attacked a bunch of other planets." Flourish, flourish.

"The Quihiri turned off the FTL drives!" the male said. Forcefully. Uh oh. I didn't want to be anywhere near an angry dragon. I took a step back.

My sldkfjfoisut friends turned darker and floated away from him.

"I told you it was them," the female said. "Those Quihiri are annoying."

The male stood up. "Maybe we should fly through this portal and wreak some vengeance on those pathetic octopus people!" Smoke puffed out through his nostrils. I got a distinct odor of sulfur.

"We don't know how to open the portal, honey," the female said. She turned to me. "Do you know how to open it?"

No. "Uh, I'm not sure, Your Highness," I said with more flourishes. Actually, if they had portal technology here, it could only help me in my quest to understand how FTL drives worked--or didn't--in the galaxy. "Do you have a portal device here? Some kind of Quihiri technology?"

"Yes!" The male stepped away from his couch. "This way." With his colossal stride, soon, he was all the way across the room.

"Slow down, please, sir!" I yelled and started running after him.

"Slow down, honey," the female said, following him, sounding a little amused.

We eventually caught up with the male by running across

the stone floor.

He walked into a stone hallway. We ran after. I guessed stone was a primo building material when you could exhale fire at any time. The hallway sloped down like a ramp. We followed.

I was just starting to run out of steam when the floor leveled off again. We were in a new hallway with several doors with bar-encrusted windows.

"Is this another dungeon, Jack?" Ted whispered. "Why are you always taking me to dungeons?"

It did appear to be another dungeon, and I didn't know how to answer him because I had already experienced more than my quota of dungeons. I ran closer to the female dragon. "Uh, madam, what are we doing here?" Not that I could stop her if she wanted to do something.

"We have some Quihiri technology," she said.

"Hello?" a tremulous voice called out from one of the cells. "Is someone there? Please?"

The dragons stopped abruptly. The male said, "Perhaps you are correct, and some Quihiri are virtuous. Perhaps not all Quihiri are evil."

"Help?" the small voice called out.

"Perhaps we were wrong to lock this one up," the female dragon said.

"Can we please meet this Quihiri?" Addie floated up near the female dragon's face.

The female dragon appeared to shrug. Then, using the ends of her wings, she plucked a key off the wall, stuck it in the lock, and unlocked the door. I stared at her wings; were those fingers on the ends?

The bulky wooden door swung open with a creak. The cell had gray stone walls, floor, and ceiling.

Inside, a three-legged, three-tentacled octopus-like Quihiri stood. When the prisoner saw us, he turned pitch-black, and his grin of relief was replaced by a frown of fear. "Uh, who or what are you all?"

The sldkfjfoisut, now looking like storm clouds, crowded into the cell, suddenly all talking at once.

The prisoner said something that sounded like, 'Ack,' and shrank back further into the cell.

"Do not kill it," the dragon said. "If you do, I've wasted a lot of time taking care of it."

"Ack!" he said. "What are you doing? I'm just here to maintain the portal. Leave me alone! Stop it! Stay away!"

"Jack!" Addie yelled from inside the cell. "Come calm the poor fellow down."

I wasn't overly excited about voluntarily entering a dragon dungeon cell, but I was a very helpful guy. I walked inside through the bobbing sldkfjfoisut, who were back to sparkly rainbow status. The cell was massive by human standards, at least fifty feet cubed.

When I reached the prisoner, he looked worried. "I don't understand what's happening. What are these creatures? What are they doing?" He looked me over. "You're a Terran? What are you doing here? You look familiar."

I stopped. Of course, I looked familiar! I cleared my throat. "*Hello, hello, hello, how low*," I sang.

"Hello?" he said.

"*With the lights out, it's less dangerous*," I sang.

"Wait. Are you a singer?" he asked.

"Of course!" I knew he would recognize me. "Intragalactic singer extraordinaire Jack Jones at your service!" I gave a flourish and bowed down in front of him.

"Uh, okay," he said. Now, he looked sick. That couldn't be right. "I feel funny."

"Poor guy," I said. "Do you want a hug?" I held my arms out and approached him.

But he stepped away. "Something's wrong." He grimaced. "What?" He hunched over and jerked his tentacles. "Ack. Argh."

Addie bobbed over to me. "I think it's his time."

"Time for what?" Ted said with horror in his voice.

Then, it was as if the Quihiri was made of rubber; he stretched first one way and then the other, his entire body distorting. His colors roiled almost too fast to register: black, gray, green, orange, black, and on and on.

The sldkfjfoisut, including Addie, rushed to him, surrounding him.

I heard Slid ask, "What should we do, Mommy?"

Addie, or someone, started singing, "*Hello, hello, hello, how low....*" It was soothing.

I reached out for Ted. I held his hand, and it felt warm and safe in mine. I joined in the singing, and after a few moments, he did as well. Soon, almost everyone was singing.

Strange fizzy noises and gargles were coming from the center of the sldkfjfoisut.

Then, suddenly, the sldkfjfoisut singing stopped. The strange noises stopped.

Ted and I stopped singing. Everything was silent.

"What happened?" he whispered.

The crowd parted to reveal a gray cloud with fireworks inside. It bobbed there inside the cell. Finally, it said, "I don't understand what just happened."

"Your true self has been revealed, Brother," Addie said.

"I think we have a new sldkfjfoisut," I said.

Chapter Twenty-Eight

After being in a hot war, traveling through a mysterious portal, meeting a dragon couple and almost getting burned by them, and helping a Quihiri transform into a sldkfjfoisut, me and my friends slept hard--or at least, I thought we did; I wasn't a hundred percent certain how the sleep of energy beings worked. Anyway, I woke up in a kitchen, on a twenty-foot by twenty-foot pet bed (presumably--what else would sleep in the kitchen?), surrounded by energy clouds and Ted. The palatial pillow was surprisingly comfortable; the sldkfjfoisut rested on it, generally showing bland colors, not sparkling or really moving at all. Ted snored gently next to me, his chest rising and falling. Was this the first time we'd slept together that he would remember?

As I sat up and stretched, it hit me, where exactly was the creature this large bed belonged to? What kind of pet would a dragon have? I scanned the ginormous kitchen, seeing a stove/oven over six feet tall, a similarly-giant refrigerator, a tremendous table surrounded by some considerable chairs, and a lot of colossal cabinets. No sign of any giant pets. Phew.

That made me think of my old buddy Max the dog. I hoped he was safe and enjoying himself with his master, no, partner, Jax. That made me think of my bosom friends, the *Shakespeare* crew, and how I'd left them all in the middle of a hot war. Yikes. The first order of business was to find out how they were doing.

Then I smelled something suspiciously like coffee. "Hello-o-o-o-o?" I called out. My greeting echoed in the vast space.

A creature walked into view; it had the torso, arms, and head of an attractive reddish-brown-skinned man and the body and legs of a handsome chestnut horse. I did smell horse. "Whoa!" He had all the makings of a centaur and appeared to be wearing an apron. This planet was crazy, crazy awesome! I was sure I was smiling broadly. Was his name Chiron? Pholos?

He wiped his hands on a giant dishcloth. "That better not be a horse reference," he said drily. "'Cuz that ain't cool, brother."

My mind was racing. Brother? I wanted to be friends, to be a brother to a centaur. Clearing my throat, I scrambled out of the voluminous pillow. "*Brother, I think it's time we talked,*" I sang as I stood on the stone floor. My head was barely even with his horse shoulder.

He snickered, which did sound a little like a whinny.

The sldkfjfoisut started stirring, by which I mean moving around and changing colors.

I skipped ahead in the song. "*Brother, oh, brother--*"

"Is it a Terran thing to sing all the time?" the centaur asked.

"No," Addie said, floating next to me. "It's a Jack thing." I recognized her voice, which was a good thing because when I glanced over at her floating and sparkling, all multi-colored, I realized for the first time, each individual sldkfjfoisut didn't have a particular look. There was no way to tell them apart unless they spoke or otherwise identified themselves.

Slid bobbed up. Ah ha. He was one sldkfjfoisut I could identify because he was smaller than the others. "What's for breakfast, Mommy?"

Another sldkfjfoisut floated up. "How do I eat?" he asked. His voice sounded familiar, but I couldn't quite place him.

Slid laughed; it sounded like bells tinkling. "It's easy."

"I can show you, Brother," Addie said. Oh, this was the new sldkfjfoisut. "The easiest thing is to absorb energy from a star. Come on, let's go outside, and I'll show you." They started drifting away.

"And you get to pick a new name if you want!" Slid said, bouncing beside his mom.

"I do like Brother," the newest sldkfjfoisut said.

The cloud of energy creatures sailed away, leaving me and the centaur standing there. He seemed a little gobsmacked. "How many of them are there?"

I wasn't sure. I shrugged. "I'm not sure." How many were there? I knew it was more than a dozen. Was it more than a hundred?

“I’m Lucius,” the centaur said.

Now it was my turn to be gobsmacked. Lucius the centaur? On the other hand, we probably couldn’t call him Black Beauty. Or Comanche. Or Llamrei. That probably wouldn’t be politically correct.

“Do you have a name?” he asked, putting the towel down on the counter.

“Yes, Lucius,” I said. “It’s a real pleasure to meet you. I’m Jack Jones, intragalactically-famous chanteuse.” And spy, but I was smart enough not to say that.

“Nice to meet you, Jackjones,” he said. “And what about you?” He pointed slightly to my left.

I turned. Ted. Oops. I’d sort of forgotten about him.

“Are you a centaur?” he whispered.

“Nice to meet you, Areyouacentaur,” Lucius said. “My mistress Nova said to give you Terrans some breakfast.” He whirled around on his four hooves and started clomping across the kitchen.

Ted stared after him. “But that’s not my name,” he said softly.

“I know, Ted.” I leaned over and gave him a quick hug.

When we caught up with Lucius, he said our breakfast choices were straw or charbroiled meat. Ted and I selected the meat; it tasted like slightly-burned chicken. There was also a hot beverage that I was choosing to call coffee; it even tasted a little like coffee.

Lucius was standing around, and Ted and I were sipping and digesting, sitting on what I was guessing were two boxes, when some of the sldkfjfoisut zoomed back into the kitchen.

“So, not to be rude, but my mistress Nova and my master Ash are eager to facilitate your exit from this planet,” Lucius said.

Slid buzzed back and forth near our chair boxes. “I feel great! That sun is buzzy.” He sparked. “And I talked to the dragon lady. She was nice!”

I felt more energetic watching his evident pleasure and turned my attention back to Lucius. “We’re happy to comply.” If only we knew how to comply. I pulled my fon out of my pocket and checked it for new messages. There were none. Why hadn’t Gina called me back? My mind galloped. Wait a minute;

had I actually called her? No. In the excitement of meeting real dragons, I'd forgotten. Shoot. It appeared that we were on our own for the time being.

"Jackjones?" Lucius asked. "What do I need to do to facilitate this complaisance?"

My mind was cantering. There was something from last night… "Did Nova say you guys had some Quihiri tech here?"

"Yes." He nodded. "It's down in the dungeon."

"Dungeon!" Brother yelped next to me, his cloud swirling black, gray, and blood-red. "I don't want to go back there."

"Did you change your name?" I asked him.

"Yes," he said. "I woke up to your beautiful song about the brother. I am Brother."

"Don't worry, Brother," I said, smiling. "Jack Jones is on the case! I'll protect you from the dungeon. But we do need to get a look at that tech."

Down in the dungeon, it smelled musty. Brother's colors remained black and blood-red swirls. He floated next to me, just above the floor.

I started singing softly, "*You've got a friend in me….*"

He moved up from the floor.

Lucius led us past Brother's cell and on down the hall. As we kept moving, I started to detect the scent of ozone.

Eventually, we reached the end of the hall, and Lucius unlocked the final cell, pointing inside. "It's in there."

"I'm not going in there!" Brother squeaked. I couldn't blame him; he'd been held in this dungeon for a long time.

"You don't have to go in there," I said. "Ted and I will bring it out. Right, Ted?" I looked around for Ted and spotted him in the back of the group.

As he approached me, he said, "I'm not happy about going into a cell either, Jack."

Sadly, I'd been in more than my share of cells in my short life. And it always seemed to work out. "Don't worry, Ted. It'll work out."

He was still grumbling when he entered the cell ahead of me. Inside, the scent of ozone was much stronger. I spied a uniform white sphere. It looked like a smaller version of the

Quihiri FTL drives.

Ted stared down at it, frowning.

I leaned over and picked it up; it was warm to the touch and seemed to thrum slightly. I carried it into the hall, setting it down gently on the floor. "Is this thing on, Brother?"

"What is it?" Lucius shuffled on his four hooves.

"We should take it outside," Brother said.

Soon, we were all outside in the bright sunshine. I wasn't an energy being, but the rays warmed my skin nicely. The sldkfjfoisut were taking full advantage, cavorting in the sunlight.

A breeze wafted the pleasing scent of freshly-mown hay our way. I sneezed as I placed the object on the dirt. We were in what appeared to be the castle's formal gardens, filled with elaborate knot gardens. The different kinds of hedges flowed together sinuously, interlacing chartreuse and jade ropes. I thought I smelled herbs. Lavender? Rosemary?

Brother sidled up next to me. "Yes," he said quietly. "It's on. It's the end-point of the FTL portal. I managed to turn it on before the dragons captured me."

"Can we use it to get back to Quihiri?" I asked.

At the same time, Ted, also standing near me, asked, "Why didn't we land in the dungeon next to the device?"

Lucius was a couple of yards away, seemingly entranced with the sldkfjfoisut dancing in the sunlight. I couldn't blame him; they resembled joyful fireworks displays.

"The beginning point of the FTL portal sets the endpoint's location," Brother said. "And yes, we can use it to go back. I just have to reset...Oh, shoot."

"What?" Ted and I said at the same time.

"I don't have tentacles anymore," Brother said. "How do I flip the switch?"

That was an excellent question, but I knew Addie could manipulate physical objects so that it could be done. "Addie?" I called out. Was she here?

Slid flew over to me. "She's still talking to that dragon lady."

I knelt over the device. Did it open the same way as the regular FTL drives? I located and pressed the slight indentations in the sphere. It snicked open. Inside it looked like every other FTL drive I'd seen: fancy metal components and tiny computer chips. I leaned over, peering at each component. Which was the switch? I didn't see it. "I don't see it."

"You see that small hole there right at the top?" Brother said, buzzing the back of my neck. "It's in there." I was reminded of the Quihiri's octopus-like agility and how they could squeeze into any space.

I stuck my forefinger in the hole with a minor amount of trepidation. It just barely fit. I stretched around for anything that felt like a switch. I found something and moved it.

Suddenly, the device's humming increased markedly in volume, and the smell of ozone increased. A tear in the sky appeared about two feet off the ground, resolving into a circular opening, obscuring some shrubbery. I thought I could see the Quihiri factory on the other side.

Hallelujah! Something I hadn't known I was clenching, unclenched. We weren't trapped here, after all.

Instantly, my pocket started ringing.

The sldkfjfoisut crowded around me in front of the portal. They talked loudly amongst themselves.

I took my fon out of my pocket and answered it.

A sldkfjfoisut went through the portal, followed by another.

The fon ringing was a message from Gina. "Jack? The fighting's over! The Quihiri had to lay down their weapons. Where are you?" She paused. "Are you okay? You're not dead, are you? Call me back as soon as you get this message."

The sldkfjfoisut streamed through the portal until only Ted, Brother, Slid, and I were standing there.

Ted took a step closer to the portal and then another. He clearly wanted to go through it.

"Gina says the fighting's over, and we won," I said. "You can go if you want."

He took another step. "Is it safe?"

"Yes. I believe her," I said. "Go ahead. And if I don't join you immediately, let her know what's going on."

"Why wouldn't you come?" he asked, edging even closer to the portal.

"Go ahead, Brother," I said to Brother. He didn't waste any time and zoomed through instantly.

"Where's my mom?" Slid whined.

Lucius' apron rang, and he took a formidable fon out of the prodigious pocket and answered it.

"Don't worry, Slid," I said. "We won't leave without her. Let's go find her." I faced Ted again. "Go ahead."

He didn't look happy about it, but Ted stepped through, leaving me and Slid there with Lucius.

Lucius walked closer to us. "My mistress says you have to come help with the mating." If they wanted me to mate with dragons, I wasn't sure even I was up for that. "But the other energy beings will arrive here soon to go through the portal." He listened a little more. "Walk this way." He started walking away. With my two little legs, I could never walk that way.

But, I hummed a little ditty about walking that way, and Slid rested on my shoulder, buzzing, as we walked away from the open portal.

Chapter Twenty-Nine

The centaur led us back into the castle and down one of its cavernous halls. I had to hustle to keep up with him. On the way, a stream of sldkfjfoisut passed us, going the other way toward the portal.

Slid called out, “Mom? Mom?” but none of them answered him.

“It’s okay, buddy,” I said. “We’ll find her.”

Ultimately, Lucius stopped at the doorway of yet another giant room and waved his hand inside. The dragon couple stood inside, seemingly waiting. Amidst the gray stone walls, floor and ceiling, a sizable jewel-toned pillow lay in the middle of the room--the dragons’ bed? I didn’t see any dressers or closets, which I guessed made sense; it wasn’t like they wore clothing. This must be their bedroom.

The colossal pillow made me wonder just how many people would fit on that pillow and what they might do on it.

Just inside the doorway, Addie floated, a rainbow of colors, including black and gray.

“Addie, the portal’s open,” I said. “We can go back as soon as we finish here. What’s going on here?”

“Mommy!” Slid cried and bounced from my shoulders.

“Hi, sweetie,” she said as Slid joined her. “There you guys are. I was explaining to Nova that I wasn’t *sure* you could make her pregnant, Jack.”

The beautiful iridescent blue dragon expelled a puff of smoke as she lumbered up to us.

I swallowed, trying not to be intimidated. “Uh, hi, Your Highness Nova. I don’t know what I can do, ma’am. Of course, I want to help you have baby, uh, dragons? Or eggs? I want to help you have little babies. But…" I did not want to stick any part of myself inside a dragon. How the heck did their procreation work, anyway? If, I mean, when I got back to Earth, I should really take an exobiology class.

Nova made a sound very similar to a growl and exhaled more smoke.

"Jack!" Addie said. "Nova and her species give live birth, obviously. Like most intelligent species." It was almost as if she didn't want me to talk more, but that couldn't be right.

"Can I speak to you for a minute, Addie?" I asked. "In the hall?"

She floated into the hall, joining me. "What?" She did sound irritated.

"What the heck am I supposed to do here?" I asked, glancing at Slid. "I'm not sticking my you-know-what into a dragon." I was an excellent paramour and inamorato--don't get me wrong--but my you-know-what and fire seemed like a bad combination.

"What's your you-know-what?" Slid asked. "And why would you stick it somewhere?"

"Never mind that, little one," Addie said. "Didn't you say you wanted to be a good singer like Jack? Why don't you practice your singing?"

I started hearing a faint humming.

"I'm sorry, Jack," she said. "Things got out of hand. I didn't stop to consider what might happen when I was bragging about how you helped me procreate. And I didn't realize how, er, eager Nova and her mate are."

"Well, what do you suggest?" I asked.

"I tried to backtrack and tell her it was your singing that calmed me and made me fertile," she said. "It's worth a try. Otherwise, I'm not sure she'll let you leave."

Sometimes my awesomeness was a curse. "Fine." I waltzed back into the bedroom.

Addie and Slid stayed where they were in the hall, lucky ducks.

Both dragons turned to examine me.

"I would be honored to sing to you," I said. "This is a special song, very famous on my planet, that will facilitate your successful mating."

The male dragon stepped behind the female dragon. As I closed my eyes, I cleared my throat. Then, I began singing, "*Puff, the magic dragon lived by the sea....*"

I heard what sounded like a snort or a quickly contained laugh coming from the hallway. Let her snort. It wasn't like I knew a lot of dragon songs. I ignored her, focusing on the song. "*... together they would travel on a boat with billowed sail. Jackie kept a lookout perched on Puff's gigantic tail....*" Something about that verse was interesting. I focused on the song, not the strange noises coming from the dragon duo in front of me. Or the smells. Was it getting smoky in here? Okay, I did peek a couple of times, but I couldn't really see anything with all the smoke. I wasn't sure if I was disappointed or relieved.

After a considerable amount of time, I felt a smoky breath of air on my face. "Enough, human," Ash, the male dragon, said in a gravelly voice. I opened my eyes to see his face right in my face. I struggled not to jerk backward. His mate, Nova, lounged on the giant cushion, as one does after successful love-making.

I debated what to say: 'How'd it go?' or 'I hope everything went well?' But decided silence was the better part of valor and more knightly.

Addie and Slid flew up next to me. "It's been an honor, sir," Addie said. Honor for what? To wait around in the hall while they got it on?

I bowed with a deep flourish. "Yes, sir. Now, we really must be getting back to Quihiri to finish quelling those evil octopi." As far as I knew, the evil octopi were quelled, but Ash didn't know that.

"Yes," Addie said. "Thank you for your hospitality."

"Thanks!" Slid squeaked as he and Addie started floating back toward the door.

"Don't hurry back," Nova said from the bed. "No offense."

I was a little offended but decided not to call her on it. (Yes, I was afraid of her.) "Thanks." I scampered after my friends before the dragons could change their minds.

Back at the portal location, a window still floated in the sky, and the device still buzzed and smelled of ozone. "Huzzah!"

"Go, go!" I yelled to Addie and Slid.

They floated through.

I stopped for a moment, surveying the castle and gardens, thinking about the dragons and centaurs. What else lived on this planet? Mermaids? Elves? Unicorns? It was little boy Jack's dream world. Maybe, someday I'd come back. I hoped so.

But, today, I needed to leave. "*What feats he did that day*." With a final sneeze, I turned around and jumped.

Back on Quihiri, in their FTL drive factory, there were a lot of sparkly sldkfjfoisut floating around. I did not see my human buddy, Ted. I did see a lot of typical orange Quihiri lighting. I held out my hand in front of me; it looked like I had some kind of not-handsome orange skin condition. I sighed. I missed the yellow sun already.

I tried to get Brother's attention. "Hey, Brother, how do we close the portal?" I said to the sldkfjfoisut next to me.

"I'm not your brother," a very deep bass voice came out of him.

Shoot. I needed the portal expert. "O Brother, where art thou?" Brother did not answer.

Who else did I know who was an FTL drive expert? That guy, Love, was one, right? "Love? Where's Love?" While that sounded like the beginning of a superb song, Love didn't answer.

"Does anyone here understand the FTL portals?" I called out. No one answered.

How did you contact energy beings who didn't carry fons?

I pulled out my fon and called Gina. She answered immediately. "Jack? You're not dead! Thank God!" It felt great to hear her voice. My heart calmed, and I felt a warm glow spread throughout my body; she cared.

"Nope," I said, grinning. "Reports of my death have been greatly exaggerated."

"What reports?" she asked. "Who's been… Never mind. We beat the Quihiri! TCC forced them to surrender their weapons. They haven't turned the FTL drives back on yet, but they will; we'll force them if necessary. Where are you?"

"I'm in the FTL drive factory," I said. Something tickled the edge of my brain.

"Well, get up here," she said. "To the ambassador's

office where we had our first Quihiri meeting. They're formally surrendering. You should be here!" She sounded giddy.

"All right," I said. "I'll be right there." All my friends should be there; it would be great to see them again. I ended the call.

All my friends but two. "Addie? Slid? Are you here?"

A sparkly rainbow cloud floated toward me. "Yes, we're here," Addie said.

"Everyone's so buzzy and happy!" Slid said, separating a little from his mom.

"I'm going to the ambassador's office," I said. "I guess there's some ceremony? You guys should come."

"Yay!" Slid said.

The three of us made our way through the Quihiri complex to the ambassador's office. What a difference a day makes; we didn't have to hide or dodge energy pulses or anything.

At the office, we had to stand in the doorway. The large room was jam-packed with three-legged, three-armed, three-eyed, three-nostrilled Quihiri, primarily a stormy gray color. Around the edges of the room, many rainbow-hued, sparkling sldkfjfoisut floated. In the middle, several officers of the Terran spaceships, the *Agincourt* and the *Shakespeare,* stood in formal uniforms. I saw Captain Gina Gomez and First Officer Carter Nillion and tried to catch their eyes, to no avail. They were paying attention to the official business, go figure.

Captain Wright stepped up to the front, clearing his throat.

I glanced around the room, taking in the groupings of three desks and chairs; this was the first room I'd been in on Quihiri. I was coming full circle. Who knew so many exciting things would happen in such a short time?

Some majestic classical Terran music with lots of strings and other orchestral instruments started playing over the sound system.

"On behalf of Terra and the United Worlds of the Galaxy, we accept the unconditional surrender of Quihiri." His voice like titanium, Captain Wright looked grim in his formal black uniform.

The Quihiri leader's color darkened, and he slumped. "I will never reveal the secret of the FTL drives," he said in a low voice. "Never." That was bad news. Some starship crews were still stranded. They might be starving or running out of air.

Truth be told, he looked so miserable I felt a little sorry for him. I scanned the crowd. All the Quhiri looked black or dark gray. Several of them looked kind of lumpy…

"Who represents the Quihiri sldkfjfoisut partnership?" Wright asked.

I beheld Addie floating next to me. "Shouldn't that be you?" I whispered.

"No," she whispered. "I've passed the torch. Look."

I turned my attention back to the ceremony.

"I stand for the united sentients of Quihiri and sldkfjfoisut," a female sldkfjfoisut said, sparkling gold and silver. I recognized that voice; it was Quinta, the former wife of the disgraced ambassador. I knew her! We'd even spent the night together.

"Woo-hoo!" I called out. "You go, girl!"

Several people turned around, giving me dirty looks. Gina's face broke out into a smile when she finally noticed me, which quickly disappeared; she gave me a business-like nod before focusing back on the ceremony.

"We welcome the united sentients of Quihiri and sldkfjfoisut into the United Worlds of the Galaxy," Wright said.

"Thank you," Quinta said. "We're honored to join you." Her sparkles got even sparklier. "On behalf of all the sentients of this world, we hold some truths to be self-evident," her voice boomed. "All sentients are created equal. They are endowed with certain unalienable rights…."

My attention wavered to some of the defeated Quihiri. Their dark lumpiness was transforming into a more multi-colored rubberiness. They moaned and groaned and made fizzy noises.

In the front, the Quihiri leader also got stretchy, his body distorting up and down. He quickly turned black, gray, green, blood-red, and black in succession. "Aagh! Help!"

Quinta stopped talking as everyone stared at the Quihiri leader.

We all knew what was happening, except maybe the leader himself and some of his oppressed followers. Most of us had seen the sldkfjfoisut transition several times now.

Gina made her way through the crowd to me. "Nice to see you made it through okay, Jack," she said quietly.

"You, too," I whispered back. "What's after this?"

"A party." She grinned.

"I meant after that?" I asked. "Back to Earth?"

Her grin faded. "No." She shook her head. "We have some unfinished business with the *Whydah* crew."

Oh. I knew what kind of business: justice.

With the speeches halted, the background music came to the fore. I enjoyed it, the rising and falling crescendos, the rhythms. Something about it, the beauty, the creativity, seemed to jump-start my mind. My conscious mind flowed along with the music and recalled other music.

...together they would travel on a boat with billowed sail. Jackie kept a lookout... All of a sudden, I had a realization. The FTL drives, the FTL portals, and fon FTL communication were all the same tech.

"I know how to fix the FTL drives!" I yelled.

Chapter Thirty

In the Quihiri leader's office, the formal surrender ceremony had stalled to a standstill while many Quihiri transitioned into sldkfjfoisut. Amidst all the commotion, my revelation that I could fix the FTL drives seemed lost among the fizzes, sparkles, and groans of fear.

I glanced at my sldkfjfoisut lover, Addie, floating next to me. "Is it just me, or are the Quihiri transitioning more frequently these days?"

"No, it's not just you," she said. "We seemed to have reached a tipping point. Most, if not all, Quihiri are transitioning."

"What's a tipping point?" Slid asked.

I was impatient to test my theory of FTL drive repair. "I'm going back to the FTL drive control center in the factory."

"Good idea, Jack," Gina said, standing near me. "Go."

Addie was turning blue, which I thought meant she was feeling thoughtful. "All these new sldkfjfoisut are going to need help. I wonder if I should hold an orientation session? Maybe in the auditorium?"

"I'll help!" Slid bounced. "I'll help!"

"Good idea," I said. "I'll catch up with you later." I started walking back to the factory and pulled out my fon again. If I couldn't call Brother or Love, I could at least call a human engineer who knew almost as much as me about the drives.

"Jack?" Olivia said when she picked up. "You're not dead?"

I paused, waiting for her exclamations of relief and happiness.

"You still there?" she asked.

"Uh, yes, still here," I said. "Still not dead. I'm on my way to the FTL drive factory. I think I know how to turn all the drives back on. Can you please meet me there to help out?"

"I've seen the tiny hole the Quihiri use to get into the factory," she said. "How does a human get in?"

"Go through the, ah, detention center," I said. Dungeon sounded bad; she might not help me if she had to go through the dungeon.

She didn't answer right away.

"You still there?" I asked.

"Yes," she said. "Okay, I'll try to meet you in the factory."

"Thanks. Bring your engineering tools," I said. We ended the call.

Back in the FTL drive factory, the sldkfjfoisut had cleared out. The space was as colossal as ever. You could fit a spaceship in here. Huh. Maybe they had. The portal to the dragon world was not open.

Over a public address system, I heard Addie say, "All newborn sldkfjfoisut, please report to the auditorium for an optional orientation session." Well, that was one way to reach folks without fons.

I made my way to the control console and examined it. Part of it was clearly a large computer and attendant screen. I knew from (bad) experience that it was password-protected, and I did not know the password.

Below that, however, was a large piece of metal with markings I couldn't read, various openings, and many unlit LED lights. Most things seemed to be powered off. "Hmm." This might be more difficult than I thought.

I pulled out my fon and started reviewing my recordings of the tech we'd found on the cat planet. That *had* to be an early version of the FTL drive.

"You made me go through the dungeon!" Olivia said, making me jump. When I turned to her, she was as lovely as ever, with her dark glossy hair and almond eyes. And a cross expression. Oddly, I was beginning to enjoy that, as well.

"Hi, Olivia. It's nice to see you. I'm glad you survived the war okay." I smiled sexily. "Thanks for coming."

She placed her toolbox on an open spot of the console. "Don't look at me like that."

"Like what?" I quirked one eyebrow up sexily.

"Whatever." She frowned and opened the toolbox. "What's the plan?"

"Can you disconnect the top of this console?" I pointed. "We need to get inside." I resisted the urge to say something flirtatious; there was a fine line between desirable and creepy.

She shrugged. "Should be able to." After studying the seam where the top joined the rest for a few moments, she reached into her toolbox and extracted a tool. She crouched on the floor and started doing something to the seam. Immediately, it widened.

She pried the top panel up as she stood. "Well, are you going to help or not?"

"Of course." I stepped around to the back of the console, and the two of us lifted the large panel off, carried it up and over, and carefully set it on the floor.

Inside, there were two separate areas. Unfortunately, several more mysterious symbols and openings were also between the unlit LEDs. "We just have to figure out which of these control the FTL drives."

"Oh?" Olivia raised her eyebrows. "Is that all?" But she said it in a way that indicated that was a lot. "What's your suggestion?"

My mind raced. "Do you have one of those multimeters?"

She nodded and pulled one out of her toolbox. "What's the plan?"

"Have you ever noticed how the intragalactic fon system is faster than light, but it's not instantaneous," I said reasonably. "Seems odd. How does that work?"

"It's Lusioturn tech," she said. What the heck was Lusioturn?

"I think," I said, "there's a network of small FTL portals that convey the electromagnetic signals, so, part of the time, they travel through regular space and part of the time through FTL space." I was proud of myself for figuring it out.

"A famous Lusioturn scientist came up with the fon tech," she said. "She yelled 'Eureka' and waggled all her eyestalks, and they have an annual celebration on Lusioturn on the anniversary." I'd never heard any of that. But, then, I was less than two years old, so I hadn't heard much.

Could the Lusioturn story be fiction? Yes. "I hypothesize it's Quihiri tech. The point is: *it's still working*," I said. "So, if it is Quihiri tech, all we have to do is figure out which part of this console controls it and then set the turned-off FTL drive controls to the same settings."

"That's not the accepted story," she said slowly. "It's too simplistic."

"So, you're saying I'm simplistic?" But I smiled to show I was joking. "I get that it's simplistic. I get that you're an engineer, and I'm not. Maybe the Quihiri don't control the FTL communication, but maybe they do. Maybe my idea won't work. But what do we have to lose? The ships' FTL drives throughout the galaxy are still off; the Quihiri refused to turn them back on."

She smiled back at me. "Okay, I'm game. Let's give it a try. What do you want to do first?"

"I'll try calling Earth with my fon, and you can see if any energy reading changes on the console. And then, we can try a similar process for one of the FTL drives here in the factory and try to open a portal. We probably need to remove more panels and covers on the console to get a clear look at everything."

She shrugged, and we got to work.

After a couple of hours, we'd identified the functioning communications portion of the controls and the nonfunctioning FTL drive portion. But we couldn't turn on the FTL drives because the panel openings were too tiny.

Olivia and I sat on the floor, staring at the troublesome tech. "I can't believe we're so close to fixing it," she said, "but we're stymied by a too-small opening."

Our fingers didn't fit. We couldn't even get any tools in there. "So near and yet so far." I nodded. "Stymied by octopi. They can reach into anything. If only they'd agree to help us."

"Honestly, I'm not sure there are any Quihiri left," she said.

"Maybe if I could reach Love," I said. "He's the sldkfjfoisut who used to be a Quihiri FTL tech."

"So, call him," she said.

"I can't call him. He doesn't have a fon," I said. "But we could try something else...."

Soon, over the public address system, we heard a voice saying, "Love, please report to the FTL drive factory."

Several minutes later, a sldkfjfoisut floated through the tiny hole in the wall into the factory. "Jack!" Love said. "It's so nice to see you again! It's the start of a new era! So exciting!"

"I'm glad you're enjoying yourself, Love," I said. "This is Olivia."

She waved.

He sparkled and bobbed back.

"We're trying to turn the FTL drives back on." I pointed at the mess we'd made of the control console.

"Oh, why didn't you just ask me?" he said. "I would have helped."

I wanted to say: 'I couldn't reach you!' But I didn't. "Can you just fix it now?"

"Sure." He floated up to the console, enveloping it in his body.

Olivia and I waited. And waited.

"Huh." Eventually, he moved away from the equipment. "I can't seem to flip the little switch in this new form."

"Uh oh," Olivia said. "Does that mean none of you sldkfjfoisut can turn the drives back on?"

"I hate to say it," he said. "But, yes." He turned a sooty-black color.

"Are there any Quhiri left?" I asked.

"Not on this planet." He slowly shook left and right. "I don't think so. "

"What if we took the rest of the console apart?" Olivia asked.

"It's extremely delicate tech. If you did that, the FTL drives might never be turned back on," Love said, drooping.

We were screwed.

We all sat, or floated, as the case may be, in misery for a few moments.

"Go ahead back to what you were doing, Love," I said. "Thanks for your help."

He floated off, somehow conveying trudging.

That reminded me of Addie. She'd been an energy being much longer than these others. If any sldkfjfoisut could manipulate physical objects, it was Addie.

I jumped up. "Call Addie to come here over the P.A.!"

Olivia worked her tech magic, and soon we heard. "Addie, please report to the FTL factory."

Several minutes later, a sldkfjfoisut floated through the tiny hole in the wall into the factory. "Jack, what is it?" Addie said. "I'm busy." Her rainbow hues swirled this way and that.

"You can manipulate physical objects, right?" I asked her.

"Yes," she said.

"Can you flip that switch in there so it's like these others?" I pointed at the console.

"What switch where?" She floated right up to the console. "All I see is a tiny hole."

"Yeah," Olivia said. "That's it."

Addie enveloped the console. After several moments she said, "I'm having a little trouble."

My temporarily-lifted spirits sank. "Well, thanks for trying."

Addie floated a little ways away from the tech. "But you know who's truly good at physical manipulations? Sldkfjfoisut who are born, not transformed. You want to try, little one?"

"Sure!" Slid said. I hadn't even noticed him. He must have followed Addie into the factory.

He floated right up to the minuscule opening. "In here?" A tiny tendril of him flowed into the opening. "Like this?"

And suddenly, the overhead lights flickered as a loud hum emerged from what was left of the console.

Slid moved away from the tech. "That was fun."

"Thanks, buddy! That was great." I was reeling. He might be the only sentient who *could* fix it. If I hadn't helped Addie procreate…

Olivia's fon rang, and she answered; she listened for a few moments. "That's great, sir! Wonderful! Thank you, sir!" She ended the call. "Commander Bello says they're getting reports from all over the galaxy: the FTL drives are back on! All of them!"

We all jumped up. "Hurray!" We all yelled and jumped up and down.

I stared at Slid. He was also the only one who could turn the drives off again. "Maybe we should keep what happened here today between the four of us?"

"Nothing happened." Addie understood immediately. "Slid was just playing as usual."

"But..." Olivia said.

I poked her hard in the stomach with my elbow.

She said, "Ow," and rubbed her belly.

"Let's go back to the party!" Slid said. "You guys should come, too! It's buzzy. We're all going outside into the sun."

"That sounds wonderful, Slid," I said. "I want to party with you, for sure!"

"Yay!" he said, sparkling silver and gold. "Let's go."

Outside, it smelled of fish and seaweed. All the sldkfjfoisut were floating and sparkling in the orange sunlight. Their effervescent joy was contagious. "Woo hoo!" I yelled. "*Be not afraid of greatness*!"

Addie said, "Come on, Slid. Let's give our new family a proper welcome." They flew off.

"*More than kin*!" I said.

Olivia turned to me. "What?"

"*More than kin*," I said. "Never mind. Sunlight isn't exactly filling. Let's find some humans. Maybe they have comestibles and libations."

"What?" she asked.

"Goodies." I grabbed her arm. "Food and drink. Come on."

We found the humans immediately; their severe black uniforms stood out in the colorful crowd. And they had loads of luscious libations...

"*We are such stuff as dreams are made on*!"

Chapter Thirty-One

I woke in my very own quarters in my very own bunk with my very own Olivia. *Hallelujah*! I stared into her beautiful face; she looked so peaceful lying there. And satisfied, she looked so satisfied lying there. I *knew* we would hit it off. My happiness balanced out my headache and nausea.

Her eyes opened. "Are you watching me sleep?" The corners of her luscious lips turned down. Bad sign. "'Cuz that would be creepy."

I could salvage this. "Of course not. Good morning, beautiful." I smiled sexily. "Thanks for last night."

She sat up and stretched. I tried not to stare. "No problem. I couldn't just leave you there lying in your drool. We were supposed to report back to the ship."

Realization slowly dawned. She was fully clothed. I glanced under the covers. I was fully clothed. The likelihood that we'd hooked up was quickly diminishing. "So, ah, why did you sleep here?"

She frowned and rubbed her forehead. "Truth be told, I think I drank a little too much. By the time I dragged your ass back here, I was too tired to find my cabin. You're heavy." She glanced around the cabin as she stood up. "Do you have any aspirin?"

"Of course, fair lady!" I got out of bed and quickly rummaged through my desk drawer. I pulled out the bottle of painkillers and handed it to her.

She popped a couple.

"*Shall I compare thee to a summer's day*?" I said.

She smirked. "Later, Jones." Before I knew it, the door was open, and she was striding down the hall.

"*Thou are more lovely and more temperate*..." I called after her. She didn't look back.

I stepped back inside, grumbling. "Shame on you, Jack. That quote was too obvious." I popped several pain pills and went into my tiny bathroom to begin my morning ablutions, including recording my memories. (Yay!)

I was all lathered up, about to rinse, when I heard Gina's voice. "Jack? Where are you? We're approaching the station and waiting for you in the ready room." Approaching the station? Why? And how long had we been en route?

I reached a soapy arm out of the shower and accessed the comms mounted on the wall. "I need five more minutes. Start without me if you need to."

Seven minutes later, I strode into the captain's ready room, shaved, brushed, washed and pressed in a fresh uniform. I'd even stopped by the mess hall and grabbed a protein bar and a coffee. I felt better than I had in I-didn't-know-how-long. Hours? Days? A lot had been happening lately.

"There you are, Jack," Gina said. "Gee, thanks for joining us." She looked freshly fluffed and folded, as well, as she smirked at me.

I nodded to her as I eyeballed her pretty pink meeting room. I caught a faint scent of Terran roses. In contrast, the TCC personnel sitting around the conference table were a bit of a motley assortment: First Officer and co-husband Carter, Security Chief Lu, former-lover security officer Ted, lover warrior princess Eva, and other-me Jax, with his best canine friend, Max.

I found a seat and sat down next to Max, gulping coffee as quickly as its heat would allow. Now, I smelled dog. My stomach did not find that particular scent appealing. Was I the only one negatively impacted by last night's raucous partying?

"So, as Jax was saying, we have intelligence that states the former *Whydah* crew is at the station. Continue, Jax." She gestured at him.

He leaned forward a little over the table. "I cannot overstate how dangerous these people are."

Ugh. We were after the *Whydah*. So much for resting on our laurels after saving the galaxy.

"We are aware." Lu's frown took over his whole face.

"They took over the *Shakespeare*. A TCC ship has never been humiliated like that before."

"Well, Jack offended them when he stole their ship," Max said. I hadn't known dogs could smirk. What was it, smirk-day today?

"Yes," Jax said. "*They* have never been humiliated like that before. Jack made them look like fools. They want vengeance. Their reputation is everything to them."

I did feel a little bit bad since my actions harmed TCC. I was the one who'd stolen their ship. But the space pirates deserved it; I had to save myself, didn't I? It was my duty.

But, consequently, I was the one who'd caused the *Shakespeare* to be overrun. I gulped more coffee.

"They're just a bunch of petty thieves," Carter said. "Surely, the *Shakespeare* can make short work of them."

I realized no *Agincourt* officers were here. "Where's the *Agincourt?"*

"They had other duties," Gina said.

"As I said," Carter said, "Surely, we've got this."

"We better got this," Lu said. "We can't let people think the TCC are pushovers."

"What do you think we should do, Jax? Max?" Eva asked, considering them carefully. "You know them."

"We need a stealth approach," Jax said.

"Yes, let's sniff them out and assess the situation," Max said.

"It would be best to take them out quickly and quietly, one by one," Jax said.

"I agree with me," I pointed at Jax.

"I can take a shuttle in with a team," Carter said. "Keep the *Shakespeare* away from the station, so it's not detected."

"I agree," Gina said. "Stealth. Lu, you're in charge. Pick your team."

"Yes, Captain," Lu said. "Everyone here, except the captain. And some additional security forces." He stood.

The others stood. I took in my fellow Shakespearians standing around the table, faces eager and determined, uniforms (except Max) pressed. Knights of the conference table! It was awesome to be on a quest with my friends again. And we would succeed--with one minor adjustment.

Still seated, I raised my finger. "*The apparel oft proclaims the man*."

Now they all looked at me with blank faces.

"*The soul of this man is his clothes*," I said.

Jax said, "Oh, yeah, we need to change our clothes."

Clad head-to-toe in black leather, I strode confidently onto the station. I looked awesome! In particular, I was enjoying my black leather wide-brimmed fedora. *O, courage, courage, courage, Princes!* The central marketplace was booming at local mid-day. It was chock-a-block full of stalls and booths selling everything you could imagine. I smelled unwashed humans, machines, and grilling mystery meat. It wasn't unpleasant.

We'd left several security officers on the shuttle. They were armed to the teeth, ready to burst into action if we needed them on the station or prepared to deal with prisoners when we brought them back.

My cohorts on the station, Jax, Max, Lu, Carter, and Ted, also sported an assortment of bad-ass outfits and lots of weapons, including guns, lasers, tasers, ray guns--basically, you name it.

Lu was busy checking said weapons. Ted noticed and began doing the same. The pair took guns and various lethal whatnot off their belts or holsters and checked the ammo. Bad-ass Ted was adorable.

"Remember, this is a stealth mission," Lu said. "The last thing we want is a firefight with these guys. It would reflect badly on the TCC." Among other things, thespians don't usually get into firefights with space pirates.

Ted nodded energetically. He was paying an inordinate amount of attention to Lu. Could it be he had a crush on his boss? I knew Ted liked men. He and I had had a romantic relationship, although he didn't remember it.

"Where to, Jax?" Carter said, also looking pretty awesome, clad head-to-toe in dark-maroon leather.

"Let's check all the bars, especially Gagopa, that karaoke bar, and that dive bar near that dingy motel," I said.

"I asked Jaxxxxx," Carter said, emphasizing the last letter.

"He's the one who's spent a lot of time here. And who knows the *Whydah* crew."

"What he said." Jax shrugged. "Jack's right. We should check all the spots the *Whydah* crew is known to frequent. Hit the bars." Of course, I was right.

"I need to do something else," Max said. "Jax, come with me."

"Is that okay?" Jax asked Lu.

"Yeah, as long as you keep your comms and your eyes open," he said. "Let us know if you see anyone from the *Whydah* crew. Let's all meet at Gagopa in two hours to regroup."

Jax and Max took a step away from us.

"And remember," I said, "we're keeping a low profile."

Someone snorted, I didn't see who, as if keeping a low profile wasn't my thing.

Jax and Max walked away from us, looking grim. I couldn't help remembering what'd happened the last time we were here: I'd euthanized Max's parents. That remained the hardest thing I'd ever done. At least the puppies, his brothers and sisters, were safe on Earth.

The *Whydah* itself was also safe on Earth since I'd left it there. "Maybe someone should check with the docking master to see if they can figure out anything about the ship the *Whydah* crew's using," I said.

"Yeah." Lu nodded. "They would have had to steal a ship to get away from here. Did the stolen ship reappear? How does that work?"

"Credits," I said. "I have a feeling anything can be bought or sold here for credits. Including info."

Lu finished messing with his guns, holstering them all. "I'm on it."

Ted said, "Should I come along, Commander Lu?"

Lu said, "No," turned and strode away. Lots of striding today.

That left me, Ted, and Carter. Fun. Ménage à trois, anyone? I grinned.

"What's that look, Jack?" Carter asked.

"Yeah, you look ...odd," Ted said. "You sick or something?"

"Hungover," Carter said. "He's hungover."

"You're right," I said. "He's hung." I smirked. If you can't beat 'em, join 'em.

Heh, heh. Beat 'em. Was it possible I was still a little drunk? That had been a great party last night. It's not every night you celebrate the end of a galactic war.

I should find a doctor and get a sober-up pill. "Why don't we split up?" I said. "We'll cover more ground that way."

"Fine with me," Carter said. "In fact, I prefer it." He instantly strolled away.

"Hey, wait up." Ted ran after him. "We should coordinate--"

So much for a fun quest with my friends. Jeez.

I pulled out the burner fon I'd bought the last time I'd been here. "If I was a doctor, where would I be?"

I successfully tracked down a medical professional and acquired a sober-up pill. He even gave me a booster shot of vitamins and energy supplements for only a few credits more.

I felt great! I sat, practically bouncing up and down, on a paper-covered table in his little treatment room. "Thanks, Doc." He looked similar (from what I could see) to a human, with two arms, legs, eyes, ears, and a nose, except for his purple skin. And the two antennas, or tentacles, or whatever they were, on the top of his head.

"What can I say?" He smirked. "Generous credits are generous for your health." He waved his fon in the air.

That gave me an idea. I whipped out my fon and scrolled to some pictures of the *Whydah* crew. I held it up. "I've lost track of my buddies." I scrolled through the pix. "I was supposed to meet up with them, but I was late."

"I might know the current whereabouts of some of those Terrans…." He paused, smirking some more.

Oh, right. Credits. I transferred another chunk of change to him.

"One of them's next door in my clinic." He stepped to the door of the treatment room. "I'll take you to him. I think his friends are visiting him."

"Uh… Wait." I jumped up from the table. Stealth, we were supposed to be in stealth mode. "Maybe just tell me where he is."

But the Doc was already in the hall and then opening a

door. “He’s right here. You’ve got a visitor, young man.”

Behind the Doc, I saw a man lying in bed with what looked like burns and bandages on his face and hands. It was Eli--a *Whydah* crewmember.

“Jax!” He croaked and started scrabbling at the small dresser next to him. “Where’s my gun? I’m gonna kill you!”

Chapter Thirty-Two

On the one hand, I was overjoyed to have completed my mission and discovered one of the evil *Whydah* space pirates. On the other hand, having him discover *me* was not stealthy. Having him shoot me would be super not-stealth. And if his fellow villains were around here somewhere, I definitely needed backup.

In the doctor's suite, I backed slowly away. "Sorry, who is this Jax?" I asked in a falsetto voice as I pulled my hat down over my face. "I don't know any Jax? Mistake. You've made a mistake."

The doc gave me a curious look but closed the door on Eli. Lucky for me, Eli was too injured to come after me. The doc and I stood in the small hall outside the door. "I thought you were looking for this guy?" he asked.

I knew what it would take to get Doc's cooperation. "How much to talk him down and keep him here?" I asked.

He named a figure, and I transferred it.

"What if his buddies come back?" the doc asked. He smirked and named another figure.

I transferred it. "I was never here."

I strode out of the doctor's clinic and walked down the larger corridor. I wasted no time in calling the rest of my team. We had a conference call over comms. "I found Eli, one of the *Whydah* crew. He's all banged up, burned, or something. I think his buddies have been visiting him, so they'll likely be back."

"Nice job, Jack," Ted said. His kudos made me feel warm inside. Even if he didn't remember, we still had a connection.

"I found their ship," Lu said. "It's the *Bullship*, docked on the opposite side of the station from our shuttle."

"Nice job, Commander Lu," Ted said. Now I felt less warm.

"Where's this Eli?" Carter asked.

"A doctor's clinic," I said. "I'll send you the coordinates." I texted them my location.

"In the meantime, get out of sight in case they come back," Lu said.

Get out of sight. That was a good, a stealthy, idea. I glanced around and realized I was standing outside another clinic promoting 'Infertility Cures!' Perfect. The *Whydah* crew would never go in there.

I opened the door and stepped inside. The generic waiting room was empty, from one dingy white wall to the other. All twenty chairs sat there by their lonesome. Perfect.

Prompted by something, a monkey-resembling sentient in soothing blue scrubs glided up to me from the back. "Welcome, Terran! What can we help you with? Are you impotent? Do you have erectile dysfunction?"

"Shh!" I said, glancing around, even though I already knew we were alone. "Shh."

He frowned, crossed his arms, and stood staring at me.

I swallowed. "Uh, yes," I said. "Of course, I have, ah, issues, or I wouldn't have come in here, right? But I need a few minutes to gather my thoughts. Can you give me some privacy?"

He sighed. "Whatever. I'll be in the back. Call out when you're ready." He turned and tramped to the back.

I texted the team my new location and sat down to wait. And think. It would be best to capture each *Whydah* crewmember stealthily and separately take them into custody. Ultimately, we should, we would, take them back to Earth for justice. *Justice, most gracious Duke; O, grant me justice!*

Carter and Ted were the first team members to poke their heads in the door of the infertility clinic.

"Why are we meeting here?" Carter asked.

The scrubs-wearing employee glided up, frowning.

"Can I interest you in some credits, sir?" I held up my fon.

He nodded and held up his fon. I transferred credits. He glided away.

I had to admit, everyone on the station being amenable to bribery was quite handy.

"We're here because it's deserted and very close to the

clinic where Eli is," I said.

Ted turned to Carter. "What's the plan?"

I tried not to be insulted that he consulted Carter. I was unsuccessful. I cleared my throat. "I plan to lure the *Whydah* crew here and take them into custody in preparation for justice back on Earth. *Justice always whirls in equal measure*."

"Huh?" Ted said. "Whirls?"

"Ignore that," Carter said. "How exactly are we luring people here, Jack?"

Just then, the door to the clinic burst open. "Jack! Jack!" Max cried, running in, tail wagging like crazy.

"You'll never guess who we found," Jax panted, lugging a man along behind him. The man was human with dark unruly curly hair hanging in front of his face, Caucasian, but spindly and unhealthy-looking. "I can't believe it," Jax said, breathing heavily.

Carter darted over to the door.

Before he could close it, Lu snuck through, and stopped, standing at attention near said door.

Carter closed the door after all the new arrivals.

Jax let go of the stranger, and he stumbled, going down on one knee before standing up.

Then, the stranger pulled the hair out of his face, and I beheld an extraordinarily compelling man. "What the hell is going on here?" he asked.

He was me.

My mouth fell open as we stared at each other.

His mouth fell open as we stared at each other.

"Is it just me, or does that guy look just like Jack?" Ted asked.

"It's not just you," Jax said.

"Yes," Max said and wagged his tail a little.

I stared some more. We were approximately the same height. Our hair color was the same. Our noses and eyes and the curves of our lips were extremely similar. But he was thinner than me and had a sallow, sickly cast to his skin. And what was he wearing? A tan tunic with nondescript pants underneath.

Finally, I said, "I don't see it."

"I was afraid of this," Max said. "Not only are they illegally cloning sentients like me here on the station, but they're also illegally cloning humans."

"You knew?" I asked him. I didn't know what to think. Maybe I was in shock. How many of me were there? I mean, I'm awesome, but good grief, enough's enough.

"How do you think Jax was born?" Max asked.

Jax was flushed and still catching his breath. "I don't know if I was cloned from him or he was cloned from me, but whichever, it's not good."

"Illegal cloning is not our mission, and you were too noisy when you dragged him here." Lu unholstered his weapon and walked towards us, pointing it at the stranger. "I heard your commotion from far away. There's no telling who else heard."

"I can't help it if he was yelling and fighting back," Jax said.

"I don't know who you people are, but I demand you let me go," the stranger said. "My mast-, er, boss is going to pissed. Let me go!"

Had he been about to say master? I involuntarily recalled that horrible dog-cloning lab I'd destroyed. "Are you some kind of prisoner or slave?" I asked softly. "Is your 'boss,'" I made the air quotes, "holding you against your will?" My heart went out to him. Had they been doing experiments on him?

The fight went out of him. "Maybe. What's it to you?"

"We could take you off the station," I said. "Would you like that?"

He seemed stunned, staring at me again, with his mouth gaping open again. Then, he said, "You'd do that for me?"

"Yes," I said.

"Yes," Jax said.

"Yes," Max said.

"But…" He trailed off.

I walked over to him and put my arm around his shoulder. "Look at me. I'm your brother. I'll take care of you. I promise." I smiled gently at him. "What's your name?"

He blinked back tears. "I don't have a name." Finally, he said, "But thanks. That would be nice."

No name? I'd never heard of a human who didn't have a name. I felt my own eyes start to fill. "You're welcome. Maybe Jax and Max should take you back to our ship."

Then, the door burst open, and a woman bounced in. "Jax!

There you are, Jax!" It was a lovely young woman with smooth tan skin, flashing brown eyes, and a healthy physique. She only had eyes for Jax.

I recognized her. Aria. My fiancée from the *Whydah*. I stepped back, pulling my hat down.

For his part, Jax seemed confused.

Max threw me a look that said, 'Stupid humans. What am I going to do with them?'

"I knew I'd find you," Aria said. "The captain is furious, but I forgive you. We can get married and run away together. Oh, Jax!" She threw her arms around him and started covering his face in kisses.

Lucky bloke. I took a step forward toward them.

The door opened again, "Aria, where are you going?" It was the male version of Aria, her twin brother, Aaron, also lovely, with smooth tan skin, flashing eyes, and all the rest. And, oh yeah, also my fiancé. "Jax?" He paused. "Wait. Aria, what are you doing to my fiancé?"

Aria moved her face away from Jax's face. "What?"

Jax had a curious expression: a mixture of wonder, confusion, and, well, curiosity.

Aaron stepped to them. "Jax and I are engaged."

"No, you aren't," Aria said. "Jax and *I* are engaged."

Jax finally said, "I'm not engaged."

"Yes, you are," Aria said.

"Yes, you are," Aaron said.

"No, I'm not," Jax said. "I would know it if I was engaged, and I'm not."

"Everyone, freeze," Lu said, steel in his voice, pointing his gun toward Aria and Aaron.

Everyone in the room froze. Yes, Commander Lu was an intimidating guy. "Ensign Jones," he said steely. "I'm sure this is your fault. Report."

"*The course of true love never did run smooth*?" I said.

Aria and Aaron looked surprised to see me, and other-me in addition to Jax, once they noticed us.

Max muttered, "*Lord, what fools these mortals be.*"

After sparing Max a glance, Lu turned and pointed his weapon at me.

"Er, uh," I said. "I was on the *Whydah.* I was trying to make, uh, allies, and I made a connection with these two fine, very fine people." I held up my hands and shrugged. "Sorry."

Aaron looked like he might cry. Aria looked like she might punch me.

I realized Carter and Ted also had their weapons out, pointing at Aria and Aaron.

Lu turned his weapon to them, as well. "If you're from the *Whydah*, you're under arrest. Ted, take them back to our ship."

"Where are you taking us?" Aria demanded, eyes flashing.

"Back to Earth for trial," Lu said.

She glared at him, her hands on her hips.

"Or, we could shoot you," Lu said drily.

"No, no," Aaron said. "We surrender. We surrender, Aria." He moved closer to her. "I don't want anything bad to happen to you."

"Something bad already did happen to me," she said, her eyes shooting daggers at me.

"Okay, let's go," Ted said, gesturing at the door with his gun.

The twins seemed to deflate. They turned and tramped towards the door.

"The three of us will go, too," Max said.

Jax nodded. "It'll be safer."

"The sooner I can get off the station, the better," no-name me said.

As the six of them exited, I heard Ted say to his prisoners, "Really? Both of you liked that Jack guy? What's so great--" The door closed behind them.

Carter and Lu holstered their guns in the now seemingly deserted fertility clinic.

"Now, what about this injured guy?" Carter asked.

"Show us," Lu said.

I tiptoed to the door, opened it, and tiptoed a few yards to the doctor's clinic. The two of them followed me silently. They were so quiet I had to glance back to make sure they were there. I tiptoed to the patient's room and, oh, so, carefully, opened the door a crack. I peeked in.

The room was chock-a-block full of *Whydah* crew.

Chapter Thirty-three

On the station, outside a sketchy doctor's clinic, I very slowly and carefully closed the door on a room full of criminals.

"What?" Lu asked, looking suspicious.

"Shh!" I said. "Most of the *Whydah* crew is in there," I whispered.

"That's good, isn't it?" Carter said.

"Shh!" I said. "Yes," I whispered. "But we're out-manned like two-to-one. And I know we're all awesome fighters...."

Lu and Carter both looked skeptical.

"But we need something to even the odds," I whispered.

"Well, they hijacked our ship," Carter whispered. "We could open the door and shoot all of them, surprise them. *A pound of flesh*."

"I like the way you think, Carter," Lu whispered. "But we are supposed to obey galactic law. Unfortunately."

I stared at the two of them. Did I know they were so bloodthirsty? "*So grace and mercy at your most need help you,*" I whispered. "Or, we could stun them, arrest them, and take them back to Earth for trial. You know, our actual mission."

They stared at me like I was the one with an antic disposition.

"Aren't they wearing armor?" Lu asked. "Stunning isn't always effective."

Carter grimaced. "Jack is right. I think we have to obey the law."

Finally, Lu said softly, "Fine. Set your weapons on stun."

The three of us checked our energy weapons. Mine had already been on stun. Theirs had not, so they spent some moments remedying this.

"I'm ready when you are," I whispered and put my hand on the doorknob.

After a few moments, they both whispered, "Ready."

I flung open the door, and we all started firing.

All the *Whydah* crew slumped or fell except Eli, who was already lying down.

The three of us stepped inside, weapons out, scanning the room. It was small, only about a hundred and fifty square feet, with a hospital bed in the center, dingy off-white walls, and no decoration of any kind. Had we gotten all the bad guys in the room? We had. "Yeah," I said. "Looks like we got them all."

"*For 'tis the sport to have the engineer hoist with his own petard, an't shall go hard*," Carter said. "*But I will delve one yard below their mines and blow them at the moon*."

I must have given him a strange look because he laughed and then said, "Just giving you some of your own medicine, Jones. Annoying, isn't it?"

It was annoying when he gave Shakespeare quotes, but when I did it, it was charming. I cleared my throat. "So, how do we get them to the shuttle now? They can't walk, and we can't carry seven guys."

"You're asking us?" Lu asked. "It was your plan!"

Shoot. I may not have totally thought this through. "Maybe the doctor has a bunch of wheelchairs or something?"

"Are you asking us?" Carter asked.

I held up my forefinger. "Just a sec." Where did that doctor get to? I stepped down the hall to his office and rapped on the door.

"Come," he said.

Before I'd opened the door fully, he said. "I have a cart you can use to transport your 'friends,'" he made the air quotes, "but it will cost you. And Eli's too injured to move."

I got out my fon and transferred the considerable funds he requested. At this rate, my balance was getting precariously low. It was a good thing I was leaving the station ASAP.

A little while later, he drove up in what looked like a glorified golf cart. He got out and tossed the keys to me. "I better get this back."

Carter, Lu, and I started dragging the still-insensate *Whydah* crew onto the cart. The captain was particularly heavy with his massive size and many muscles. We managed to shove the six of them inside, except Eli. I still wasn't sure what to do about him.

"Let's take these guys to the shuttle," Commander Lu said. "Carter, I'll need your help unloading them.

"We only left room for the driver," Carter said.

"Can't you get the folks on the shuttle to help you unload?" I wasn't nervous about being left here alone.

"Hop on the bumper, Carter," Lu said, getting in the driver's seat. "We'll be right back, Jack. Guard the sick guy. For security, stay off comms."

Right. We were still trying to remain stealthy.

Carter jumped on the back, and they quickly zoomed away.

I stepped back into Eli's room and sat gingerly on his bed. I wasn't scared or even nervous. Nope. Not a bit. Everything would be fine. They'd be right back, and we'd figure something out about Eli. I shifted on the bed, and it moved a little. I leaned down. This bed had wheels.

I sat back down. *Not afraid of greatness.*

Not afraid, not afraid at all. *The noblest Roman of them all.* Quotes were lovely.

The doc strolled into the room, purple face scowling. "You owe me more remuneration for all this extra trouble. How much longer will you be? Stonewalling station security is expensive." I didn't know the station even had any security. And he'd changed his tune.

I smiled at him, took out my fon, and checked the balance. Not much.

On the other hand, I could wheel Eli out of here right now and meet up with everyone on the shuttle. "I hear what you're saying. How about we get out of your hair immediately?"

"I guess," he said.

That sounded like a plan. I jogged to the head of the bed and started shoving Eli, bed and all, toward the door. The bed just barely fit through the door. I pushed it down the hall, picking up some speed.

"I better get that bed back!" he called after me.

I kept going, leaving the medical area of the station.

I pushed Eli in his hospital bed through one of the shopping districts towards the spaceship docking area. People were staring at him as we wheeled by.

Then, in the distance, I heard, "Eli? Eli, is that you? Where are you taking him?"

Shoot. We hadn't gotten all of the *Whydah* crew. I pushed the bed faster.

"Stop, or I'll shoot!" the man said.

I ran, pushing the bed in front of me.

Pew, pew! Energy bolts zoomed past me, hitting the wall, sizzling, and lighting small fires.

So, not on stun. Weren't they worried they'd hit Eli? Or bystanders? Or didn't they care? Space pirates were not nice.

People screamed and ducked and ran.

I ran as fast as I could, now, in the central atrium outside the docks. It was chaotic as other people darted this way and that, trying to escape.

Pew, pew!

"Stop!" some other men near my destination shuttle yelled, "Stop immediately, or we shoot."

Pew, pew! Pew, pew!

Pew, pew!

Now I was getting it from both sides! I ran the only way I could, into the docking area, but away from my shuttle. I ran and ran, pushing Eli in front of me.

I paused for a moment, trying to catch my breath. When I looked up, I realized I was standing outside the *Whydah* crew's new ship, the *Bullship*. In terms of size and design, it looked similar to the *Whydah,* small, like a classic flying saucer.

I pushed Eli right up to the door and tried to open the external hatch by grabbing the handle. No go.

Sometimes ships had verbal passwords. "Open sesame." Nothing happened.

"*Whydah*." Nothing.

"Password." Zip.

"*Bullship*." Nope.

"Now I've got you!" someone yelled.

Pew, pew! Pew, pew!

I felt a lance of pain stab through my left arm. It burned like it was on fire.

Time seemed to slow down. *P-e-w-w.*

Think, Jack, think. If I didn't open this door, I was probably dead. If I didn't open this door, Eli might be dead…

P-e-w-w.

Eli!

Often ships had biometric scanners. I grabbed his hand and pressed it up against the handle.

P-e-w-w.

The light turned green, and I heard the door snick open.

I pulled open the door, shoved Eli inside, followed close behind, and then slapped the door closed.

The sudden silence was jarring.

My arm felt like it was melting. "Shit!" I clutched it in my other arm.

Through the small window, I could see a man clad in black leather run up, energy weapon pointed forward. A group of five uniformed men ran up after him. Station security?

The leather-clad man took a step towards the ship. Oh no! He could probably get in here!

One of the uniformed men grabbed his arm, yelling at him.

No time to waste! I punched the inner airlock door and wheeled Eli inside the ship proper. It was much more difficult to push the bed with only one good arm.

I closed the inner airlock door.

I ran in the direction I thought the bridge would be, leaving Eli there in the corridor.

I found the bridge, but I couldn't get anything to work.

I had to run back to Eli and wheel him to the bridge. I pressed his hand to the main control panel, which lit up, green by green.

I fired up the main engines.

The comms sputtered to life. "*Bullship*, you are not cleared to depart. Stop and prepare to be boarded."

"No, thanks!" I engaged the sub-light engines and tried to back away from the station. Unfortunately, the docking clamps were still engaged.

"*Bullship*, stop!"

I gunned the engines, and it burst away from the station

with a loud rending sound reverberating through the ship. I flew away from it and stopped still in visual range, but, hopefully, out of its weapons range.

I took a deep breath. Phew. I did it. I escaped. Yay, me!

I paused, glancing around the empty bridge. I had been in trouble, but I wasn't anymore. I grinned.

I should rendezvous with the *Shakespeare*. But my left arm was still killing me, and my left hand was useless at this point. I very, very carefully took off my shirt (difficult to do one-handed) and almost fainted when I saw my mangled arm. It looked like it'd been pulverized by an energy weapon.

I glanced over at Eli. Suddenly, his constellation of injuries, including burns, made much more sense.

I had to get some treatment, at least some pain meds.

I got up. If I was the med bay, where would I be?

Several minutes later, I sat on a cot in the med bay. I'd just finished putting some topical pain-killer on the wound and started wrapping it in gauze when the ship jerked, making me drop the gauze. I leaned over to pick it up, and the ship jerked again.

Hey, wait a minute. That shouldn't happen. We were in outer space; there was no way the ship could move unless…

I dropped the gauze and ran to the bridge.

Through the main viewscreen, I saw what looked like a missile headed straight for us!

"Evasive action!" I yelled. Nothing happened.

I sat down in the captain's chair and accessed the engine controls. Nothing happened. Then, I saw, 'Engines off-line.' The control panel was covered in red lights.

The ship shuddered again.

A red light started blinking. "Hull breach on level 1! Hull breach on level 1!" the ship said.

"This is bullship! Er, bullshit! This is not how Jack Jones ends!"

I accessed the ship's communications system. "I surrender! I surrender! Stop shooting at me!"

But it said, 'Comms off-line.'

Time seemed to slow down again as another missile approached.

My heart thudded, *ba-boom, ba-boom*. My arm throbbed. A bead of sweat rolled down my forehead. *Ba-boom, ba-boom.*

Was this how I died? "*To sleep, perchance to dream*," I whispered, blinking back a tear.

Would they bring me back as a clone?

When was the last time I backed up my memories? "Shit!"

Then, Eli said, "Ffff--" I glanced at him, and he had one eye open, staring at me.

"The FTL drive!" I accessed the FTL control; it was the one green light on the board. My right-hand shaking, I input the course and immediately engaged the drive.

"I wish I was on Earth!"

I spied a beautiful blonde goddess leaning over me, my lady love Sophia. "There you are, Jack." She smiled. Unfortunately, besides being my lady love, she was also a duplication engineer. Shit. They did clone me.

How many memories did I lose? What was the last thing I remembered? Dying on a spaceship…

Huh. That didn't seem right. Shouldn't the last thing I remembered be recording my memories?

She caressed my left arm.

"Ouch!"

"Oh, I'm sorry, honey," she said. "I'm just so glad to see you. Aren't you glad to see me?"

"Of course, Sophia," I said. "It's always nice to see you." I pulled her face to mine, and we shared a delectable kiss. She smelled faintly of roses. "Mmm. Why don't you lie down next to me?" My functional hand explored all her alluring parts, and I lost track of time…

Wait a minute. My left hand didn't seem to work, and my arm hurt. That meant they hadn't cloned me. "Am I a clone?" I looked around and saw what appeared to be an ordinary three-hundred-square-foot hospital room with soothing pastel-colored walls, pastel-cushioned chairs, and lots of medical equipment. I was not at the duplication center.

"Yes." She nodded solemnly. "My favorite clone. But no, we didn't *just* clone you."

"Jack!" A deeper female voice, Gina's voice, said. "Are you

coming to the ceremony or not?" She was also my lady love. She strode to my bed in her full-dress captain's uniform, looking captivating. Her TCC uniform was midnight blue with a silver image of the Milky Way galaxy and the blue-white marble of Earth superimposed in front, and she filled it out perfectly.

Sophia jumped out of bed, rearranging her clothing. "I didn't tell him about the ceremony yet. Sorry, Ms. Gomez. I got distracted."

"I can see that." Gina frowned. "And it's Captain Gomez."

Sophia sort of curtsied to her as she finished buttoning her shirt. "Yes, ma'am."

"Aw, Gina," I said. "You could lie down next to me if you wanted...."

She looked tempted for a few moments. That's my story, and I'm sticking to it. "So, how far did you get, Ms. Olsson?" she asked.

"Uh," Sophia looked like a dear caught in headlights. "Not very far."

"What's going on?" I asked, rubbing my arm.

"The *Bullship* appeared out of nowhere on the green in front of the Eiffel Tower," she said.

Yay! My special skill worked! I nodded like that was obvious.

"Only you and that Eli were on board," she continued. "He's under medical care in custody. All the people captured on the station are in TCC custody except for Max, Jax, and that other one. Max and Jax got a deal by informing on the others."

I was glad Jax and Max weren't in trouble. "What other one? Ohh...that other me? What's up with him?"

"It's a legal nightmare." She shook her head. "How would you feel about being part of a triplet?"

Not the Quihiri kind of triplet, a regular Terran kind of triplet. "Okay, I guess?" I said, mind reeling. Brothers, two brothers. That would be great, wouldn't it? "They're not going to be in TCC, are they?" That might get confusing.

"No." She shook her head again. "So, the *Shakespeare*'s crew is being recognized by Earth. Are you coming?"

"Recognized? How so? I thought our spy status was secret?"

She nodded. "We're outstanding thespians. The medal

ceremony will be private at TCC headquarters."

"Medal ceremony?" I asked. "Will I be getting a medal?"

She smiled. "You'll have to come to the medal ceremony to find out." But her smile said I was.

I smiled back. "What does this thespian ceremony consist of?"

"Well, first, we're in a parade through Paris," Gina said. And then she said some other stuff, but I wasn't paying attention.

"A parade!" I said. "Count me in! Is my uniform here?"

A few minutes later, I was in my captivating TCC midnight blue uniform, striding out of the medical center with a lovely lady on each arm. (Sophia was appropriately gentle with my injury.) "Hurray for us," I said. "We saved the galaxy."

"Saved is a strong word, but basically." Gina grinned.

"You're my hero, Jack!" Sophia said.

"That's what I thought." I nodded. "Jack Jones, saver of galaxies." I grinned at each lady in turn. "Singer-, spy-, lover-extraordinaire."

Right outside, we jumped into an open-topped conveyance with the rest of the *Shakespeare*'s senior staff and my buddies, including Ted, Carter, Eva, Olivia, Jax, a bunch of adorable puppies and Max. He barked happily when he saw me--Max, I mean. The car took off immediately and soon joined a procession of other vehicles.

As we drove past the Eiffel Tower, the crowds lining the sides of the street cheered, and confetti rained down from on high. It was magnificent. I breathed deeply, drinking it all in.

But, as I glanced around, the best part was being reunited with my friends, everyone safe and sound, and all the peoples of the galaxy saved from the scourge of war.

My eyes filled. *We are such stuff as dreams are made on.*

"What's wrong, Jack?" Sophia sitting next to me, asked, squeezing my hand.

"Nothing's wrong," I said, squeezing back. "Everything's right."

Jack's special skill enables him to take advantage of probabilities from the quantum FTL drive. If you think I stole this idea from a certain famous British SF author associated with the number 42, you would be correct. Let's look a little closer at probabilities in quantum mechanics...

Science Fact: Probabilities in Quantum Mechanics

Quantum mechanics is the branch of physics focused on the smallest things. Atoms are made of electrons, neutrons, and protons. Neutrons and protons are made of quarks. Electrons and quarks are believed to be indivisible and so are among the smallest things in the universe and hence, called elementary particles. Thus, the behavior of elementary particles is described by quantum mechanics (QM).

QM has been extensively proven via experiments. For example, it explains the periodic table of the elements in chemistry and how atoms bond together to form molecules. In fact, the term 'quantum leap' comes from an electron in an atom jumping from one discrete energy level to another. Such a transition involves the electron emitting or absorbing a particle of energy called a photon. Thus, a quantum leap is the smallest possible leap.

In QM, the quantum state of a particle is mathematically described by a wave function. Wave functions are considered the set of all probability amplitudes. Notice *all* probability amplitudes correspond to infinite probabilities. These probability amplitudes provide a relationship between the wave function of a system and the results of observations of that system. Thus, QM says that everything can be described in terms of probabilities.

This idea seems to conflict with our everyday reality. For example, in my experience, there is a one-hundred-percent probability that I read this book--not a fifty-percent chance I read the book and a fifty-percent chance I played a video game instead. I either read the book or I didn't read the book. Even famous physicist Albert Einstein said about QM, "God doesn't play dice with the universe."

The resolution of this seeming paradox is humans live in the macroscopic world, not the sub-atomic quantum world. Everything we directly deal with is made of many, many fundamental particles. The mechanism(s) of how we get from infinite quantum possibilities to one macroscopic reality is described by the field of QM interpretations--and still contains many mysteries.

For more information and details about these and other topics, check out the Physics Is Fun website: www.physicsisfun.net

Thank you for reading *A Jack For All Seasons.* I hope you enjoyed it!

- For more info about me or my work, please visit my author's website, http://www.lesleylsmith.com/. Sometimes, I post links for free fiction downloads!
- Please check out the Physics Is Fun website www.physicsisfun.net for lots of information about fun physics topics.
- Reviews help other readers find books. I appreciate any and all reviews.
- Please check out an excerpt from the next Jack short story, "Jack Daddy," on the following pages.

–Lesley L. Smith

Jack Daddy excerpt

I had some vacation time coming to me on account of how I'd saved the galaxy (again), but I'm a super modest guy; I don't brag about my daring dos, so you'll have to take my word for it about the saving. Yes, I'm that Jack Jones, renowned throughout the galaxy as the best singer, the best spy, and, yes, the best lover.

Anyway, I planned to go to Earth to see my dear Sophia, a bodacious blonde Scandinavian goddess, and also, by the way, a duplication engineer. She'd cloned my body in a big vat for the Terran Cultural Committee when my original body was cruelly and evilly murdered. But that's another long story you'll have to take my word on. Sophia was a dear because not everyone who'd seen you as a seemingly giant bloody red worm in a tank would want to make love with you afterward. But that's my scrumptious Sophia, a real peach.

I'd hitched a ride on the freighter *Ship Happens,* and we were supposed to go straight to Earth; that's what they'd told me at any rate. I was sitting in the mess hall, a twenty-foot-cubed space with metal walls, floor, and ceiling, sipping on a bulb of hard cider (appropriate any time of day, and on a spaceship, who really knew what time it was anyway?).

One of the crew approached me and said, "Hey, Jack, we're taking a detour to The Station."

I'd been to the unimaginatively-named station before, and it was a real wretched hive of scum and villainy, so, my favorite kind of place. On the other hand, sumptuous Sophia was waiting for me. "You guys promised to take me to Earth."

"Sorry," he said. "You can come with us to The Station, or we can let you out the airlock anywhere you'd like." Since, despite the name, the other side of the airlock was no-air-whatsoever, this didn't sound like a great plan.

"No," I said. "The Station's fine." Of course, the last time I'd been to The Station, there had been some trouble along the lines of space pirates trying to kill me and me blowing up some illegal genetic labs and pissing off their criminal owners, but that was all over and done now, so I should be safe, right?

I believed in the power of positive thinking. I just had to believe in, and expect a positive outcome, and it would happen. And in this particular case, it worked, sort of. My troubles didn't have anything to do with space pirates or evil genetic experiments, at least.

Soon, we disembarked at The Station. I'd debated staying on the ship, but, ultimately, that wasn't any fun, was it? What decided me was I hadn't made sweet, sweet love in days, so I was on the lookout for sexy sentients to spend some time with. No doubt The Station would be chock-full of lonely ladies, or gentlemen, of some species or other, who would be thrilled to get to know the famous Jack Jones very, very well.

The massive disembarkation area contained hundreds of sentients headed for The Strip or elsewhere in The Station. It was spacious enough that several spaceships could have fit inside. I stood outside the door of the *Ship Happens* and watched the commotion for a few moments. There was a group of Alpha Catoblepans (2-legged human-sized 'mice' famous for loving my music); they did all usually want to have sex with me. And over there, a group of Tau Cetoans (2-legged human-sized 'turtles' famous for wearing tunics); their big humped shell-covered backs didn't do anything for me. I spied a couple of Keplarrians (human-sized snake-like creatures) slithering along; I had no idea how they even had sex. I observed a triple-triple of Quihiri (three-legged 'octopus' creatures); truth be told, I had had sex with a Quihiri to two in my day; they were sweet and very flexible. I even spotted a kaleidoscope of rainbow-colored sparkly sldkfjfoisut, energy beings, who'd I'd procreated with in the past.

Someone punched me lightly on the shoulder. "Jones! I'm talking to you." It was the crewmember, a Terran, I'd talked to earlier. He wasn't bad-looking; I liked the sprinkling of freckles across his nose and cheeks. Terrans were a little dull, but at least you knew what you were in for.

"What?" I asked brilliantly.

"Be back here in twenty-four hours," he said. "We're taking off then with or without you."

I smiled sexily. "So, where are you going? Can I join you? What's your name again?"

But he was already marching down the walkway.

I watched the crowd a little longer, almost overtaken with an inkling of something, apprehension? But that couldn't be it; I didn't get uneasy. I was a paramour, a troubadour, a jongleur. I was up for anything!

I opened another button on my shirt and strode stout-hearted into the crowd, ready for adventure.

I decided not to hit my usual spots, just to be on the safe side, so I ended up in Schrodinger's Bar—where anything can happen, a watering hole catering to oxygen-breathing species (my favorite kind). Schrodinger's Bar looked like just about every gin joint in every town on every planet. Sentients sat at mismatched tables and in chairs in a large room, with a considerable counter to one side, behind which was a bartender, behind which were many colorful bottles containing many presumably delightful substances.

I sidled right up to the bar and sat down on one of the stools. I pounded the plastic (?) surface with my palm. "Barkeep, a mug of your best suds."

The bartender, a Yeblypson, who looked like a large brown-furred chimpanzee, frowned at me. "You want to drink soap?" Of course, I knew he wasn't actually a chimp; he only looked like a chimp because of convergent evolution.

"Nay! Ale, brew, lager, malt, stout," I said. "Beer, man! Pour me a beer."

I thought he muttered, "Stupid humans," as he placed a mug of amber deliciousness in front of me, but that couldn't be right.

So, I sipped my elixir and perused the opportunities for love.

Sadly, folks in the bar were all sitting with extant friends; no one seemed to be looking to make new friends. I quaffed my first beverage and procured a second.

About then, a very intriguing creature, resembling a cloud of golden glitter, entered the establishment and glided to the bar. S/he was some kind of energy being. Floating next to me, s/he said, "I'll take a mug of your best beer if you please." His/her English was like the tinkling of ethereal magical bells. Energy beings were very good at speaking different languages in my experience because they could make any sounds they wanted.

The Yeblypson placed a beer on the bar in front of him/her and quickly backed away.

I hummed the musical overture of Phantom and then sang the first couple of lines. "*In sleep, he sang to me...*" I smiled sexily.

He/she said, "What's that? It's pretty. A Terran song?"

I nodded. "Yes." I made a flourish with my hand and bowed down. "My name is Jack Jones, and I'm a balladeer, a bard, at your service."

To Be Continued…

www.ingramcontent.com/pod-product-compliance
Lightning Source LLC
Chambersburg PA
CBHW060414180626
46817CB00007B/2577